Seasons' Beginnings

Book One of the Season Avatars

Sandra Ulbrich Almazan

Sandra Ulbrich Almazan, Solar Unicorn Publishing
www.sandraulbrichalmazan.com/solarunicornpublishing.com

Book Layout © 2014 BookDesignTemplates.com

Seasons' Beginnings/ Sandra Ulbrich Almazan. – 2nd edition.
ISBN 978-0-9838903-8-6

This book is dedicated to all my friends and family members who have supported my writing efforts over the years.

CONTENTS

Part One: The Magicians

CHAPTER ONE

The Meeting

Kron Evenhanded was packing up his many unsold artifacts when a woman in a scoop-necked dress pushed her way through the crowd and halted in front of him. She had a grim expression on her face and one hand behind her back. "I hear you're a magic-user, stranger." Her tone made it clear she didn't think much of his kind.

"I'm an artificer," he replied. He waved his hand over his collection: scraps of wood embedded with pebbles, a couple of bronze mirrors with words carved into the handles, soapstone figures, cloth bags, and more. He had the most eclectic merchandise in the city—and the most misunderstood. She didn't seem like a customer, but he had to treat her like one. "Each of these items is enchanted. Do you want me to demonstrate what they can do, Dame, or should I make an item just for you—"

"Can any of your items do this?"

She thrust a white, bloodless chicken a thumbspan from his nose. Kron blinked as he stared at the carcass. Its head was on backward, melded smoothly to the neck as if the bird had been born like that.

Kron had only arrived in Vistichia a few days ago, but he hadn't encountered any other artificers—or other magicians, for that matter. Many people blamed magicians for the recent plague of disasters that had inspired Kron to return to his own family in Delns. What if they blamed him for this? He could end up as dead as the chicken.

He smiled at the woman while wishing his tunic and leggings were less torn and stained. "That's not my type of magic, Dame. I work with made objects, not natural creatures."

"Well, could this be a side effect of your magic?" she asked.

Kron shook his head. "None of my artifacts can do that to a living thing. Where did you find the hen?"

"In my henhouse. She was one of my best layers." The woman shook the carcass at him. "We have laws in this city, magician. There's a fine for destroying someone else's property."

"But Dame, I didn't—"

"Phebe, that's enough." Another woman, younger than the first, stepped forward, her arms draped with baskets full of bread, vegetables, and fish. "He's not that kind of magician. Can't you tell from looking at his wares that he doesn't practice magic on animals? Someone else was cruel to our poor Mama Hen." Her gentle voice became grieved at the final words.

"She was an egg-layer, Bella, not a pet." But Phebe looked down and stepped away from Kron's temporary shop as if ashamed by her earlier accusation.

He turned to the other woman. She wore a simple white tunic with a matching headcloth covering her dark hair. Her large eyes, flecked with green and gold like gems, would have made deer envious. As Kron met her gaze, she smiled and looked away. He couldn't blame her; he was hardly as lovely to look at as she was.

"Thank you, Dame." He honored her with a slight bow.

"It's Dama." Bella smiled at him again, making his stomach feel like a thousand butterflies were trapped inside. If he remembered the title correctly, "Dama" meant she was unmarried. The men in this city were fools to overlook someone this kind and pretty.

Phebe cleared her throat. "I still want to know what happened to my chicken and who did it."

Without looking away from Bella, Kron heard himself saying, "I'm done with the marketplace for the day, Dame and Dama. Perhaps I might be able to find out who killed your hen." He picked up a finder. "With this, I can track magic."

Phebe didn't seem impressed, but Bella stared at the finder, a silver arrow mounted on a wooden base with a cat's eye gem embedded in a corner. Kron wondered if she was sensitive to magic. Only one person in a hundred possessed enough sensitivity and power to use magic. No wonder he'd always been so isolated.

Kron packed all of his artifacts except for the magic finder into his sacks, then followed Phebe and Bella out of the marketplace. A white-haired woman wearing a midwife's orange dress waved to Phebe as she passed, while a youth with a strong resemblance to the midwife winked at Bella. Kron grit his teeth, but Bella barely glanced at the other man. She stopped instead at a weaver's booth to finger finely woven wool. The weaver, short and dark-haired, seemed even shyer than Bella.

"Not now, Bella," Phebe said before Bella could ask the weaver the price.

Bella's shoulders drooped. Even though Kron already carried a heavy load, he took a basket from her. Relief shone in Bella's eyes.

"Who is she to you?" he asked Bella when Phebe was halfway up the street from them. She led them to an area neither markedly rich or poor. The houses here were mostly two-story and made of fired brick strong enough to endure harsh weather, but they shared walls and had small dirt yards.

"My sister."

She seemed like a bossy sister. "What about your parents?"

"Both dead in the last plague."

"I'm sorry." Kron wondered if that was why Bella wasn't married yet.

"I was lucky to survive myself," she said. "Phebe nursed me through it, even though she has her own husband and children to look after. So now I'm helping her care for her family until I have a chance to sing at the palace. I missed my audition because of the plague."

Kron tried not to wince. He might be a stranger in this town, but even he'd heard that the palace wasn't the safest place for young, attractive women.

Bella snuck a sideways glance at him. "What about you? I don't think I've seen you in the marketplace before. You're not from Vistichia, are you?"

"No, from Delns, northeast of here. I'm on my way to see my family. I haven't been back there for twenty years." Normally Kron could have created a portal to travel instantly to a place he'd been to before, but his family home must have changed too much with the recent wars and other catastrophes all over the known world. Although he'd resented walking from the Magic Institute across the Western Mountains, then sailing down the Chikasi River to Vistichia, he'd had more adventures by traveling like a person without magic than he would have otherwise.

Phebe led Bella and Kron around one house, indistinguishable from the rest, to the back. Part of the area was paved with stone, while a chicken coop and a small garden of vegetables occupied the rest of the space. Although Kron cautiously picked his way through the dirt and droppings to the henhouse, something disgusting splattered into his sandal.

"Bella, go put our purchases away, then start preparing dinner." Phebe began weeding, but she positioned herself so she could watch Kron at the same time. He suspected she was more worried about what he might do to the rest of her hens than interested in his magic.

"Good luck," Bella mouthed at him before leaving.

Kron would have liked to linger—perhaps Bella would find a reason to come outside—but he could feel Phebe's stare boring into his back. Ignoring her, Kron brought out the finder he'd shown the women earlier, then circled the henhouse. He was three-fourths of the way around before the arrow jerked and swung off in another direction. Before he could follow it, the arrow spun and landed in the opposite direction. Either the magician was transporting him or herself around, or else the finder was picking up more than one source of magic. Kron hoped it was the former.

For the next few hours he wandered all over Vistichia, following his finder to ripe-smelling midden piles, windowsills of homes and bakery shops, and the harbor where the Chikasi met the Salt Waters. Each time the finder brought him to a place where someone could hide, although some of the places, such as a wine barrel or a nook in a wall, were too small for Kron to enter. Perhaps he was following the traces of a magic spy, someone or something sent to learn the weaknesses of the town before invaders arrived. But the spy avoided the gates and other sources of military information; very strange. And what kind of spy would mutilate a chicken? Kron drummed his fingers on the finder as he tried to make sense of it.

By sunset, the traces became clustered in the northwest section of the town, near the forest. As Kron followed the finder to the edge of Vistichia, the cat's-eye embedded in the base began to glow, a sign he was coming to a stronger source of magic. The arrow pointed to the forest. To get there, Kron waded through knee-high grass that poked through his leggings.

The finder pointed him to a tangle of undergrowth. Kron pushed sticky branches away from his face as he squeezed through the brush surrounding the narrow path. The glow from the cat's-eye provided much-needed light. What sort of magician could use a trail like this? Perhaps he or she had shrunk in size or changed into an animal. Or perhaps....

"From north to south, you are dead! Wash your face and go to bed!"

The cat's-eye scorched the finder as something dropped from a tree into the bushes. A brown bear rose and roared, jaws gaping and sharp claws extended. Kron's heart raced even as he realized it was an illusion. He tried to banish it but failed. How could this unknown magician be so strong? He hadn't met anyone of this caliber since leaving the Magic Institute. Was this a peer, a rival, or an enemy?

Kron ripped a white thread from his tunic and enchanted it to turn strong and sticky, then threw it at the other magician as a distraction while he prepared another weapon. To his surprise, the illusion of the bear dissipated, and a high voice cried out, "That's not fair! Let me go, or I'll call my mother!"

"Your mother?" Kron pushed through the branches to reveal his captive: a boy, about six or seven, with apple-round cheeks and dark brown hair dappled by the sunlight pouring through the half-grown leaves. He had an extra finger on each hand, and as he squirmed, his joints bent backward as naturally as they did forward.

"What's your name, son?" Kron asked.

The boy stopped struggling and looked at him, dark eyelashes shielding his fearless eyes, so green they made the leaves above seem dull. "Are you my father? Mother never told me who he was, but I know he can't be a Nil."

"A Nil?"

"You know, one of them." The boy's voice dripped adult scorn on the last word. "The ones without magic. Mother says the only thing they're good for is serving us magicians."

Kron frowned. Didn't this child know any ordinary people? Why wasn't his mother teaching this child more respect for others? Kron knew only one magician who was so contemptuous of those without magic, but she was nowhere near here. Still… "Is your mother's name Salth?" Kron asked.

The boy nodded. "My name's Sal-thaath. What's yours?"

"Kron Evenhanded. I'm a … I knew your mother. We studied magic together about ten years ago."

He couldn't really say he had been a friend of Salth's; he didn't remember her having any friends at all. She had spent all her time at the Magic Institute studying. She'd done well on her own but refused to perform group magic, saying she couldn't trust anyone. Rumor had it that she was the sister of a city-king far to the east. When he summoned her home to be his personal magician, she'd sent the messenger back in animal form, though no one was sure exactly what type of animal. Had she thawed enough to take a lover since leaving the Magic Institute? Kron wouldn't have believed it, but Sal-thaath's existence proved otherwise.

"Sal-thaath," he said, "if you don't like ordinary people, why were you spying on them?"

"I wanted to see what they were like. We don't have any close to home."

"And the chicken?"

The child's expression never changed. "Oh, that. I was just playing around."

"Playing around! You can't do that. You could hurt someone."

A puzzled look appeared in the boy's eyes. "What does hurt mean?"

Kron frowned. "Haven't you ever fallen, or cut yourself?"

"No."

Further questioning revealed he'd never been hurt at all; his potent magic had always protected him. Kron wondered how Salth disciplined him—if she even did. She had to know that a powerful, untrained magician with a child's impulses could wreak an unimaginable amount of damage.

"Where's your mother?"

"Back near the mountains." He said it casually, as if the mountains were next door instead of close to the Magic Institute. Sal-thaath tried to break free. "Can I go home now?"

"Only if you take me with you. I need to speak to your mother."

"Does this mean you're going to be my father?"

Kron didn't know how to answer that question. He didn't want to take responsibility for this child, but someone had to tame him before people were hurt. He broke the thread. "Let's go."

CHAPTER TWO

Salth

Sal-thaath took Kron's hand, but he didn't lead him to a portal. Before he could blink, they arrived at the foothills of the Western Mountains, thousands and thousands of furlongs from Vistichia. Pine trees scented the air, and an eagle plunged into a nearby stream, emerging with a fat fish. "Your country is beautiful," Kron said, wishing privately that Sal-thaath would stay here instead of traveling to Vistichia at will. "I didn't know you can travel without a portal."

"It's easy." Sal-thaath danced, crushing delicate wildflowers underfoot. He gripped Kron's hand with all six fingers. "This way, behind the trees."

Salth's home looked as if a stone house from Thaume, the city near the Magic Institute, had swallowed an abandoned farmhouse. Kron wondered why she'd bothered to graft the two together. There was no one here to appreciate her magical talent. Perhaps she'd done it for the challenge. She'd always been like that, as if she needed to prove her worth by seeking out the most difficult tasks.

Sal-thaath led Kron inside the farmhouse section. The single large room was cluttered, with dirty dishes of various types piled in the dusty hearth. The room smelled moldy, and flies buzzed everywhere. Salthaath raced through the room to the marble section. "Mother," he called, "come see! I've found a father!"

"I'm not your father, child," Kron muttered under his breath.

The marble section of the house was as neat as the farmhouse was chaotic. Shelves of scrolls and tablets lined the walls from floor to ceiling. Water clocks, sun dials, and striped candles formed an obstacle course. Salth herself hadn't changed. She aimed a sight-enhancer—Kron recognized the piece as one he'd made—out of the window as if searching for a new star. Next to the sight-enhancer was a scroll with marks arranged in an uneven circle. Salth's limbs were as thin and angular as ever, though she had gained matronly curves. Her reddish-brown skin looked sallow, as if she hadn't been outside in moons. Her only feminine traits were her luxurious hair, caught in a jeweled hair net, and the twisted lines tattooed on her cheeks and hands. Despite the noise Sal-thaath made as he brandished a stick and knocked over scrolls and tablets, his mother didn't look away from the sight-enhancer.

It must be working well. Kron itched to inspect his old artifact, but he said nothing and waited for Salth to look up.

After a hundred or so heartbeats, Sal-thaath swung his stick so that it struck the sight-enhancer. Kron leaped forward, arms extended, to catch it, but Salth maintained her firm grip. "Sal-thaath, be more careful!" She finally turned her head, blinked a few times, then started as she stared at Kron.

"I know you," she said. "You were at the Magic Institute, weren't you? Who are you again, and what are you doing here?"

"I'm Kron. Kron Evenhanded." He dipped his head. "My specialty is enchanting objects."

"Ah, yes, I remember. Knickknack work."

Kron's smile slipped. "Like the sight-enhancer you're using? I made it."

"Is that true?" She examined the bronze tube, decorated with a scene of boats in a harbor. "Pretty shell, simple magic."

"If it's so simple, why not make your own sight-enhancer?"

She sniffed. "I have more important things to do than make tools. If you'd actually bothered to use your sight-enhancer to look past the clouds, you'd know something is coming that will affect us all."

Kron didn't respond. Salth liked to think she knew more about magic than even her instructors. That was why she'd chosen to leave the Magic Institute—that, and her refusal to teach, claiming only slaves taught others.

"Don't you even want to know what I'm talking about?" she asked.

"If it's that important, I'm sure I'll find out eventually."

Her frown hardened. "You don't believe me, do you? Never mind, then. Talk is a waste of time. I never have enough time for all I want to study. There must be a way to find more time. Look at how much of it Nils waste, and they seldom make it to forty or fifty years when they could live much longer."

Nils? Does she mean people? Ordinary people, like Phebe and Bella?

Sal-thaath took a few steps forward. "I thought you said Nils don't have magic, Mother, so how could they live longer?"

"They do have some in their souls. Not much, a few drops compared to the double-mighty waterfalls we carry. But there are so many of them that they would make a nice source of magic for the magician double-smart enough to figure out how to collect it—or their time." Her eyebrows knitted together as she glowered at Kron. "What are you still doing here, Kron?"

"We need to talk." Kron tilted his head at Salth's son. "Sal-thaath, why don't you go play for a while so I can talk to your mother?"

"Will you play with me afterwards?"

"We'll see."

Sal-thaath disappeared. Kron waited until he could no longer feel the boy's magical residue in the air before saying, "Salth, you have to do something about your son."

She had already returned to her scroll. "Why? He's a fine boy, double-strong, double-smart, and many-powerful," she said, not even looking up at him.

We're equals out here, no matter how strong she thinks her magic is. She has no right to treat me with more contempt than I'd give a first-

year apprentice. And she's not going to listen to me if she has a scroll in her hand. Kron strode to her and jerked her scroll away. She shrieked and reached for it, but he held it out of her reach. Only when hostile magic built between them did he say, "Sal-thaath is too powerful, and he has no sense of right and wrong. He's more powerful than I am; he could destroy a city."

"So? What are a few more or less Nils? They breed like animals."

"Is magic all you care about? Don't you care about Sal-thaath?"

The anger in Salth's eyes softened. "He's many-talented. I've learned much about time from watching him grow. And when he grows up, he and I will study magic together and peer into the heart of it."

"Maybe, but even you can't teach him everything. The Magic Institute won't take him if he can't tolerate others. Then how will he master his magic?"

"Master his magic? He *is* magic." She leaned forward, her eyes gleaming with green light. "I always wondered if it would be possible to breed without a partner. It took several tries and a lock of my favorite brother's hair, but I managed to create life in myself."

Kron wondered if Salth's brother had had six fingers instead of five. Maybe Salth hadn't been as successful as she thought. Instead, he asked, "Your favorite brother?"

"There were many of us in the harem—too many. Most of them were cruel, caring only for power, seeking favor with our father. Only Tham looked out for me when I was Sal-thaath's age. He was pushed down some stairs when I was eleven. I still think Aksam did it, that bastard. No wonder he won the throne. A plague to all who sit on it." Although her voice had remained even and calm, she turned her head away for a moment before continuing, "Anyway, I wasn't going to mate with any-one weaker than me, Nil or magician. That includes you." Glancing away from him, she crooked her forefinger. The scroll in Kron's hand tugged at his grip like a fish on a line. He tried grasping it with both hands, but the pressed plant leaves seemed to exude grease. The scroll slipped away and sailed back to its mistress's hand.

Salth's eyelids lowered in satisfaction before she glared at him again. "You've wasted enough of my time. Go, and leave us alone!"

She didn't gesture, so Kron was unprepared as she transported him out of the room and dumped him into the river. Cursing, Kron leapt out before the tools and powders in his belt pouches were ruined. The cold water made his tunic cling uncomfortably. He'd never been good at cleaning with magic, so he had to brush off the mud by hand.

High-pitched laughter from overhead startled him. "That was funny. Do it again," Sal-thaath said as he floated down to Kron's eye level.

"No." The soft grass was cool, but the soil crumbled under Kron's feet; he'd lost a sandal. "Go find my other sandal, please."

"Please? What does that mean?"

Did Salth teach her child anything besides magic? "It's a nice way to ask someone to do something for you."

"Oh, I've never heard that before." Sal-thaath whistled, and Kron's sandal plopped next to him.

Kron wiped off both sandals on the grass, then picked the laces out of the leather soles. In bare feet, he trudged along the river until he found a few suitable pieces of driftwood. While it would have been easier to ask Sal-thaath to send him home, Kron preferred to leave using his own magic.

"What are you doing?" Sal-thaath asked as Kron lashed two branches together.

"Making a portal back to my workshop."

"Aren't you staying?"

"I can't." He had to decide what to tell Phebe about her chicken, then he had to warn the other residents of Vistichia to avoid any strange six-fingered boys they saw.

"That's all right. Mother never has much time for me either." Sal-thaath's shoulders drooped as he turned away.

Kron couldn't help but feel sorry for the child, unnatural or no. He had no one else for company besides a magic-obsessed mother. Kron searched through his sack until he pulled out a flat cloth ball. "Come here."

The boy backed up, passing through a stump without bumping into it. "Why?"

"I have something for you, but you have to grab it with both hands to key it to you."

Sal-thaath took the cloth and stared at it. "I feel magic in it. What does it do?"

"Drop it, and you'll find out." Kron grinned.

Sal-thaath dropped the ball on the ground, where it inflated and bounced up to him.

"It'll always come back to you now," Kron said. "Toss it to me."

Sal-thaath's throw was so far off Kron couldn't move to intercept the ball in time. It rolled into the river, but then it rolled back out, leaving a trail of mud as it returned to Sal-thaath. By the time he picked it up, the ball was dry and bouncy again.

Sal-thaath beamed. "Thanks, Kron!" He floated off, bouncing his ball.

With a sigh, remembering his boyhood in Delns, Kron finished tying the portal together. He willed it to open onto a hidden spot by the docks, crawled through, and collapsed it from the other side. No sense making it too easy for Sal-thaath to return to Vistichia.

CHAPTER THREE

An Apprentice?

The next day, instead of selling artifacts in the marketplace, Kron prepared more of them in his makeshift shelter. Rather than paying for a room at the inn, he'd twined sticks and boards together, then enchanted them to keep him safe, warm, and dry. While he needed to barter his wares for meals and a better place to sleep, not to mention passage to Delns, he wasn't ready to encounter Phebe in the marketplace. What should he tell her about Sal-thaath? She had no magic to keep him away. Even the city-king's magician wasn't powerful enough to control—or destroy—Sal-thaath. Kron certainly wasn't.

"Kron! Here you are!" Sal-thaath's voice made Kron drop his chisel. A heartbeat later, the boy appeared and squatted next to a pile of driftwood. "I've been searching all over the city for you! Is this a game?"

"A game? No. I'm making finders." Maybe if he talked to Sal-thaath and showed him interesting things, he could keep the boy from playing tricks on Phebe again—or Bella.

He showed Sal-thaath the finder: a finger-length ash arrow pinned to an oak base. A quartz crystal nestled in an indentation in the base.

Sal-thaath splayed his thumb and five fingers over the finder. He touched first the arrow, then the crystal. "There's no magic in here."

"I haven't put it in yet. Watch." Kron unpinned the arrow and took it in his left hand. He grasped the base in his right, then he moved his arms straight out to each side. He closed his eyes to focus his will. *The ash to seek and the oak to know. The ash to seek and the oak to know. The ash to seek...*

Kron's arms were trembling by the time the pieces of the finder grew warm. He plunged them into a bowl of water and held them there until the quartz glowed. He dried them off, then pinned them back together. "Now the arrow will always point to the nearest source of water, no matter who holds the finder." He gave the finder to Sal-thaath. "Go on, try it."

Sal-thaath floated around the shelter, testing the finder. No matter where it was, the ash arrow always pointed towards the bowl. "Double-clever!" he said as he dropped the finder on the ground. "This is a kind of magic Mother and I never used before!"

Kron smiled. It felt good to have another magician praise his work. And if he impressed Sal-thaath with his magic, maybe he could teach him some respect for others, even people without magic. Then he wouldn't have to worry about Phebe's temper and could visit Bella again.

"Sal-thaath, if you promise to be careful, you can stay and watch me make other magical instruments. You might even be able to help me."

"Could I! I promise; please let me stay." The boy's eyes shone with excitement. "This is more fun than catching birds in the forest."

And safer for the birds too. "All right, but remember not to hurt anything – or anyone. Now, let's start by sorting out the pieces to these finders you jumbled together."

For the next week, Sal-thaath visited Kron every day. Sometimes he stayed for only as long as it took for water to drop a level in the water clock, sometimes all day. Sal-thaath was always willing to do whatever Kron asked, whether it was to fetch wood or water or organize his materials. But instead of physically hauling the wood or water, he transported it from the closest source. "This is easier," he said when Kron tried to explain the value of physical labor. In return, Kron shared his meals with him, taught him how to make a few simple magical instruments, and listened to him chatter. Kron only sold his artifacts in the marketplace when Sal-thaath wasn't with him. Word had spread about what his finders could do, so he now sold a couple of artifacts each time he visited the marketplace. But instead of moving into the inn, Kron stayed in his shelter, not only to save for more supplies and passage to Delns, but to keep Sal-thaath away from other people as much as he could.

"You haven't told your mother you visit me, do you?" he asked Sal-thaath once.

The boy shrugged. "She's been very busy looking at the stars. That's all we talk about lately, besides magic."

Kron didn't know whether to be relieved that Salth didn't know about their association or sad for Sal-thaath that he didn't have other company.

One morning Sal-thaath arrived as Kron was gathering some of his finders and other magical tools into a sack. "Are you leaving?" he asked, his eyes shadowed with worry.

"Today's a market day. I'm going to trade these for supplies." Kron hesitated. Was Sal-thaath ready for the marketplace? He'd been very good with Kron; perhaps it was time to see how he behaved with ordinary people. He knelt and looked the boy in the eye. "You can come with me…if you promise to be the best you've ever been." He shook a finger in the boy's face. "No leaving my side, not for a heartbeat, no getting angry at people, and no using your magic. Do you think you can do that?"

Sal-thaath stuck out his lower lip, so Kron added, "And if you do, I'll buy you a sugared pastry afterwards."

"I'll be good! I'll be good! Of course," Sal-thaath said hopefully, "I'd be even better if I had the sugared pastry first."

Kron laughed. "After the market, not before. Now, help me decide which pieces to sell and which ones to keep."

The market was less than ten furlongs from Kron's shelter, in the town square. Kron chose a secluded, shaded spot next to a low stone wall. Customers would find him once the word spread, and he could keep a better eye on Sal-thaath in a quiet area. Together, they spread their wares on the dusty ground, then Kron boosted Sal-thaath to a seat on the wall. He sat next to him.

"Now what happens?" Sal-thaath asked.

"Now we wait for people to come talk to us," Kron replied.

He had been worried that Sal-thaath would find this part of the market boring, but for all the boy's spying, he didn't know much about towns. Obediently remaining on the wall while craning his neck in all directions, he asked about everything from the types of buildings surrounding them to the horses and donkeys pulling wagonloads of goods. Kron patiently answered each string of questions as best as he could before Sal-thaath found something else to distract him.

A few customers stopped by, more of them browsing than buying. Still, Kron managed to sell two finders before he spotted a pair of familiar faces: Phebe and Bella. Bella was just as pretty as before, her hair escaping from her head covering as if it knew life was too short to spend it under restraint. His heart beat faster at the sight, then sped up even more when Phebe frowned and turned sharply in his direction. Although he'd thought about visiting Bella, he didn't want to lead Sal-thaath to her house to cause more problems.

"So, magician," Phebe said as soon as she'd worked her way around the crowd, "you never came back to tell me who or what killed my chicken. I guess you never found him, did you?"

Sal-thaath giggled, but the women paid him no attention.

Instead of answering, Kron glanced at Bella to see if she was as upset with him as her sister was. She still smiled at him, but her lips trembled. What should he tell them? Should he pretend he'd been unsuccessful, or tell them about Sal-thaath? The boy would never learn if he was never corrected for his mistakes. He had to convince Sal-thaath to confess and apologize. It was too bad he hadn't thought to discuss this with Sal-thaath before coming to the market.

He drew Sal-thaath off. "Sal-thaath, do you remember using magic on a chicken and twisting its neck backward?"

The boy nodded.

"Well, that chicken belonged to that woman. It laid eggs for her, but your magic killed it. You should tell Dame Phebe you're sorry for hurting her chicken and that you won't do it again."

"Why would I say that?"

Kron stared at Sal-thaath for a few heartbeats, speechless. How could a child be so callous? "Aren't you sorry?"

"It was only a double-stupid chicken, Kron. It bothered me, and Mother always says I should try new things with my magic. Why should I be sorry that bird can't peck at me anymore?"

The women had advanced into Kron's space while he'd talked with the boy. Now Phebe gasped. "This boy...this boy killed my chicken? And you're sheltering him?"

Kron stepped between Sal-thaath and Bella, who stood there quietly, but with such sadness in her eyes Kron longed to comfort her. "Dame, I'm not sheltering him. I'm trying to teach him why what he did was wrong!"

"I don't care. You owe me for that chicken!" Phebe's face grew red as she shook a fist at him. "If you're his master, it's your fault—"

"My master!" Sal-thaath laughed scornfully. "Oh, Kron knows a few things I don't, but I'm much stronger than him. When I grow up, I'm going to be the double-strongest magician ever — Mother said so."

Phebe drew back, eyes wide. Sal-thaath wasn't done, though. "And when I'm a double-strong magician, all the Nils will do whatever I want." He approached her like a wolf stalking a deer. It should have been funny to see a grown woman frightened by a boy half her size, but it wasn't.

Kron eyed his stock, but finders and enhanced tools wouldn't stop Sal-thaath from using magic. All he could do was bluff. "That's enough, Sal-thaath," he said, grabbing at the boy's shoulder but missing. "Leave her alone."

Sal-thaath didn't even seem to hear him. He stared straight at Phebe, who didn't move despite the fear in her eyes. "What's the difference between a Nil and an animal?" Sal-thaath asked softly, almost to himself. "I don't know. Do you?"

Phebe shrank between one heartbeat and the next, her market-day dress collapsing around her. A russet chicken poked her head out of the neckline, clucking confusedly and cocking her head at Kron and Sal-thaath. Bella gasped.

"Sal-thaath! Change her back this heartbeat!" Furiously, Kron started to shake the boy, then stopped. His hands clutched air.

Sal-thaath was gone.

CHAPTER FOUR

Breaking the Spell

Kron made sure the door to Bella's house—actually, her sister and brother-in-law's house—was closed before opening the basket with Phebe. Still a chicken, she poked her head out, but then cowered inside.

"It's all right, Phebe. I'm here. I won't let anyone hurt you." Bella crooned a lullaby as she held her hands out, inviting her sister to hop into her embrace. When Phebe finally fluttered out of the basket to her sister, Bella turned to Kron. "Kron?" She spoke his name hesitantly. "Why didn't you do something to stop your apprentice?"

Kron sighed. "Sal-thaath isn't really my apprentice. I know his mother from the Magic Institute, and he likes to visit me because I pay him more attention than his own mother does."

"So, he learned how to change people into animals from his mother?"

"I think so." He didn't want to reveal Sal-thaath's origins to Bella unless he had to.

"But who's going to change her back?"

"I will." He smiled reassuringly at Bella. "Can you keep her calm while I prepare an artifact? It may take me a while to decide which materials to use and how to combine them." He felt in his pouches for supplies. "Actually, I may need to use some of your own things. My inventory is limited."

"Just do whatever you have to do to make Phebe herself again." Bella glanced at the water clock in the corner. "But hurry. Troge will be back soon for dinner. He'll be angry enough if the meal is late. I don't know how I'll explain what happened to his wife."

Kron examined the household furnishings, weighing what would make an effective artifact against what the family could spare. They were neither extremely poor nor extremely rich. The whitewashed walls were plain, but embroidered pillows and blankets covered the wood table and chairs. A few children's toys occupied one corner of the main room, while a couple of bronze pots, clay jars, and piles of dried food surrounded the fireplace. Bella mixed ground corn and a ladleful of water for flatcakes, shooing Phebe away as she pecked at seeds on the floor. All of these objects would have human associations for Phebe, but most of them were so ordinary they would be hard to enchant.

"Dama?" When Bella didn't look up, he said, "Bella? Does your sister have any jewelry?"

She wiped her hands on her dress. "A few necklaces of copper and beads. But she won't like it if they're ruined."

"A necklace would be perfect. And it should survive being enchanted and disenchanted."

Bella climbed to the upper level and returned a few heartbeats later with a necklace. Most of the beads were clay; only the center one, turquoise, was valuable. Kron wondered if Bella's family was really this poor or if she'd chosen one of her sister's least favorite necklaces on purpose. He hoped not, as something she loved would be more effective.

"Thank you. Now, may I have a few strands of your hair?" he asked. "Since you and Phebe are sisters, something from you will make the artifact stronger."

"Of course."

She didn't flinch as she yanked a few wandering strands out by their roots. She had to be very fond of her sister. Kron told himself to be more courteous to Phebe in the future—if his artifact worked.

He wrapped the hair around the necklace. He still needed something else. He could sense intuitively when his artifact wasn't complete, but he couldn't always tell what he needed to add. Perhaps a container to hold Phebe...no, he didn't have anything big enough to hold a human. A covering, maybe?

"Perhaps a blanket. Yes, a blanket sounds right. Something she made herself would be ideal."

"I know just the thing," Bella said. She climbed up the ladder again and returned with a wool blanket. "She made it for her wedding."

Kron laid the necklace and hair in the center of it, then stepped back, judging what else he needed to do to bind everything together. He found the spot where the necklace had been joined and broke it apart with a touch of his finger. Then he wove the string through the blanket and tied the beads into the fringes in random patterns to disrupt Sal-thaath's spell. He inspected the blanket a final time, adjusting beads and hair, infusing them with his will, until they crackled with magic. "Set her down in the center of the floor," he told Bella. While he was tempted to chant or gesture the way other magicians did, Bella would be more impressed by the swift recovery of her sister than by showmanship. So as soon as Bella stepped away, he dropped the blanket over Phebe.

The blanket didn't move, and she didn't make a sound. Was Phebe frozen in fright, or was this a stage in her transformation back to normal? Beside Kron, Bella watched the blanket. Kron couldn't resist a glance at her, even though he worried the artifact wouldn't break the spell—or have an unintended side effect.

"How long will it take to change her back?" Bella whispered.

"Any heartbeat now." *If it'll work at all.* Kron frowned, studying the artifact. It seemed complete to him. Maybe he needed to try something else with it, like rub Phebe with it. She probably wouldn't tolerate such indignity. Instead, Kron draped the blanket around her like it was a dress.

The blanket clung to the contours of her chicken body—and then she was changing, shedding feathers and growing taller. Bella shouted with delight, but Kron studied Phebe, looking for any residue of Sal-thaath's spell. As her beak changed into lips and her eyes became less beady, she turned her head from side to side as if searching for something. Her breathing became rapid. As soon as the change was finished, she dove under the table and curled up around herself, making clucking noises.

Bella squatted next to the table and reached out to her sister. "Phebe? It's over. You're human again."

She squawked.

Bella looked up at Kron with such worry his heart wrenched. "What's wrong with her?" she asked.

Kron brought out his magic-finder, but it didn't flicker when he held it next to Phebe. "It's not remnants of Sal-thaath's spell."

Phebe clucked again and crawled about as if searching for a place to hide.

"Phebe, you're safe, you're home." Bella tugged on her arm. "Troge will be home soon. Won't you help me with dinner?"

She pecked at the ground.

"It's like she thinks she's still a chicken, Kron," Bella said. "What should we do now?"

Why were humans so much more difficult to fix than artifacts? This wasn't his type of magic, and Kron knew he couldn't restore Phebe's mind on his own. That meant taking Phebe—and possibly her sister too—to the one place he'd never expected to go again.

He sighed. "We go to the Magic Institute."

CHAPTER FIVE

The Magic Institute

Kron left Bella to dress her sister and keep her calm while he prepared a portal to the Magic Institute in the courtyard behind the house. When she came out to ask if she should pack supplies for their trip, he shook his head.

"How long will it take?" she asked. "What do I tell her husband and her children?"

"The trip will be shorter than the time it takes me to put this together." Kron heaped more soil around the base of a pole. "But I have no idea how long we'll have to stay there. It depends on who's left at the Magic Institute."

"Is that where you're from?" Bella glanced back toward the house, but she didn't return to her sister.

"I grew up near the Northern Salt Waters. I used to repair my family's fishing net and boats so that they were better than new. After I survived twelve springs, a passing magician realized I was using magic. He persuaded me to leave my family and join him on his travels."

"And he took you to the Magic Institute so you could be trained?" Bella asked.

Kron frowned at the memories. "No. He kept me with him to make magical artifacts he passed off as his own. He barely gave me enough food to fuel both my body and my magic, and while he did teach me things I hadn't learned on my own, he usually delivered his knowledge with a slap."

"You poor man." Bella crept closer to him. "How did you get away?"

Kron had wished for her attention, not her pity. He sat up straighter, trying to make light of his years with Eldhid. "My so-called teacher met up with another magician as we sailed up the Chikasi River. They'd both studied at the Magic Institute together. The other magician, named Milas, knew Eldhid, the one I was working for, wasn't capable of making artifacts like mine. So one night after dinner, as they emptied a couple of jars of wine, Eldhid let slip to Milas that I was the one making the artifacts, not him."

Bella smiled. "And then Milas rescued you and took you to the Magic Institute so you could become a magician yourself?"

If only it had been that easy. "Close, but not quite. I'd overheard them talking about me, so I eavesdropped on them when I was supposed to be sleeping. When I heard Eldhid tell Milas about me, I hoped that he would take me away from Eldhid. But all Milas did was laugh and offer to swap me for the secret to making portals like the one we'll use. I realized then if I wanted to get away from Eldhid, I'd have to do it on my own. But I also knew I didn't want to spend the rest of my life repairing boats and nets. I wanted to learn more about magic, but I didn't know how to get to the Magic Institute. And from what I overheard, I knew neither magician would take me there, since then they would have to turn me over to the other magicians so I could be trained properly."

Kron got up to search for another suitable pole for the portal. Some loose branches were piled behind the henhouse, so he borrowed one.

"What did you do then?" Bella asked.

"I listened to Milas' instructions on how to make a portal, but I soon realized it would only take me to a place I knew well, not somewhere I'd never been before. All I knew from what I overheard was that the Magic Institute had the most powerful magic and magicians in the known world. If I could only figure out the direction with the strongest sense of magic, I could find my way there on my own." Kron took a deep breath. "That's when I created my first finder. Then, when they'd passed out from the wine, I stole some supplies, enchanted a cloak so no one would notice me, and ran away."

"How brave!" Bella said. "I've never even been out of Vistichia."

Kron, busy fusing the branches together, couldn't respond at first. He supposed it had been brave for an inexperienced youth to travel all the way up the Chikasi River on his own, but at the time he hadn't known how long the journey would take. He didn't want to relate to Bella everything he'd done on that trip either.

"Well, as soon as the portal is ready, you'll see the Magic Institute," he said. "It's not something many Nils—I mean, people without magic—get to see. Do you think Phebe will go through the portal on her own?"

Some of the excitement left Bella's eyes. "She won't even come out from under the table. I hope Troge and the boys don't see her like this. They won't believe what happened. I'm not sure they would have believed it even if they were there."

"I don't know how long we'll be gone," Kron said. "Travel will be quicker than anything you can imagine, but healing her mind may be difficult. If we're not here when Phebe's family returns, they won't know where she is. That could be a problem."

Bella chewed her lip for a moment before saying, "I guess we'd better wait for them, then. I'll finish supper."

Kron decided it would be better to finish charging the portal when they were ready to leave. Otherwise, stray animals—or children— might find themselves in the Magic Institute. He followed Bella inside. While she baked the flatcakes and fried slices of cured ham, Kron examined Phebe again. Still acting like a chicken, and still no sign magic was causing this. Maybe taking her to the Magic Institute wouldn't be helpful, but this wasn't something an herbalist or surgeon could cure. Besides, the fewer questions raised locally, the sooner he would be free to resume his journey.

Bella draped the blanket over the table, creating a shelter for her sister. She had just finished cooking the last flatcake when a heavily muscled, bearded man tromped in, followed by a pair of youths who were obviously his sons. All three of them dropped carpenters' tools by the door. "Phebe, is dinner ready?" the man asked. "We're starving. Bella? Where's your sister?" He turned his head toward Kron and merged his bushy eyebrows. "Who are you, and what are you doing in my house?"

Sweat trickled down Kron's back as if to point out how dry his mouth was. This man, though not much taller than him, possessed enough bulk to make two of him. "I'm...I'm Kron Evenhanded." His voice retained its normal pitch, but it wavered. "And I'm here..."

"Because Phebe isn't feeling well," Bella continued. "She needs a healer. He's going to help me take her to one."

"You mean Galia? Is Phebe with child again?"

"I don't think so. This is different. She needs another healer." Bella peered into a jug. "Troge, could you get more beer? We're out."

As soon as he left, Bella ducked under the table and grabbed Phebe. Kron copied her, and they pulled her out. "Mother?" one of the boys asked. "What were you doing under there?"

She clucked at them and tried to gather them under her arms.

Bella, pressing her lips together, gestured toward the courtyard. They had to haul Phebe there, as she didn't move no matter how much they coaxed her. Once they were outside, Kron left Bella to handle her sister while he activated the portal. He grabbed the supports, closed his eyes, and brought up the memory of the receiving area: a square with a fountain in the center surrounded by walls with a mosaic of the sun, moon, and stars. It was an image that was meant to be easy to remember, so magicians could always return. Not all of them used portals the way Kron did, but everyone who could transport themselves needed land-marks.

Once the fountain was visible through the portal—the bright sun in-dicating it was still mid-afternoon, not early evening—Kron stepped back. "This portal is too small for all of us to go through at once. Do you want me to go first, or are you willing to try it?"

Bella walked around to the other side of the portal without answering. Many people did that the first time they saw a portal, as if they had to see for themselves that the portal only worked from one approach. She bit her lip again when she returned. "I'm sorry, Kron, but could you please go first? I've never seen anything like this before."

How sweet she made his name sound. "Many people feel that way at first, Bella." Did she like it when he dared to use her name? "There's nothing to fear. It's just like walking through a door."

To prove it, he stepped through. Warm sunlight made him realize how cool Vistichia had been, and as he approached the fountain, the water shifted to pour over chimes, an alert that a magician had arrived. Kron turned back to see if Bella had followed him. She and Phebe were still on the other side of the portal. Bella stared at him with a curious look on her face, while Phebe pecked at the ground.

Kron approached the portal and extended his arm through, hoping it wouldn't startle her. "Come on, I'll help you through."

Taking a deep breath, Bella grabbed her sister with one hand and took Kron's with her other one. He guided her through first, then, before Phebe could struggle too much, helped Bella pull her into the courtyard. Once there, Phebe shook herself before continuing her hunt for food. Bella walked to a mosaic and traced the pattern of stones.

"Kron Evenhanded?" a familiar deep voice said from behind him. "I thought you were returning to your family. What brings you back here?"

Kron turned to see Pagli, one of his teachers, striding toward him, wearing the traditional lavender tunic over black wool leggings and boots. It had only been a few moons since Kron had left the Magic Institute, but Pagli's red braids had faded slightly, and his smile didn't match the rest of his serious expression.

"This dame here," he gestured at Phebe, "was the victim of a magic prank. I did what I could to reverse the spell, but she's still not acting like herself. I thought maybe Valadia or Utho might be better suited to help her."

Pagli hesitated for a few heartbeats before saying, "Neither of them are here, but I'll summon another healer to examine her." He gave Kron a heavy look. "In the meantime, you'll have to tell me more about what happened—and who did it."

He beckoned all three of them past the fountain into one of the Institute's private nooks. Bella had to urge her sister to sit on a stool next to a fireplace. Pagli poured a handful of a blue powder into his palm and tossed it into the fire, which flared for a heartbeat before returning to normal. Bella flinched, but Kron told her, "It's a way of passing a message through the chimneys. A novice will come here soon to find out what we want and who we need to see."

Pagli didn't bother to sit. "And while we wait, Kron, tell me what happened."

This was the moment Kron had been dreading. He had to tell Pagli about Salth and her son, but part of him wanted to protect the boy. It occurred to him that perhaps Pagli would blame him for not reporting Sal-thaath's existence sooner, or doing more to control him. While he didn't fear censure or loss of his gift, he didn't want his former teacher to think less of him.

"The tale would be easier to tell with a flagon of wine and some cheese," he said. "I've performed a lot of difficult magic today."

Pagli nodded slightly. "Have you come all the way from Delns?"

"No, I wasn't able to portal home, so I've had to sail down the Chikasi. I met these women in Vistichia while earning passage to Delns."

"And what have you seen?" Pagli asked. Unvoiced was the question, "How are the lands recovering from the recent spate of disasters?"

Kron shrugged. "Farmers farm and traders trade, though there's less of the latter these days, and more robbers. That's why I'd rather sail up to Delns than make the overland passage north to the strait."

Pagli glanced at Bella. "And what do you think of your city's king?" When she didn't speak, he added, "His ears don't stretch this far. You can speak freely."

She stared at the floor and whispered, "I want to sing, but not for him. He's cruel. Why can't you magicians do something about that?"

"Rulers? How do you change their nature?" Pagli threw up his hands. "Some things even magic can't fix, Dama."

"Well, someone should try." A fierce light gleamed in Bella's eyes. "If I had your magic, I would do something."

"Knowing what is the best thing to do is always harder than finding the power to do it." Pagli spoke with authority, as if he'd told this to many other magicians before.

A novice arrived with refreshment, followed in a few heartbeats by a woman in blue robes and a collection of crystals. "You summoned me, Pagli?" she asked.

He gestured at Phebe, who hadn't touched her bread or wine. "This one was enchanted in body and mind. Kron broke part of the spell, but apparently not all of it."

The healer asked Kron and Bella a few questions before taking one of her crystals and passing it in front of Phebe. She repeated the process with crystals in different colors before saying, "Fear is keeping her mind imprisoned, but I think I can soothe her." She looked at Bella. "Are you her sister? Will you come with me? I'll need your help."

Bella nodded and urged Phebe to follow the healer.

When they had left, Pagli said, "Now that the Nils are gone, you can tell me what really happened."

Bracing himself, Kron summarized how he'd first met the women, his encounters with Salth and Sal-thaath, and the disaster in the marketplace. "I don't know what disgusts me more," he said. "Salth's raising of the boy, or her insistence she can harvest magic from non-magicians."

"A harem-raised woman like Salth would have grown up wild herself," Pagli said "It wouldn't matter as long as the children were secluded. I'm sure spending time with you would only help Sal-thaath, Kron." Pagli leaned forward. "Anyway, I want to hear more about what she told you. What does she think is about to happen? Why is she watching the sky?"

"I don't know. She didn't give details."

"Could you find out and report back?"

Kron tensed. "Why? Do you think there's something to what she says?"

"I might not have thought so before, but if she's discovered a way to create a child with magic, she needs to be watched. Power on that level can only cause problems."

Kron wondered if that applied to the Magic Institute. Some magicians left the institute to serve kings—or to try to become rulers themselves. Many other magicians remained at the institute to teach or study magic, each one as independent as a cat. Even getting them to work together to build something like the Magic Institute required much persuasion. If they all banded together to work in concert, how much power could they wield, and what would they do with it? It was a question Kron didn't want to consider.

"Salth has always been one of those to study magic for magic's sake," he replied. "Even if there is some magical event about to occur, why would she change?"

Pagli shook his head. "Think, Kron. She's the mother of a half-magical being."

Kron's eyes widened. "So, this event—it could affect Sal-thaath?"

"It's possible."

Kron couldn't think while he was sitting, so he rose and paced the length of the alcove. A magical event could change Sal-thaath's power—or even his nature.

"I should probably tell her what Sal-thaath did, though I doubt she would care," he said.

"Excellent." Pagli studied his wine. "And then you can report back to me."

"Then what will you do?"

Pagli lowered his glass. "Obviously, Kron, it depends on what you tell me."

* * *

The water level in the jar dropped two holes before the healer returned with Bella and Phebe. Bella was smiling, and Phebe walked normally instead of hopping, so the healer must have been successful. If only Kron's effort had worked completely, so this trip wouldn't have been necessary and Bella would be grateful to him.

"Kron! She's better! Phebe's herself again!" Bella danced forward, face extended toward his. For a wild moment, he thought she might be bold enough to kiss him, but she pulled back before committing herself. "Thank you, thank you for all you've done for us!"

Phebe gave her sister a sharp look before giving Kron a tight smile. "Yes, Kron, thank you. I would like to go home now, though."

"I'll guide you back to the portal, Dame." Kron suddenly remembered Phebe's family might have found it. While he didn't think they would go through on their own, he hoped they hadn't destroyed it. He didn't know the courtyard well enough to make another portal directly to that location.

"I'm glad your mission here was successful, Kron," Pagli said. "And don't forget about what I said."

Kron led the women back to the portal. Before crossing through, Bella asked, "Kron, will we need to bring these magicians any goods in trade for their help?"

He shook his head. "No, that won't be necessary. I'll pay them back in information."

Which meant he had to return to Salth as soon as possible—tonight—whether she welcomed him or not.

CHAPTER SIX

A Midnight Visit

At Bella's insistence, Kron paused long enough to eat with Phebe and her family—a tasty meal, but one made uncomfortable by everyone staring at him and asking him questions about magic—before taking down the portal in the courtyard. Then he returned to his shelter and studied his collection of materials. Salth wasn't likely to be forthcoming with information, so he might learn more by studying her unobserved for a while before revealing himself—assuming she didn't detect him first. Maybe he should bring some protection along too in case she became hostile. Weaving cotton into his sandals ensured no one would hear his movements, and he already had a cloak enchanted to make him difficult to see. He renewed the spell on it, then, for good measure, swept a collection of nails, pottery shards, and other small items into a pouch, which he tied at his waist. If he needed to, he could enchant them into weapons or something else that was useful.

When Kron couldn't postpone his departure any longer, he created a secret portal to the spot where Sal-thaath had taken him. The sun had set, so it was difficult to make out landmarks, but the river's murmuring and silhouettes of trees helped to orient him. Kron crossed through the portal, then paused to consult his magic-finder. Traces of magic everywhere, most likely Sal-thaath's trail. He couldn't tell if Sal-thaath or his mother had set up magic wards to detect another magician—or any human, for that matter. It was safer to assume they had done so. Kron felt through the items he'd brought with him, enchanted a pottery shard to magically resemble a human, and threw it toward Salth's house. When nothing happened, he felt his way forward, then repeated the process. If he was going to trip a ward, better to let a shard do it. However, he made it to the threshold without incident. He backed off, then circled the house. Salth would undoubtedly have set up some protection or ward here. He tried to locate the ward with his magic-finder, but again he couldn't tease it out from Sal-thaath's own magic.

Kron scratched his chin as he thought about how to outwit the ward when he wasn't even sure what or where it was and what it would do. *Whatever artifact I use, it has to keep things exactly the same so the ward doesn't warn Salth or Sal-thaath. Perhaps a mirror would work, to reflect the magic back at the ward. Do I have any polished bronze or glass?* He searched his pouch by feel. Eventually he found a silver coin. Under his touch, the metal warmed, spreading out and softening, erasing the king's seal. He took the metal out of the pouch and let it expand until it formed a ring large enough to go around his waist. He slid it over his head and pushed it down until it fit snugly around his waist without hampering his movement. Taking a deep breath, Kron crept, a step at a time, up to Salth's door. When nothing happened, he pushed at the door. It was blocked on the other side, but Kron coaxed the bar to slide back and let him in.

The fires had been banked for the night, but light still glowed from Salth's study. Kron listened over his unnaturally loud heartbeats. Two sets of faint, regular breathing, one lighter than the other, answered him. He smiled; even Salth had to rest sometime.

Salth and her son slept on a pile of reeds next to the fireplace. Sal-thaath clung to her as if she was the only source of safety in the world. Kron had never seen her look so peaceful, and he watched the pair for a moment, wondering if Bella would be so tender to a child of their own someday, before remembering his mission.

The sight-enhancer was still aimed out of the window. Kron crossed the floor and peered through it. Stars beyond number revealed themselves to him. He blinked, about to look away and examine Salth's scrolls, when something else caught his eye. Beyond the stars was a golden haze, like a shower of sunshine in the middle of the night. Kron didn't spend much time using his sight-enhancers or viewing the night sky, so he wasn't sure if this was normal or not. But when he shifted the sight-enhancer to look at another group of stars, he didn't see the golden shimmer. Frowning, Kron returned the sight-enhancer to its previous position and unrolled the scroll Salth had been writing in. She'd first noticed the golden glow in the sky last moon. It had been so faint at first she'd thought it was a mistake, but every night, it grew a little stronger. She predicted that if it kept getting brighter, it would be visible without the sight-enhancer within a moon.

"As to what happens then," she wrote in her tightly cramped symbols, "no one can know for sure. But I suspect what we see is magic, or a source of magic, and if so, I mean to study it and use it for my own."

What for, Salth? What do you need so much power for? Do you want to lead the Magic Institute, or your own country? You don't even like being around other people!

Kron unrolled her scroll to see what else she'd written, but he bumped into the sight-enhancer and knocked it into the wall. Salth jerked in her sleep, then sat up. Panic filled Kron's belly with a storm, and he wrapped the cloak around himself. He must not have covered himself completely, for instead of settling back down to sleep, Salth blinked her eyes.

Maybe I can convince her this is just a dream. Kron felt in his pouch for something suitable for charming, but the clinking of his materials made her blink more rapidly.

"Kron? Are you real?" She extracted herself from Sal-thaath's grip. "What are you doing in my house in the middle of the night?"

Kron took a deep breath, trying to calm his inner storm. Maybe he could distract her. He did have another reason to be here besides spying. "It's Sal-thaath."

The boy stirred, but he didn't wake.

"What about him?" Her voice was sharp now; she was awake, but not hostile—yet. "He can't be hurt. He's never been hurt."

"He hurts others, Salth! He cast a spell on a woman earlier today, making her a chicken in mind and body. It took us two separate attempts to break his hold over her."

She grinned as she gazed at her son. "Yes, he has strong magic."

Kron slapped the table, making her inkpot jump. "Is strong magic all you care about? What about control? Sal-thaath is a menace. No child should have so much power. He has to be contained before he kills an entire city with a thought!"

"And here I thought you liked the boy." Salth trudged over to the farm part of her house and returned with a shallow bowl of a bitter-smelling drink. She drank half of it, stared at Kron for a few heartbeats, and slowly offered it to him. Coming from her, it was a generous gesture, but the unfamiliar beverage made him refuse.

"I've heard nothing but 'Kron says this' and 'Kron says that' for days," Salth continued.

He has been listening to me? Kron struggled to keep his surprise and delight from showing on his face. If that was the case, why hadn't Sal-thaath listened in the marketplace? Something was off here, like trying to assemble an artifact without some vital component. He'd have to talk to the boy later and try to figure out why he was acting like this.

"And while I do appreciate you keeping Sal-thaath company," Salth continued, "I don't want you teaching him things I don't agree with."

"Such as compassion and respect for other people?"

"People who will never be able to do what he can, people whose only purpose in life is to work for others greater than themselves and to make more servants?" She touched one of the tattoos on her cheek. "Such people die faster than flies, Kron. One of them isn't worth much. Only when you have many of them do they add up to something with value."

She sounded as if she was already a city-queen. If she really had been a ruler, some of the places Kron had traveled to would consider it blasphemy or treason to contradict her. Kron hadn't been born to a ruling family, or even a magic one. He'd spent much of his life with what Salth would call ordinary people and couldn't dismiss them so easily. But he knew he'd never convince Salth of that while she isolated herself in her house-palace.

"How many ordinary people have you met, Salth?" he asked. "If you walked through a marketplace, or sat in a tavern and listened to musicians and storytellers, you might see they have their own gifts too."

"I don't have time for that." She glanced sideways at the sight-enhancer. "I'm busy with a very important ... project."

The golden haze. Even if she's right that she can sip magic from the stars, is it worth trying? How could she control such power? And if she can, what would she do with it?

This was definitely something that Pagli would want to know about, but Kron couldn't wait to report back to him before doing something. If her project did involve the golden haze, then perhaps if he altered the enchantment in the sight-enhancer, she wouldn't be able to claim this magic from the stars. All he had to do was touch the instrument for a moment to make whatever she saw through there appear farther away than it was.

"Do you want me to check your sight-enhancer then, to make sure it's working properly?" His conscience stung him a bit, since he'd be ruining her equipment instead of repairing it, but Salth and her son didn't need more access to power.

Salth shook her head, then narrowed her eyes. "Perhaps you should first explain how you managed to enter my house uninvited."

It would be hard to veil his true intent from Salth now that she was fully awake. Kron tried anyway. "I told you before, Sal-thaath caused mischief in the market earlier, so I thought you needed to hear about it—"

"But how did you enter my house?"

For a moment he was tempted to say Sal-thaath had let him in, but he didn't want to see the boy punished unjustly. Kron raised his head proudly. "Maybe artifacts are more powerful than you realize."

"Really? Then why did you join the fishes last time?" Salth's eyes turned blood red, a trick that might have terrified someone unaccustomed to magic. "You're annoying me. I think it's time you joined the little people you're so fond of."

The air battered down on Kron as Salth attacked. He pushed back with all of his magic, drawing on skills he hadn't used since he left the Magic Institute. He had to do more here than defend himself; he also had to sabotage the sight-enhancer without letting Salth realize what he was doing. His body burned with pain as Salth shrank it several inches and he forced it back to its normal size.

Maybe I don't need to defend against this spell; I can use it. Kron reached into his pouch and grasped a chunk of porous stone. *Perfect.* As Salth's spell continued to work, he allowed its magic to flow through him into the stone. The stone absorbed most of it, then started to shrink itself. That alone was proof that Salth already controlled more magic than all the other magicians Kron knew.

When the stone was so tiny he could conceal it by pinching his fingers around it, Kron pulled it out of his pouch, along with a more-impressive but unpowered crystal. He raised it over his head with both hands, taking the opportunity to transfer the pebble to his other hand, closer to the sight-enhancer. "Prepare to feel your own spell, Salth!" His voice was higher-pitched than normal. He lunged forward, but he must have shrank more than he'd realized, for he fell short of the sight-enhancer. Kron clenched his hand into a fist so he wouldn't lose the pebble. Salth cowered for an instant before spreading her hands as wide as she could. Guessing she had cast a shield over herself, Kron didn't press his attack. Instead, he touched his hand to the sight-enhancer, allowing the pebble to melt inside. Then he turned and bolted out of the house, not stopping until he was winded. He staggered to a tree and leaned on it, panting. If Salth wanted to send another attack after him, now would be a good time to do it. When no fantastic animals or blasts of power erupted from her house, he backed away, keeping a magic-finder out in case she decided he was a threat after all.

He'd never thought of Salth as a threat before, even if she was too obsessed with power. But if she wanted to use it against others—that was another matter. As for the golden haze she found so fascinating, was that her own desire speaking, or the truth? How could she be so sure something so far away was so powerful, or that it would ever come within anyone's reach? This haze was too insubstantial to bother Pagli with. Kron had to focus on finding some way to make Salth and Salthaath leave others alone. He couldn't return to Delns knowing that Bella—and Vistichia—were at risk.

* * *

When Kron returned to Bella's house late the next morning to check on Phebe, he found himself greeted by a crowd of people so thick he had trouble pushing through them. As he attempted to maneuver around a bulky matron, she grabbed his arm. "I found him! It's the magician who turned Phebe back into a person!"

"I thought he'd turned her into a chicken," a man said. "Didn't the city-king's magician change her back?"

Kron gritted his teeth. He'd hoped they could avoid this kind of attention, but more people must have noticed them than he'd realized. Poor Phebe and Bella must be embarrassed by all the attention. Then he spotted a city guard blocking the entrance to the house. What if more people believed the man's story instead of the woman's? What if the official magician of Vistichia wanted Kron out of the city, or wanted to cause trouble? He wasn't equipped to make up more defensive artifacts on the spot. Maybe he could bluff his way through.

"Let me go," Kron said in his gruffest voice. "I need to check on Phebe."

"Check on her, or cast another curse on her?" another man asked.

"I never cast a curse on anyone!"

"Your boy did," the first man said, "and that's the same thing."

"He's not my boy, not my son or apprentice," Kron declared in his loudest voice. He scanned everywhere he could see, from the flat rooftops to the barrels of rainwater beneath the houses, searching for Sal-thaath. If he should appear now and hear him, it could be complete disaster for everyone here. But perhaps that could be a way to disperse the crowd.... "In fact, Sal-thaath is under no one's control. If I were you, I'd get away from here in case he returns. He might want to create more chickens...."

The woman holding his arm, shrieked, released him, and bumped into several people as she fled. Others copied her, and soon Kron was alone. Well, almost alone. The guard hadn't deserted his position, and a second man, tall, rail-thin, and ornately dressed and jeweled, stood next to him, scowling at Kron.

"We don't need more magicians in Vistichia," he said. "The king will tolerate none who oppose him."

Kron shrugged. "I'm not here to oppose him or do anything more than pay his fees with the artifacts I sell. I'm simply traveling home and need to earn passage back."

The man sniffed and stepped away from Bella's door. "Then see that you do so quickly, stranger."

Kron waited until the guard and the king's magician departed before knocking on the door. He had to wait for an agony of heartbeats before Bella finally opened it. Dark circles under her eyes showed she must have had trouble sleeping. Kron wished there was more he could do for her to ease her worries.

"Is everything all right?" he asked. "How's your sister? Nothing...else has happened, has it?"

"Not yet." She opened the door a little wider. "But she had poor dreams all night. No one slept well."

"But she's acting human now, isn't she? Do you want me to check her?"

"Troge won't like it. He thinks you changed her in the first place, even though I explained you were the one who changed her back." She glanced around. "His head's as thick as the wood he chops. Come on in, just for a few heartbeats. Phebe can't complain after all you did for her."

And Bella couldn't help her family. Kron slipped in to find Phebe huddled near the fireplace, grinding corn so furiously kernels flew everywhere. She started as Kron approached.

"Good morning to you, Dame. How are you today?"

She glanced everywhere before replying, "He's not with you, is he?"

"Sal—the boy?" Kron didn't want to say Sal-thaath's name out loud in case the child was listening in magically. "No, I haven't seen him since the marketplace yesterday. He comes and goes as he pleases. I can't stop him."

"But you must, Kron!" Bella said. "What if he comes back? What if he does something worse next time?"

"That's what I want to prevent." He sighed. "I'll talk to the boy— once I find him."

Phebe looked up from her grinding to glare at him. "Just talk to him, magician? Can't you do more than that?"

"Dame, he's just a boy. A very powerful boy, but not taught properly. If I can correct him—"

"Boys do need a firm hand," Phebe said. "I could never get my sons to listen to me half as well as Troge does."

Bella frowned. "That's because he beats them senseless."

"Wait until you have your own, Bella. Then you'll understand how hard it is to keep them out of trouble. Speaking of trouble, magician, you should leave before more of it follows you." Phebe finally looked at him. Her expression still wasn't welcoming compared to her sister's, but the hostility had melted away. "And ... for your trouble before...I thank you. You're welcome to stop by any time my husband's working for a quick meal."

Bella's expression brightened, as if she was being rewarded too.

"Show him out, sister, before more gossips stop by. There's much work to be done to make up for yesterday."

Bella pressed a cooked flatcake filled with pickled vegetables into his hand as she led him to the door. "She is grateful to you, even if she doesn't show it," she whispered. "She's just fearful of saying too much."

"She has reason to be frightened of Sal-thaath," he replied. "His mother has no respect for anyone who can't perform magic, and I'm afraid he feels the same way. If you see him, try to make sure he doesn't see you."

"What will you do if you can't change him?" she asked.

Kron gazed at her face for a few heartbeats before replying, "Then I'll have to find some way to keep you, your family, and everyone else safe from him."

She smiled at that, but when he reached for her hand, she ducked away and closed the door. He tried not to take her rejection personally. Of course a maiden would avoid contact with a strange man. But they shouldn't be strangers to each other by now, should they? What would it take to make her more comfortable with him, a betrothal? Would she be willing to leave her family behind and come to Delns with him?

Bemused, Kron shook his head. He needed to avoid crowds until people forgot about him, so he headed for the city gates. If he wandered by the banks of the Chikasi River, he would find materials, like branches, stones, and various items dropped from boats, he could use later in artifacts. And if Sal-thaath sought him out—though Kron suspected he might have to hunt for the child this time—no one would be around to suffer another of his spells.

Kron passed fishermen and washerwomen standing on the rocky banks of the river. Other people gathered driftwood or birds' eggs. The sun was close to the zenith by the time he found a small curve in the river, obscured by willow trees, where he was certain he was the only other person within shouting distance. Using an enchanted thread from his tunic, Kron lured in a pair of fish for lunch. He cleaned them, stuffed them with wild herbs, and set them on a thin flat rock over a fire to roast.

While the meal cooked, he found a few snail shells and feathers that might be useful. Kron braided a grass rope, but he knew no matter how much enchantment he poured into it, it wouldn't last a heartbeat against Sal-thaath's magic. He'd studied magic for nearly twenty years, and a child young enough to be his own easily mastered him. Kron let the rope fall apart. Toys weren't the way to make Sal-thaath treat others with respect, and threats would be useless, since both of them knew Kron wasn't powerful enough to take action against Sal-thaath. What else could he do?

"I'm hungry," Sal-thaath said from behind him. "When do we eat?"

"How did you know I was expecting you for lunch?" Kron asked.

"I was watching you, and you caught two fish."

"Can't you feed yourself with your magic?"

"I like it better when someone else cooks. Sometimes I take sweet bread or fruit tarts from a baker. Or sometimes when Mother is busy studying, I bring her back a meat pie."

No need to ask if the boy paid for the food. Kron simply nodded and prodded one of the fish with a stick. "They're done. Help yourself."

Sal-thaath reached out with his bare hands for the closest fish, yelped, and snatched up a pair of sticks to hold his meal. Kron claimed the second fish before the boy ate both. He was definitely hungry; maybe Kron could use that to reach him.

"Does your mother ever cook?" he asked.

"She never learned how. She said when she was growing up, they had servants and slaves to cook and make their clothes."

"She's the daughter of a city-king, isn't she?"

Sal-thaath shifted as if the ground had become uncomfortable. "Mother says she'd rather be on her own, owing nothing to anyone, than be a city-queen."

"But people need each other," Kron said. "How can you grow crops and build a house and cook your meals and weave cloth all by yourself?"

"With magic, of course."

"But someone had to figure out how to do those things without magic first before magician could create spells and artifacts to warm food or keep it from spoiling. And what would you do if your spell failed?"

Sal-thaath glared contemptuously at him as though he were the teacher and Kron the student about to be forced out of the Magic Institute. "Magic doesn't fail any more than the sun does, or the rivers. In fact, Mother says soon we'll have a brand new source of magic to draw on."

"The golden haze in the sky?" Kron asked.

Surprise broke out on Sal-thaath's face. "How did you know about that? You must be more double-clever than Mother says you are."

"I did create the sight-enhancer she's using."

Sal-thaath frowned. "But it broke. Maybe you should come fix it. Then Mother would respect you, and you could live with us forever."

"But I don't want to." At Sal-thaath's stricken expression, Kron quickly added, "I mean, I like your company, Sal-thaath, but I need to return home to Delns and visit my family. It's been a long time since I've seen them, and I don't know how they're faring."

"Why don't you portal to them?"

"I can't. My home has changed out of my memory—"

"You could find a way to do it, if you really wanted to." Sal-thaath's voice rose from its childish treble to a grating pitch. "But you don't. You like that pretty woman who lives with the chicken dame."

Kron gaped at the child. "How...how did you know?"

Sal-thaath grinned. Was it remnants of his meal stuck in his mouth, or did he have pointed teeth? "I go everywhere and see everything, Kron Evenhanded. I could portal you to your country if you wanted me to."

Delns! The smell of the sea, the cold breezes in the morning, the taste of his mother's flatcakes, unlike any he'd found no matter where Kron traveled. Longing flowed through him for a tide of heartbeats. Perhaps he should accept the boy's offer. He could always portal back to Vistichia afterwards to make sure Phebe and Bella were well...but did he dare leave them alone that long?

How well could he trust Sal-thaath? Would the boy even keep his word, or would he find a way to harm Kron? He couldn't leave Vistichia vulnerable to the child; the king's magician had no idea what Sal-thaath was capable of.

Kron shook his head. "I still have business in Vistichia."

Sal-thaath glared at the fire, which shot up as tall as a full-grown man. Kron scooped a handful of water out of the river, but the flame died down before he could quench it.

"I still have business in Vistichia too." The menace in Sal-thaath's tone belied the softness of his face. "Farewell, Kron. I'll see you there—soon."

Sal-thaath disappeared as silently as he'd arrived.

Kron moved like an ancient man as he put out the fire and tossed the leftovers of the meal into the river. He should have known he couldn't get a child, no matter how magical, to listen to him. Maybe he should have lectured Sal-thaath more about the harm he was doing, but the boy would have disappeared the heartbeat Kron raised his voice.

He's too powerful. I can't do anything with him like this. I can store magic in artifacts, but that will never bring me up to his level. He needs to have his magic neutralized for a while, long enough for him to understand what it's like to have no magic. It wouldn't have to be a long time, maybe less than a day.

Kron looked up at the sky, as bright blue as ever. It had to be his imagination that the blue was a little lighter, a touch more yellow, than it normally was this time of day.

However I do it, I'll have to do it soon. If Salth is right and she can harvest magic from the golden haze, then she and Sal-thaath will control more magic than a dozen Magic Institutes put together.

But what could absorb all of that magic?

Kron stared at the river flowing past him until the sunset turned the sky pure gold. He portaled home, still without an answer.

* * *

Kron spent the next several days wandering through Vistichia, collecting every discarded item he could find, then taking them back to his room at the inn—while he loathed the expense, sleeping in a rough shelter grew less appealing when the nights became colder—and enchanting them until he ran out of energy and collapsed onto his pallet. But it was a futile effort. No single item was strong enough to siphon off a tenth of Sal-thaath's magic, and his artifacts were too varied to mesh well.

Desperate, Kron portaled to the Magic Institute for another meeting with Pagli. He held nothing back, not even Salth's speculations about the golden haze. At that, Pagli shook his head.

"Magic in the sky? What a strange notion, especially since everyone knows it comes from living things. While I have noticed the sky is more yellow these days, it's probably due to something we don't understand yet."

Kron discreetly checked to see how much Pagli had watered his wine. Perhaps he added one drop of water to every bowl. "Then it could be anything, Pagli."

"Or nothing at all." He waved his hand. "Anyway, it's too far away for any of us to feel, so we don't need to worry about it."

"What about Sal-thaath? I still have to worry about him. How do I contain his magic?"

"You can't, Kron." Pagli became serious. "Be grateful he's leaving you and your friends alone."

Kron couldn't be grateful. Sal-thaath was too intelligent to forget about Phebe and Bella, let alone Kron. If he was ignoring them, it was only temporary, while he was distracted by something else, perhaps something in the sky.

"Do you have any new materials I can experiment with?" he asked as he rose to leave. "My selection in Vistichia is limited, despite the trade."

"I have a pair of attracting stones, though they don't always work. Sometimes they repel each other. You can have them if you fix the fountain in the courtyard. Its aim is off."

Kron agreed. The fountain was easily fixed—something had clogged one of the nozzles—and soon he found himself in possession of two chunks of black rock. He played with them after returning to Vistichia and discovered they could attract or repel each other depending on how they were oriented. He marked the sides so he would know how to hold the stones. That was minimal work, barely enough to turn natural materials into artifacts. He would have to shape them more in the morning. Between the lack of sleep and the magic he'd poured into his failed artifacts, Kron was too weary to let the music and talk in the inn's common room keep him up. He barely remembered to hide his new stones in his enchanted pouch before falling asleep.

* * *

Kron roused as someone shook his shoulder. "Kron, Kron, wake up!"

Still weary, he opened his eyes. Phebe, her husband Troge, and several others surrounded him. Their angry expressions sent him reeling backward. "What's going on?"

"Where's your apprentice?" Troge asked. He shifted benches and chairs as if he thought Sal-thaath was hiding under one of them.

"Sal-thaath?" It took him a few heartbeats to make the connection; when he did, a flood of anxiety reenergized him. "What has he done now?"

"He took Bella!" Phebe said between sobs. "We were mending clothes when he appeared in our house. I didn't even hear the door open. Before I knew it, he put his arms around Bella, and they both disappeared, like they'd become air." She looked pleadingly at Kron. "Do you think he's going to change her into a chicken too?"

No. Whatever he has planned for her, it'll be something worse. He couldn't say that out loud, though, as that would only send Phebe into further hysterics.

"When did it happen?" Kron asked. The common room was brighter than it'd been when he went to sleep, but the light didn't seem as clear as morning sunshine. How long had he slept, and how close was it to nightfall?

"It was after the noon meal. We looked for you in the marketplace, but we couldn't find you." Some sharpness returned to Phebe's tone, as if she couldn't understand that someone who worked when others slept would have to sleep when everyone else was awake. "It's close to sunset now."

"Kron? Do you know where they are?" An edge in Troge's voice warned Kron he'd better give them an answer they wanted to hear.

"Yes, I do. But I'll need to portal there." Normally he wouldn't portal indoors, but it sounded as if he'd already lost too much time. He needed to improvise a portal from whatever he could find in this room. Kron whipped his cloak into the air. Before it could fall to the floor, he touched it, freezing into half an arc. Phebe gasped. He completed the rest of it with a remnant of wool thread. The portal was so narrow he'd have to suck in his breath to pass through, which meant he'd be limited in the supplies he could carry. At least his small pouch wouldn't be a burden.

Kron took a bottle of a restorative from his pouch. The potion smelled like lemons and tasted a little like chalk, but drinking it restored him to full magical reserves—still pitifully small compared to what Salth and Sal-thaath controlled. "I'm sorry, but none of you are powerful enough to deal with the boy or his mother. Don't follow me through the portal. I'll return with Bella as soon as I can." He hesitated as he faced the hope and fear in their eyes. "If I don't return, you'd better flee the city."

"But why—"

Kron didn't respond as he collected beads, pieces of string, and a few splinters of wood. He wasn't sure what he could do with them, but perhaps he could use them as distractions.

He touched his stiff cloak and closed his eyes. Focusing on every detail he could remember of Salth's room—every book cover, every cobweb—he forced his will past all of her protections. Then he dove through the portal.

CHAPTER SEVEN

The Golden Haze

Magic was thick in the air, aiding him as much as it strengthened Salth's spell. For a moment, Kron thought he'd be caught in some space between the portal and Salth's house, and the fear made him push through with all of his might. He landed roughly on Salth's marble floor, scraping his skin and shredding his tunic in a score of places.

"Kron! You're always interrupting me!" Salth shouted.

He pushed himself to his knees, then to his feet. Shimmering golden light obscured the objects in the room. Kron waved his hand in front of his face to clear the light away. Bella had been laid on Salth's table as if for her funeral. Her chest heaved up and down, but otherwise she didn't move. Kron sensed two spells at work: a spell to paralyze her and another one encapsulating her like a cocoon.

"I knew you'd come if I brought this Nil, Kron!" Sal-thaath appeared next to him, eyes bright with excitement. "Mother says if we kill a Nil, we get more magic from its soul than if it dies naturally. We can then bring the magic of the stars down to us. Are you here to watch? I think you'd have to be very, very nice to Mother if you want some of our magic. She's very angry with you."

When Sal-thaath finally ran out of words, Kron said, "You shouldn't kill Bella or any other person without magic, Sal-thaath." To his mother, he said, "Let her go, Salth. What do you need magic from the sky for, anyway? You're already the most powerful magician I know!" He fingered the items in his pouch, searching for anything that could break Salth's spells on Bella.

"You can never have too much power. Power protects you." She tapped the cocoon-like spell with a finger, then folded her arms and glanced at Sal-thaath. "It's almost time. Sal-thaath, be a dear and kill this woman for me so I can take the magic from her soul. You can do it any way you like."

"Sal-thaath, no!" Kron shouted. The pair of magnets grew warm in his hand, and he clenched them as if they were his only hope. "You didn't like it when I caught you with my thread; think how she must feel!"

Sal-thaath glanced back and forth between Kron and Salth. Except for their breaths, the room was silent. Then Sal-thaath drifted closer to the cocoon. "Aw, I could've broken free of you anytime I wanted, Kron," he said. "I just stayed cause I've never met another magician before. But you're as dull as a Nil, always telling me I can't do this or that. And Mother says Nils are like animals anyway, so it doesn't matter what we do to them."

No child should be this callous. Maybe if Kron could permanently separate him from Salth and send him to the Magic Institute, Pagli and the other instructors could teach him empathy. But for that to happen, Sal-thaath's magic had to be drained off enough so he couldn't portal away. The magnets might be able to do it, but Kron needed more time to shape them into an artifact.

"Pagli doesn't believe the golden haze in the sky is magical, or that you or anyone can bring such magic down to Earth." Kron rubbed one of the magnets, willing it to attach itself to Sal-thaath and stay there no matter what he did. *Cling to his very nature, his essence. The more he tries to rid himself of you, the more secure you'll be.* "And he won't approve of you kidnapping an ordinary person to fuel your own magic. He'll punish you even if it takes the entire Magic Institute to do it."

She laughed. "Then when I'm done here, I'll have to pay him a visit, won't I? The Magic Institute always tries to restrict magic, not free it. That's why you're limited to working through your artifacts. Deep down, you're afraid of handling magic directly. And that's why you'll never be able to do this."

She crossed her fingers as she glared at him. Kron felt his tunic and trousers tighten around his limbs, but after a couple of heartbeats, his clothing loosed as they neutralized the magic she'd thrown at him.

Kron grinned at Salth. "Sometimes I don't need to wield magic on the spot." Maybe that would confuse her enough to let him enchant the second magnet.

She narrowed her eyes. "Pre-set spells won't protect you against everything."

The air in front of him thinned so much he could no longer breathe. Kron fought down his panic and grasped the other magnet in his pouch. *Feed what your mate takes from Sal-thaath into...into the ground!* The ground had to be immense enough to absorb the magic of one small child, no matter how powerful he was.

"Mother, what are you doing to him?" Sal-thaath asked.

"Taking away the air he needs. He should pass out soon. Then we can use his power to help us capture the magic of the golden haze."

Kron obligingly collapsed, making sure he fell next to Sal-thaath. How would the child react to his mother's plan? Would he object? They were supposed to be friends....

"That's a good idea," Sal-thaath said. "He always wanted me to do things I didn't want to anyway."

Even though Kron had expected the betrayal on some level, it hurt more than he'd expected. He didn't dare speak or react, but he squeezed his eyelids tightly, trying to hold his rage and grief inside. Maybe this child was unreachable. If so, draining his magic was the best thing Kron could do.

Salth grumbled. "The magic in Kron's clothes won't let me lift him magically. You'll have to help me."

"I'll grab his arms," Sal-thaath said.

Perfect.

Kron continued to lie still and fight off his growing dizziness until Sal-thaath grabbed him under the armpits. His hand was still inside his pouch, so he opened it, allowing a passageway for the first magnet to fly out and attach itself to the boy's forehead. Kron's pouch ripped, spilling everything as the second magnet broke a hole in the floor and disappeared.

He roused himself enough to say, "This is for your own good, Sal-thaath. "

Sal-thaath screamed and fell to the floor, landing on his side. The cloth ball Kron had given him escaped from his tunic and rolled into a corner. The boy didn't appear to be hurt at first, but then his face aged until he appeared older than Kron's grandfather. His body withered, his hair fell off, and his skin darkened. Kron stared in horror. This wasn't supposed to be a side effect of his artifact. The swollen magnet emitted a mosquito-like whine as it turned red. Sal-thaath drowned out the whine as he howled. He rolled from side to side and pulled at the magnet with all twelve digits.

"What did you do to him?" Salth screamed.

Kron gasped for air. "I just neutralized his magic."

"You fool! He *is* magic! You're killing him!"

Sal-thaath shifted back to normal, then aged again. What did growing old have to do with his magical legacy? Kron would have liked to question Salth about that, but there wasn't time. He'd created the enchantment; he should be able to banish it. But as Kron reached for the artifact on the boy's head, it pushed his hand away. *What? This shouldn't be possible.* Kron tried to mentally pull the magnet off of Sal-thaath. Again it didn't respond.

"Salth, a magnet, a crystal, anything else I can use on that artifact?" He felt around in his pouch but found only the hole made by the other magnet. "I can't touch it directly."

Sal-thaath's convulsions ceased.

Salth was instantly at Sal-thaath's side. "Get it off of him!" She reached for the magnet and scowled as her hand stopped before she could grab it. Her arm trembled as she pushed forward, but it didn't budge.

Sal-thaath opened yellowed eyes. Some remote part of Kron's mind noted the child now had only five fingers on his hand.

"I…I hurt, Kron," Sal-thaath whispered. "Why did you hurt me?"

"I never wanted to hurt you, Sal-thaath. I just wanted you to be someone I could be proud of. "

A final breath left the boy's mouth, then he fell still. The magnet dropped off.

Salth keened as she picked up the body of her son. "There must be a way to undo death!"

Kron numbly reached for the magnet, so warm he could feel its heat a foot above it. Sal-thaath had been malicious, but he hadn't deserved to die in pain and confusion.

"Sal-thaath, my son, forgive me," he whispered.

Salth's keens stopped. "Your son? He's my son, all mine! I'll take your life for his!"

She dove at him, but Kron gripped her arms and kept her from clutching his throat. Her eyes glowed, and she whispered a few syllables in a language he didn't recognize. Air fled from his lungs and out of his mouth. When he tried to breathe, nothing entered his nose.

What did she do? How did she bypass my protections? Panic made it hard for Kron to think of a way to counter whatever spell Salth had managed to work on him. Perhaps she would succeed in killing him and sending him to the next world. Would Sal-thaath be there, or would his unnatural origins mean he lacked a soul?

The light in the room grew brighter. A sign of his approaching death, or something else? Salth seemed to notice the light too, and she let her attention slip from Kron long enough for him to let him put his hand to his throat. Salth's spell weakened enough for him to gulp in a mouthful of air.

"I knew it!" Salth turned her face upward and raised her hands as if she meant to grab something sent from the heavens. Light collected around her. "But you're too late. Is this enough magic to turn back time…time…time…?"

She knelt and draped herself over her son's body, covering him completely. More light gathered around her until it seemed to form a shell over Salth and Sal-thaath.

What is she doing? Kron found himself able to breathe normally again. However, he'd attracted a few particles of light. Fearful they would harden around him too, he tried to swat them away. His hands passed through them—or did they pass into him? If they did, they were more intoxicating than the finest wine. His head buzzed with ideas for artifacts more complicated than anything he'd ever made. If he were back at the Magic Institute or even Vistichia, he could spend all day contemplating these ideas. But he needed to rescue Bella and portal away while Salth was distracted—or disabled.

Kron retrieved the magnet and used it to remove both spells on Bella. The greedy artifact reached out for the golden light next. *Enough of this.* Kron attempted to deactivate the spell he'd placed on the magnet, but it proved harder to disrupt than he expected. He had to reach out for the rest of the golden magic to disable the magnet. Despite the difficult task, his own internal store of magic seemed replenished. Strange, but useful.

Come with us, Artificer, a strange voice whispered in his head. *Come with us to See the Unseeable.*

Not now! I have to rescue Bella.

The voice didn't respond.

Bella blinked and moved her head from side to side, as if searching to see where Salth and Sal-thaath were.

"We're safe for now," Kron whispered, "but we need to leave quickly. Can you stand?"

She nodded, and he helped her to her feet. She clung to him tightly, but he didn't mind. No matter what Sal-thaath, Salth, or any other magician thought about Nils, he had saved someone precious.

Some of Kron's guilt and grief for Sal-thaath faded. He had protected those who needed him. And he'd do it again if he had to.

Holding Bella close to protect her from the cold, Kron pushed again though the portal to Vistichia.

Part Two: The Avatars

CHAPTER EIGHT

Pagli

Once again, Kron sat in the marketplace at the end of the day by himself, but that was because Bella had gone off to barter her duck eggs for a shawl. He only had a few unsold items to pack, so while he waited for Bella and any final customers, he set a ward on his selling space and crossed to the other side of the square. The woman who brewed and sold beer smiled at him as she strained it into a drinking bowl.

"You're lucky I have anything left," she told him. "It's been a busy day for me too. Thanks to the God of Summer, though, my hops and barley are growing splendidly. I can hardly wait to harvest them so I can brew my best batch ever."

Kron sipped his beer. "This is already good. But what do you mean by the God of Summer?"

She laughed, not unkindly. "You don't pay any attention to anything other than your lovely young wife and your artifacts, do you? You should come over here and gossip more often, so you can learn what's going on in Vistichia."

"I'm not that isolated. I see how everyone is happier now that the old city-king is gone. The council takes less tribute from everyone, so people have more to barter with." Kron swallowed some more beer. "It's good for all of us."

Crows-feet crinkled in the corners of her eyes. "Do you know why they reduced the tribute?"

Kron shook his head.

"The Four appeared to the Council and demanded it."

He handed the bowl back to her. "Who are the Four?"

"I thought you might know, seeing as They can do magic. They might even be stronger than you."

It was a good thing he'd finished his drink, or he'd have spat it out in surprise. "They are? Who are they, and where do they come from?"

"That's the thing. No one knows. No one even heard of them until last moon. But then, They're gods and goddesses, not humans, so I suppose They came from somewhere beyond this world." She gestured toward her jar of beer. "More?"

"No, I'd better stop. What do you mean, they're gods and goddesses? How do you know they're not just powerful magicians?" Kron spread his hands. "My teachers at the Magic Institute said until we could figure out the limits of human magic, we would never be able to tell where magicians left off and gods began."

"They can do miracles, Kron. Oh, I know your finders and other artifacts are marvelous, but you can't make seeds sprout and bloom in an instant, can you?"

"My magic works best on manmade things—"

She continued as if he hadn't spoken. "And the God of Summer certainly doesn't look like a normal person, what with His green skin and all."

Kron felt like he might turn green himself, but with worry, not envy. How had he not noticed the presence of such powerful magicians sooner? What did they want here? Was Bella safe?

His ward pealed an alarm as a familiar but unexpected voice called out, "Kron Evenhanded, what are you doing here? I thought you'd be in Delns by now!"

Kron turned. Pagli waited at the boundary of his space as if he came to the marketplace in Vistichia all the time.

"Pagli!" Here was one magician he didn't have to worry about. He crossed the square to greet his friend. "What are you doing here? I didn't even know you knew this city well enough to portal over! How long are you staying? You have to come to my house and have dinner with us! My wife—" Kron still enjoyed being able to say that—"bakes a fine flatbread!"

"I'd love to." Pagli glanced at the artifacts set out on a blanket—and sniffed. Illness, or contempt? He'd never disdained Kron's magic before. "Though with your magic, I'd have thought you'd be living in the palace complex by now, serving the city-king."

"You know I never sought to serve power. Common people need my talents too."

The air stirred at Kron's words. His magic-finder, which had started glowing with Pagli's arrival, flared, then cracked.

"I need you too." Pagli reached under his cloak. "I found an artifact unlike anything I've ever seen. Could you identify it for me?"

"Of course. Where did you find it?"

"Someone dropped it off at the Magic Institute."

"Dropped it off? They didn't want to trade something for it?"

"Oh, of course they did." Pagli spoke quickly. "First they asked for healing. Then they wanted a love potion, even though I told them no one actually made such things. Then they asked for a gold nugget the size of your thumb. I finally gave them that to get rid of them."

Kron raised his eyebrows. This wasn't how Pagli usually spoke. What kind of artifact could excite—or upset—him so much? "Show me this valuable artifact then."

Pagli stepped forward with a smile that didn't reach his eyes. He smelled as if he hadn't bathed in days. "Come, take it and find out."

He pulled out a small, black sundial and thrust it at Kron. Hostile magic roiled off the object strongly enough to make him step back.

"I'm not touching that." How could Pagli handle that safely? Kron would have to sacrifice a square of silk from Kin to neutralize the sundial's magic. Thankfully, Bella hadn't returned yet, so he didn't have to worry about her getting hurt by the sundial. Yet, Pagli, who wasn't an artificer, seemed unaffected.

"Why not?" Another step forward by Pagli. A few passersby stopped to see what was going on. "Think your magic isn't strong enough to master this artifact?"

Anger surged within him, but caution restrained him from blurting out a response. Pagli had never been to Vistichia before, wouldn't know how to find Kron so easily, and wouldn't treat him like a foolish novice. What if this wasn't Pagli, but someone pretending to be him? How could Kron tell for sure? His magic-finders would only get confused by the sundial. What Kron needed was a way to see through the magic to the truth beneath.

He glanced at the unsold artifacts, trying to determine what could be used as it was or if he could modify something quickly. Too bad he didn't have the far-seer he'd made for Salth. Only a couple of magic-finders today; most of his items were things ordinary people would find practical: bowls and jars enchanted to keep food fresh and pest-free, tools that wouldn't break, and even a few toys that could move on their own. None of those would help him. His most ingenious creation, a carved bird that could fly, was back at the workshop. He could summon it to bring him something small, but nothing useful came to mind.

Kron kept eye contact with Pagli—or whoever was pretending to be Pagli—and said, putting as much scorn into his words as he could manage, "What, this thing? This is nothing next to all the traps I set on the tomb of that queen three years ago. Do you remember?" At the same time, Kron searched in his pouch for something, anything, he could enchant. His fingers touched the rough edge of a broken chain link, discarded as useless. All it was now was a hole surrounded by metal. But maybe a hole wasn't useless….

"The queen's tomb. Ah yes, I remember. There was a pit trap at the entrance, right?"

"No, Pagli." Kron willed true vision into the chain link. "There was no pit trap, or queen, or tomb. But the real Pagli would know that. So, by my true love's eyes, who are you?"

He drew the chain link out of the pouch and held it up to his right eye. Kron closed his left eye and peered through the link. Pagli's image wavered for a couple of heartbeats, but it didn't disappear. Instead, his skin took on a waxy sheen, his eyes developed a glazed-over look, and his body odor became more prominent—and more rotten.

Kron dropped the chain link in horror. This was the real Pagli, but he was dead. How could he still be moving and talking? Had Pagli's ghost come back to wreak revenge on Kron for some forgotten crime, or was somebody abusing his corpse?

"Get away from me, abomination!" Kron grabbed a bowl and altered its enchantment to create a fuelless fire in the bowl. It wouldn't last for long, but it would destroy poor Pagli's body and hopefully bring peace to his spirit.

Pagli—or whatever force was animating his body—hissed, then threw the cursed sundial at Kron. It happened so quickly he didn't have time to dodge, only attempt to catch it in the bowl. The flame leapt higher to consume the sundial, but although the sundial was wood, it resisted the fire and passed through to graze Kron's hand. It felt like ice in his veins. Kron dropped the bowl, letting the flame die, and cradled his hand. Liver spots bloomed on his skin, and his hand grew thin and skeletal. *They won't be calling me "Evenhanded" anymore.* Was it going to spread?

Foreign magic passed through his defenses and surged within him like a wave. The advancing signs of age disappeared.

"Hold. Who defiles the dead in Our domain?"

A man and woman materialized next to Kron. There was no sign of a portal opening behind them; they seemed to form from the air itself. Although the man was white-haired, he stood tall as someone in his prime. The woman's hair was yellow, and her skin was paler than Pagli's. However, she glowed with health and warmth, making the corpse appear even deader.

The jewels on Kron's magic-finders blazed, cracked with soft popping sounds, and died.

The corpse flung its arms to the sides, and a translucent blue bubble appeared around the four of them. Then it straightened up, and a new light shone in its eyes.

"You two have many-strong power," it said in a new voice.

Only Salth speaks like that.

"You may claim this land as Yours, but I have claimed time itself as My domain," the new voice said. "Can You challenge Me for that? I could scramble the seasons of this land until not a blade of grass lives."

The man smiled thinly, his eyes hidden from Kron's gaze. "No, you can't. We are the Seasons themselves."

"Then You are below Me, under My control."

"After seeing what no one else has ever seen, We are under no one's control." The man advanced fearlessly toward Pagli's corpse. "Can you say the same, you who send a dead person to speak for you? Have you Seen the Unseeable?"

A pause. Then the corpse said, "I've seen what I need to see."

"Then you haven't seen the Unseeable, then."

"I don't need to!"

The woman opened her mouth as if to say something, glanced at the man who'd accompanied her, and shut it again.

"Never mind the power," the man said. "Tell Us why you've sent this shell of a man here."

Please say it has nothing to do with me.

The corpse said, "I have a grievance against this man here." Its eyes narrowed. "Why are you still breathing, Kron? That sundial was supposed to claim all of your remaining time!"

Kron rummaged in his pouch, looking for something to enchant. String might hold one of them for a heartbeat, but he didn't have enough to restrain all of them.

The golden-haired woman played with a stack of bracelets on her wrist as she regarded Kron. "He isn't one of Us, but he's no longer completely mortal, either."

"What? How can that be?" he asked.

Ignoring him, the woman continued, "Even if you two weren't on the same level, We would disapprove of you coming here to harm one of Our own."

The corpse eyed Kron. "I know he wasn't born in this region, so he's none of Yours. He doesn't intend to stay here."

"Maybe that will change, now he's married."

Pagli's corpse grinned. "I'll take his wife, then. She's completely mortal."

Kron gasped. "No! Take me instead!"

As the woman's bracelets clinked, she said, "Actually, Fall is interested in Bella as an Avatar, so she is under Our protection."

Kron wasn't sure whether to be relieved or worried if these strange people could protect Bella—and what it meant for her to be an Avatar.

The corpse crossed its arms and glared at the woman. "You can't claim them both."

"Of course We can. This is Our domain, and We Ascended to help the inhabitants, not treat them like cattle."

Treating people like cattle sounded like something Salth would do. Kron focused on the corpse of his former colleague. Could Salth be behind this? If so, how? She had broad knowledge of magic, but she'd never practiced it on the dead before.

The corpse—or Salth—frowned, and the bubble trapping them constricted. "What do You call Yourselves?"

"I'm Spring," the woman replied, "and this is Winter."

"You said there was a Fall. Don't tell Me there's a Summer too." The corpse sneered. "How clever."

"Since you're so *clever*," the man said, "then you can figure out that there's four of Us, and only one of you."

"You mean, it takes four of You to equal one of Me?"

Spring and Winter glared at the corpse with enough heat to cremate poor Pagli. Then They spoke in eerie unison. "For the last time, you are in Our domain. We decide what happens to the people in this land, not you. Leave Our domain, and stay in your own."

"Oh, I shall," Salth said. "But that doesn't mean You've heard the last from me. I don't enjoy having neighbors. As for you, Kron," Pagli stared at him with an evil grin. "You can't hide from me forever. I'm the one who controls time now. You'll never know when to expect me to come after you—or anyone you care about."

With a cackle, Pagli disappeared, but the blue bubble remained.

"Does Time actually think she can keep Us trapped in Our Domain?" Winter asked. He laid his hand on the side of the bubble and pushed, then frowned when nothing changed.

"Technically, this time bubble is her domain. She may not have a Goddess's full power, but she wields what she has with skill. Even so, there must be a way out." Spring raised an eyebrow as She glanced at Winter. "Perhaps with death?"

His death? Then why protect him from Salth, or Time, or whoever it had been? Kron eyed both of the so-called gods warily. He was outnumbered and low on artifacts, but there had to be some way to defend himself....

The woman laughed, a gentle sound. "No, Kron Evenhanded, We are not interested in sacrifice, human or otherwise. And We apologize for not seeking you out sooner, but there are many others who need Us more."

Kron straightened. "And why is that? Who are you, exactly?"

"We already told you. We are two of the Four Gods and Goddesses of this land. We claim as Our domain all the land between the Western Mountains and the Salt Waters, from the Northern Sea to the Southern."

"Actual gods? What makes you different from a very powerful magician?"

"What makes Us different?" Winter repeated. "We're not bound by mortal limits. We do not need to eat, or sleep, or even breathe. We do not age or die. And while Our magic may be specialized—" he said this with an ironic edge—"We can do things with it that ordinary magicians can't."

He turned away and placed both hands on the bubble. Its blue color faded, and it became translucent as it thinned out.

"Don't destroy it just yet, Winter," Spring said. "This is an excellent opportunity for Us to talk to Kron."

"It is?" He didn't think so. "But my wife must be worried about me."

"We're still outside of time," Spring said, "so no time is passing for her. It's best for now if We don't draw attention to you."

"But do We really want to be talking about Time in one of her bubbles?" Winter asked. "She may be listening in."

"Good point. Your cabin, or My meadow?"

He smiled at her, his face tilted so that Kron couldn't get a good look at his eyes. They seemed too dark for his complexion. "Your meadow is a better choice for someone who still has more in common with humans than with Us."

"Agreed. Break this bubble, and I'll take Us there."

CHAPTER NINE

The Four

The blue surrounding them faded away, to be replaced by a glorious meadow bounded by forest. Flowers from all seasons bloomed in the grasses, creating a perfume no master blender could achieve. A river small enough to step across burbled as it ran through the meadow. In the center of it all, four benches covered with cushions sat in a square. The grass here was thick and short, like a carpet. Spring and Winter sank onto two of the benches, but Spring gestured Kron to a smaller seat, still comfortable but less lavishly decorated. He barely had time to wonder where the seat had come from—he was certain it hadn't been there a heartbeat before—when two more individuals appeared. One of them was a youth with green skin and hair; the other, a girl who scowled at him and took the bench farthest away from him, covering herself with a blanket.

"Fall! That's no way for a Goddess to behave!" Spring said. Kron repressed a grin at the scolding. "You have nothing to fear."

Why would a goddess—if She really was one—fear him? No matter what Spring and Winter had said, Kron was still human. Wasn't he?

Fall peeked out from under Her blanket, but She seemed disinclined to give it up. Spring cleared Her throat, as if to draw attention from the girl goddess.

"You are in a dangerous position, Kron Evenhanded, and you put Us in a delicate one." She plucked a few daisies and wove them into a chain. "I admit We favor you over Time, but she has more magic than you."

Time seemed to hold Salth' grudges; it was almost enough to make Kron believe Salth was Time. But Salth wasn't capable of manipulating time. No one was. Was this a joke? It couldn't be; she had no sense of humor. Besides, why would these strange magicians be part of it?

"Is Time—or whoever spoke to us through Pagli—really Salth?" Kron asked. "How did she get time magic?"

The Four raised Their eyebrows. All of Them had exceptionally dark eyes, eyes that made Kron uncomfortable.

"Perhaps you should portal—is that what you call your mode of instantaneous travel?—to Salth's house and see for yourself," Winter said.

"Without preparation? Are You trying to collect his soul, Winter?" Spring shook Her head, and the flowers in Her hand drooped. "I doubt Time would let You keep him. She'd prefer to put him on display, or torture him for eternity."

Kron tried not to squirm. Yes, that sounded like something Salth would inflict on him. Sometimes when he saw a young boy that resembled Sal-thaath, he had to restrain himself from calling out Sal-thaath's name—or using a protective artifact. He reminded himself he'd had to stop the pair of them from hurting other people....

He sat upright. "But if Time is really Salth, what's to stop her from hurting people? She thinks she can harvest magic from them!"

"She hasn't Ascended, so she's not as strong as one of Us. We can prevent her from directly harming someone in Our domain," Spring said. "However, within her realm..." She let the dead flowers fall from Her hand.

Kron hoped Salth's domain was smaller than an urn.

"How did Salth master time?" he asked. "Does it have something to do with the golden haze that fell from the sky last year?"

The Four exchanged glances, as if They were holding a conversation on some level he couldn't hear.

"Have you noticed any changes in yourself in the last year, Kron Evenhanded?" Spring asked.

"Well, since marrying Bella, I've been happier, and eating much better—"

"That's wonderful." She smiled. "But what else has changed? Is there anything different about you, or your magic?"

Magic did seem easier these days, not just in terms of putting artifacts together, but coming up with new ideas. But he'd thought that another happy benefit of being a married man and looking at life through Bella's eyes. As for himself, he didn't need as much sleep as he used to, so he sometimes crept from the bed and worked on a new design or prepared materials. And his beard grew so slowly he only needed to shave once a moon. Was that what she meant?

"Those could be part of your transformation," She agreed as if he'd spoken his thoughts out loud.

"Transformation? What do you mean, transformation? I'm still human!"

Spring sighed. Even Her disappointment created beautiful songs. "You were born human, Kron Evenhanded, but when you absorbed star magic last year, it made you into something more."

He reluctantly remembered the night he'd killed Sal-thaath and rescued Bella. He wouldn't have been able to do that if Salth hadn't become distracted by the star magic and wrapped herself and her son's body into a cocoon. "I remember some of the magic came to me as if it wanted me to take it in, but I refused it. I thought it was dangerous."

"But it still wanted you," Spring said gently.

Kron studied the grass. "What would have happened to me if I'd embraced it, the way Salth did?" He tried staring at Spring, but Her gaze disturbed him so much he had to look away.

"That would have been entirely up to you, Kron Evenhanded, and how much you were willing to … embrace," Winter replied.

Kron shuddered. "I could have become a corpse-molester like Salth?"

"Star magic can only change your nature, not your heart. And I don't see it in you to desecrate a corpse, especially a friend's."

Kron wondered what was in Salth's heart now, if she still grieved for her son. *Of course she does. Why else does she seek vengeance on me and Bella?* "Can these changes be undone?"

Spring raised an eyebrow, as perfectly formed as a petal. "Why would you wish to do that? The star magic not only enhances your own magic, but your health. You can live much longer now than you would have as a human."

She must be forgetting about Salth's plan for vengeance.

"But if he were to complete the Ascension, or Time does…"

Kron started when the green-skinned youth spoke. The other three glared at Him as if he should have remained silent. Winter rubbed his bearded chin.

"There isn't enough star magic left over for both of them to manage it," He said. "In fact, the only way one of them could do it now would be to drain the star magic from the other one."

"Another reason we should protect Kron," Spring said. "Salth—or Time, as she calls herself now—has more star power, but Kron seems better able to cope with Ascending."

"Ascending? What's that?"

The Four glanced at each other and remained silent.

"Well, if you're not going to tell me that, could you at least tell me what Salth would be like if she succeeded? Would she gain even more power than she has now?" Kron wondered how she could even measure her strength. Magic couldn't be heaped into baskets or weighed on a balance.

"Her magic would never be exhausted," Spring said.

Winter lifted a finger. "It can be temporarily drained if, for instance, She created Avatars as We plan to do, but Her weakness wouldn't last long."

"Then how do we stop her from gaining such power?" Kron asked.

"Keep her far away from you." Winter slowly brought His hands together, but a sheet of ice crystalized between them before they could touch. "Or drain her own power. I would prefer that. She's already tipped her domain hopelessly out of balance, to the point where it could affect Ours."

"You expect me to drain her? How?" Kron asked testily. "Better yet, why don't you do it? You seem to be more powerful than her."

"It's because We're so powerful that We can't do it Ourselves, Kron Evenhanded. There would be too much backlash, both in Our domain and with others like Us, with domains throughout the rest of the world. That's why We need to create Avatars, humans who share in Our power and serve Us in protecting Our domain."

There were more powerful magicians like Them in this world? More importantly, hadn't They admitted They planned to recruit sweet, innocent Bella, who wept when she had to sacrifice her birds for food, as One of Their avatars? How could They expect her to defend herself against Salth? Kron grabbed everything in his pouch, heedless of what it was, and let it fuse together. "You'd hide behind someone weak? Shame on you!" He pulled his impromptu artifact out of his pouch, intending to do something threatening with it if necessary. Instead, the clump of wool, wood, beads, and clay fizzled, emitting an unpleasant burnt odor. Apparently his magic hadn't been enhanced as much as these Four claimed.

Spring held out Her hand. "I'm afraid you misunderstand, Kron. When we gift Our Avatars, they won't be helpless. Even so, We hope you'll help them learn how to use the magic We share with them."

"But Bella—"

"Will be happier with magic than without it in the long run. We see this, Kron Evenhanded."

He struggled to keep his feelings off of his face. After the wedding, Bella had borrowed the family cradle from her sister and filled it with swaddling and baby blankets. But every moon, when she bled, she wept. Last moon, she'd angrily covered the cradle and placed it in the back of the storage area, as if it had been meant to hold food instead of a child. Maybe learning magic would distract her from her empty womb—or help her find a way to fill it. But Kron had other reasons to reject this task.

He crossed his arms. "How can you expect me to teach anyone when I failed with Sal-thaath?"

"Sal-thaath wasn't ready to learn what you wanted to teach him, especially with his mother telling him something else." A breeze touched Kron's cheeks. "The Avatars We pick will be older, but still able to learn."

"My earlier advice stands," Winter said. "Protect yourself with every artifact you can create, then portal to Salth's domain and see for yourself what she's doing."

"We will have a formal ceremony granting Our Avatars their magic in four days," Spring continued. "I hope by then you'll be more willing to help Us—and them. In the meantime, be careful." She raised Her hand. "Farewell until We meet again, Kron Evenhanded."

Kron found himself back in the market with his collection of artifacts. A faint stench of something rotten lingered in the air, but there was no sign of Pagli or his cursed sundial. Kron pinched his arm. The pain proved this wasn't a dream. How could he dream up walking, talking corpses and green-skinned gods anyway, let alone the notion that he wasn't human?

I'll portal to the Magic Institute first before I visit Salth, Kron decided. *I need to find out if Pagli really is dead, and if so, what happened to him. Maybe someone there can tell me more about these super-magicians and Salth. Maybe they'll have something I can enchant into protective artifacts for Bella and me.*

Bella came into view, her hands empty but a broad smile on her face. "Kron, you're never going to believe what happened to me!" she said. "I was bargaining with a weaver for some cloth when I saw a man pass by with a wriggling bag. It was full of kittens, and he wanted to drown them in the Chikasi River. I told him he shouldn't do that, that kittens can grow up to be good mousers, but he said this litter had all been born deformed. I told him it was still cruel to drown kittens. Then he turned into a young girl, about ten or eleven, and She told me She was the Goddess of Fall and animals!" Awe filled her voice. "She wants to grant me magic to heal animals and have them do my bidding, and I said yes! Now I'll be able to help animals—and people." Her eyes sparkled. "What do you think of that?"

Stunned, Kron felt his legs give out, and he sat down heavily, smashing several enchanted cooking pots. "That's…that's amazing, my dear."

If the young girl he'd seen was a genuine goddess, then Salth—or Time—was too. And so was the threat to Bella. Could the Goddess give her enough protection from Salth? Kron couldn't take that chance. He'd have to prepare his own protective amulets and portal to the Magic Institute as quickly as possible.

CHAPTER TEN

Timeless Artifacts

Kron found he and Bella couldn't even return home without encountering other new Avatars. There was Galia, an elderly midwife; her son Janno, a carpenter who leered at Bella; Caye, a petite weaver who did little more than smile at Bella and gift her with a shawl before scurrying away as a noblewoman named Domina proclaimed she was going to be the most gifted Winter Avatar of them all; and others with names Kron forgot as soon as he heard them. Bella, however, seemed to know several of the Avatars already. She hugged Galia and whispered something in her ear, ignoring Janno's attempts to flirt. When Domina ran Caye off, Bella looked after the weaver as if she wanted to talk to her instead of the sharp-nosed woman wearing more jewelry than both Bella and her sister possessed. By the time they finally made it back home, all Kron wanted to do was retreat into his workshop and develop protective artifacts. But first he had to explain to Bella why they needed such artifacts. Hopefully there wouldn't be more Avatars banging down their door during their conversation.

Kron made sure the door was latched and that Bella had calmed down before saying, "Dearest, there's something you need to know before you agree to become an Avatar." He sat at the table and indicated she should do the same.

Bella brought some peas over to shell before complying. "What do you mean, Kron?" She gave him a sharp glance. "Don't tell me you don't approve!"

"Of course not."

She raised her head and stared at him.

"I mean, of course, I'm not going to tell you to turn a goddess down."

"It's not just a role, it's a calling." She beamed. "Fall says once I pledge myself to Her, I'll be reborn with magic in each new life. I'll be able to help all types of animals, everything that lives in Her domain. Did you know Vistichia is just a small part of the domain the Four Gods and Goddesses care for, Kron? Oh!" She popped a couple of peas so hard they fell on the floor. "Have you heard anything about the Four? You spend so much time in your workshop I doubt you've seen Them yet."

Kron would have liked to have asked some more about new lives and being reborn with magic, but she'd given him the perfect opening for what he had to tell her. "Actually, I met all Four of Them today. Two of them appeared in the marketplace and took me to a meadow, where I met the other two. Then they sent me back to my stall heartbeats before you arrived."

She gasped. The basket of peapods fell on the floor. Feeling like it was his fault, Kron helped her pick them up, then related the whole story. Bella absently reached for the peas once or twice, but she stared at him the whole time, opening her mouth as if inviting him to toss peas between her teeth.

"So, Salth isn't really...gone?" she asked when he finished. "And she's using dead people to threaten you?"

"And you too," he reminded her. "You need magical protection." He'd be the one to provide it, not that timid young girl. How had she ever found the courage to speak to Bella if she cowered from him?

Bella shivered, and her face went pale for a few heartbeats. Then she bit her lip and put a determined expression on her face. "When Fall grants me my magic, I'll be able to defend myself."

"Against Salth? Dearest, I've practiced magic for twenty years, and I've come closer to losing against her than I like to admit."

"But I won't be alone. I'll be working with the other eleven Avatars."

There were only twelve of them? Kron had thought there were more.

"Twelve magicians might have been able to defeat the Salth we knew," he agreed, "but remember, she's gained even more magic since then. And she seems to have time magic now. I don't know what that allows her to do, but she did capture Two of the Four in her time bubble."

Bella shook her head. "They only let her do that so They could speak with her, I'm sure of it!"

"I hope you're right." The room dimmed as daylight faded. Kron activated an artifact that gave off heatless light and set it in the center of the table. "The question is, can I protect us against time? If Salth can play with time, she could undo anything I do, or prevent me from doing it. Can she?" He frowned. "I'm not sure what the rules of time magic, are, or how powerful Salth is now. The Four said she wasn't as strong as They are."

Bella glanced at him through a lock of hair that had fallen over her face. It made her expression seem guarded. "And...you said They said...you're different too, didn't They?"

"It doesn't matter if I only have to shave once a moon instead of once a day." Kron crossed to her and pulled her into his embrace. "I'm still the same person I always was."

Bella let him hold her for a few heartbeats before pulling away. "I better start supper."

As she hurried to the fireplace, back turned to him, she brushed her hand over her stomach for a heartbeat. He knew her well enough to guess what she was thinking: would he be able to give her a child if he wasn't fully human anymore?

Kron ground his teeth together. His magic dealt with artifacts, not living things. If their childlessness was his fault, he didn't know how to fix it.

If I can't create a child, at least I can make artifacts. He left the house to go to his workroom in the back. *Maybe small sundials can be enchanted to protect us from Salth....*

He busied himself with his artifacts until Bella silently fetched him for dinner.

* * *

Kron found his services much in demand the next day, as people brought him items to repair, not just enchant. As he was eating lunch, a servant came by and promised him a bag of gold if he would enhance his master's house so the walls wouldn't crack or let out heat. That job took him most of the afternoon. By the time he returned home for dinner, the sun had set, leaving him no time to finish the protective artifacts he'd started.

"I wish there was a way I could test these artifacts before I portal into Salth's domain, or even the Magic Institute," he told Bella over a meal of flatcakes, baked fish, and roasted vegetables.

"You think the Magic Institute isn't safe anymore?" she asked.

"It must not be, if Salth was able to murder Pagli and take over his corpse."

Bella pushed her plate away. "Maybe that part wasn't real. Or maybe she found him outside the Magic Institute. That must be what happened." She shook her head. "The Institute seemed like a wonderful place when you took me there. Wouldn't they have enough magicians there to protect the Institute?"

"Normally they do." Did he dare go there without the artifacts? Kron considered the matter as he finished the fish, garnished with salt and herbs grown near the Chikasi River. It was disturbing enough to think of Pagli's fate, but Kron might be in danger if he went there. Worse, he'd be too far from Bella to protect her if Salth sent another corpse after her. If the Four had given Bella Their protection, Kron hadn't detected any signs of it yet.

He activated the light artifact. "I'm going to work on the protective artifacts some more, Dearest. I won't be able to sleep well until I know for certain we're both protected from Salth—or Time, or whoever she is now."

"What about the Four?" she asked. "They promised to protect us."

He leaned over and kissed her. "I'd feel better if you had one of my artifacts too."

"Why?" Her eyes seemed to get even bigger. "Don't you trust the Four?"

Why should I, when I know how cunning magicians can be? He held his words inside, where they wouldn't hurt Bella. Instead, he smiled. "Don't you think the more protection, the better?"

She studied him for a couple of heartbeats before clearing the meal off the table. He must not have been convincing. But Kron didn't know how else to prove himself to her, so he drank the last of the beer, then retreated to his workshop.

Kron had assembled his workshop out of driftwood. Inside, baskets, clay pots, and shelves held goose feathers; wool dyed and undyed, combed or spun; polished stones; a few carefully guarded bits of gold and gems; and many other items. None of these seemed suitable for the sundials that would protect him and Bella from Time. Wood and leather could rot, clay could crumble, and jewelry could break. Anything that could shelter him from time had to be made of something that wouldn't be easily destroyed by time. But what? Ancient bones? Petrified wood? How would he obtain such rare materials?

Kron thought longingly for a few heartbeats about all the materials he would like to use for the sundial, then gathered up the most likely materials he had on hand—stone, gold and gems, and a bronze hammer—and added them to sundials. Then he enchanted them to be stronger, less likely to change, and impervious to magic other than his own. By the time he was done, no light shone from his house—or any others. Everyone else must be asleep. But despite all the enchanting he'd done, Kron wasn't tired. Maybe Spring was right, but he didn't want to think about that. He'd rather test his sundials. He could portal to Salth's territory and be back before Bella could worry. But…what if his sundials didn't work and he couldn't make it back? She'd never know what had happened, and she'd be unprotected herself.

Kron debated on whether he could attach the sundials to wild animals, portal them to Salth's realm, and let them test his sundials. But Bella would never talk to him if she ever found out. Besides, would Salth bother practicing her magic on animals? She was after him and Bella; she had no reason to attack a wild deer or fox. Her time magic might not trigger at all unless she detected him—or what she thought was him.

Kron snuck into the house and brought out his spare clothing—three robes. Bella didn't wake as he kissed her cheek. He knotted a sundial into each robe, then enchanted some of the spun wool to stick to the robes so he could throw them through a portal and drag them back. Next, he created a portal to Salth's house. At least, he tried to; the portal didn't open where he'd planned it to. Instead of showing him her house, the portal displayed the river bank where he'd played with Sal-thaath. Even in the moonlight, the river appeared—wrong. Where were the cattails and other tall grasses? Although it was early fall, the ground was as bare as midwinter. No other signs of life—no mice searching for seeds, no fish creating ripples in the water or owls flying overhead—were apparent. Kron frowned. Had Salth done this? If so, why? She'd never resented nature as much as she did people.

Well, let's see if she's awake. Grabbing the robe with the stone sundial, Kron held the wool string with one hand while tossing the robe through the portal. It landed in mud. Bella wasn't going to be happy with him the next time she did laundry. Kron waited for a few heartbeats, then wriggled the string before pulling the robe back toward the portal, as if he were fishing.

Just as the robe drew close enough for him to reach through the portal and grab it, the knot he'd used to fasten the stone sundial to the robe came undone. In an instant, the robe ripped, frayed threads pointing in all directions. The brown dye faded to tan. Kron yanked on the robe, and it split in half. By the time he dragged the remnant of his robe through the portal, it was a rag so holey Bella wouldn't use it for cleaning.

"She's not going to be happy with me in the morning," Kron muttered as he tested the iron sundial. This time, he made sure to enchant it so that it magically clung to his robe and wouldn't fall off. Despite his precaution, the iron quickly rusted and fell apart, and the second robe met the same fate as the first.

If Salth breaks down everything, soon there will be nothing left in her self-appointed realm but dust. Kron's hands trembled as he checked the final robe, the one with a gold sundial, before tossing it through. Then he waited, still as the portal. A bat swooped through the portal so quickly he didn't have time to react. Would it die too? It squeaked and fell, splashing in the river. Kron shivered, and not from cold. The Salth he knew hadn't been so desperate for life that she'd take it from everything.

He waited until the sky started to lighten, but his robe didn't disintegrate. Then he pulled it back through the portal and inspected the robe. This one seemed unchanged. Perhaps he could wear it tomorrow night, when he visited the Magic Institute to find more answers.

***

Although Kron seemed to have more stamina these days than he did when he was a youth, he realized he still needed a few hours of sleep when he found himself nodding off in the market that afternoon. A pair of boys attempted to snatch some of his artifacts, but they tripped on his blanket, and their cries roused him. A guard with a dog held tightly on a leash asked Kron if he wanted the boys arrested, but Kron shook his head. The last time he'd attempted to correct a child had been a disaster. Why would this time be any better?

His sales picked up after that, but he trudged home to Bella, reluctant to portal to the Magic Institute and learn what had happened to Pagli. Bella's enthusiastic kiss cheered him up, and they enjoyed a supper of fresh bread and baked fish stuffed with river greens.

"The Goddess of Fall returned to me this morning," Bella said as she poured more beer for both of them. "The day after tomorrow, She and the rest of the Four want us to pledge ourselves to Them."

Kron struggled not to spit out the beer. When he could speak, he asked, "So soon?"

Bella's eyes were solemn. "She wants us to be ready if Salth—I mean Time—tries something. Which reminds me." She leaned forward, letting her shift gape open at the neck. "The Four think we'll be safer if all twelve Avatars remain close together. Kron, dear, would you mind moving?"

"Moving?"

"Into a larger house. A palace that used to belong to a judge." She shook her head and let out a laugh. "Can you imagine it, people like us living in a palace? I'm sure it will be beautiful!"

And I'm sure it's been half destroyed by looters. Kron couldn't bring himself to say the words out loud and take the excitement from his wife's face. Instead, he reached over and took her hand. "Anywhere with you is beautiful, my love. Have you told your sister yet?"

"Not yet. She may be jealous, but I'll still come to visit. It's not that far away."

As she would be if she traveled to Delns with Kron. He supposed that once Bella tied herself to the child goddess, she would be forbidden to leave this region, and he'd never return to Delns. Perhaps he should discourage her from becoming an Avatar, but he didn't have the heart to deny her. If he'd changed to the point where he could no longer give her a child, then at least he should let her find some other way to spend her time. Perhaps, if Bella served the gods well, they would grant her–and him–what she wished for.

With that hopeful thought in mind, Kron smiled at his wife and caressed her hand.

They went to bed early, and Kron fell asleep after they made love. But bad dreams roused him in the middle of the night. He lay there, listening to water drip out of the clock, until he realized sleep wouldn't grant him more peace tonight. He might as well visit the Magic Institute and learn more about what was going on.

He dressed, collected the light-producing artifact, the gold sundial, and a few other items that might be useful, then stepped outside. The air was cold, although it wasn't yet Frostmoon. Kron felt his way to the place where he'd set up the test portal last night and rebuilt the arch. Then he rested his hands on the wood and remembered the mosaics and the fountain in the institute's courtyard. He knew them well, yet he had trouble bringing them into focus. The mosaics were still present, but they were missing stones, and some of their colors had faded. The fountain held no water, and part of the basin had chipped away. Leaves littered the courtyard, along with animal droppings and small bones. It didn't look as if anyone had cleaned the courtyard in moons. The only possible good point about the situation was that it didn't appear Salth had been here recently either. But if no one was at the Magic Institute, would Kron learn anything by portaling there? Or what if this was a trap, some illusion Salth had cast to lure him somewhere she could ambush him?

"You won't get me that easily, Salth," he muttered. He brought out a magic-finder, gave it a taste of Salth's magic signature, and tossed it through the portal. As he'd suspected, it flared, though the stone flickered as though it was uncertain what it detected. Maybe Salth had altered so much her magic core had transformed too. Would he know if his had changed? She hadn't had any trouble finding him, so maybe it hadn't.

You're wasting time, he told himself. *Either head through the portal or close it before something comes through after you.*

The sundial was small enough for Kron to wear on a chain around his neck. He checked to make sure it was secure, both physically and magically, squared his shoulders, and stepped through.

Nothing pounced on him as he arrived, but Kron moved as silently as he could and strained to listen for any signs of life—or unlife. He picked up the magic-finder and swung it in a circle around him. Its glow didn't change. The fountain couldn't betray his presence without water, but he edged around it anyway as he approached the Magic Institute. Before entering the building, he waved the magic-finder in front of it. It seemed to brighten for a heartbeat. If Salth had been here, any traces of her presence would most likely be inside. Kron dug a tuft of undyed wool from his pouch and enchanted it to soak up magic. Then he pushed the door open with his foot—something he shouldn't be able to do if someone was here to defend the Magic Institute.

Kron used the glow from the magic-finder to explore. He found the first body in the reception area. A female in an apprentice's robes lay on the floor. Unbound dark hair spilled down her back. When Kron turned her over to see if he recognized her, her wizened face belied her apparent youth.

Salth must have drained all of her remaining years from her, but why? If she's mastered time, shouldn't she be able to create more for herself? But if Salth wasn't mortal anymore, she didn't need to steal time for herself. Kron frowned. The only person she would give more time to would be Sal-thaath. Had she managed to resurrect him?

Kron needed answers, and he didn't think he would find them here. However, he searched every room in the Magic Institute, hoping to find a survivor. There were none. Every body that he found had been aged, sometimes so much that he wasn't sure if he recognized the individual.

He didn't find Pagli's body; he wasn't sure if that was a blessing or a curse.

When Kron had finished searching, he returned to the courtyard. Numbness made it difficult to think. Should he attempt to warn the other magicians he knew? Was anyone else even left? No word from his family in years, his second home forever haunted by this tragedy—if something happened to Bella, he'd have no one left to love.

The cold breeze on his neck brought him the scent of decay. Kron spun around and raised his magic-finder. Pagli's body shuffled forward, but not toward him. Toward the still-active portal.

"No!" Kron yelled. He threw the enchanted wool toward his former teacher. The breeze caught it and brought it back toward him. The wool wouldn't work on him because he'd enchanted it, but he instinctively dodged it anyway. Pagli halted, then turned toward Kron. He raised his hands. Did he intend to throw another black sundial at Kron? He moved his hands in a pattern Kron recognized, even though he'd never mastered it himself. Pagli—or Salth working through him—was summoning a fireball. Kron's robe was enchanted to protect him against fire, but he'd never had to test it against someone this strong. Where was that wool? If he could touch Pagli with it before he completed his spell—

Pagli finished his spell with a flourish, pointing all of his fingers at Kron. However, only a few sparks dribbled out of his fingers. Apparently the corpse's ability to wield magic on its own was limited. Kron seized the chance to dart forward and snatch the wool off of the pavement. Before using it, however, he halted and stared at Pagli's face. "Pagli? Are you still in there?" he asked. "It's me, Kron Evenhanded. You don't have to do this. You can resist Salth. Just show me a sign that you don't want to hurt me or my wife...."

As if he'd remembered he had a more urgent task elsewhere, Pagli turned back toward the portal.

No. Not Bella. You won't hurt Bella. Grimly, Kron tackled the corpse. There couldn't be any part of Pagli's soul still trapped in there.

Nonetheless, Kron's hands trembled as he knocked Pagli's body down to the ground and pressed the wool on his forehead. The body jerked a couple of times, but feebly. Kron knelt on Pagli's chest. He gritted his teeth and forced himself to watch as the light faded from Pagli's eyes for the last time. Perhaps he was providing relief for his mentor, but he couldn't tell. The corpse didn't bother taunting Kron, which was very unlike Salth. Perhaps she was too busy planning mischief back at Kron's house. Instinct urged him to hurry home, but he wasn't finished here yet. He couldn't let Salth take control of Pagli's body—or the others—again. The easiest way to do that would be to burn all of the bodies. But instead of preparing a fire, Kron peered through the portal, trying to tell if anything was amiss at home.

An owl hooted behind him, making him jump. Perhaps this creature was under Salth's control too. But when he turned around, the owl transformed into the woman-child who'd distrusted him so much during their encounter in the meadow. Her hair bounced as if She'd just tumbled out of bed, and She held her hands out as if preventing Kron from coming any closer. Her face wasn't visible, making it difficult to guess her intentions.

When She didn't speak, Kron asked, "Bella?"

"She's safe. I have owls and wolves surrounding your house, watching for any sign of Salth." She jerked Her head toward the Magic Institute. "Go and do what needs to be done here. Take anything you need for your own magic. You will need it for tomorrow night."

With that, She disappeared, leaving no portal or other sign of her behind.

Kron waited a few more heartbeats, but Fall didn't return. He appreciated the reassurance that these new magicians were keeping their promise, but that didn't make this task easier.

Kron entered the Magic Institute for the last time and collected as many gold objects as he could carry. He stopped at each of the bodies to straighten them out and close their eyes. He also collected the records of the Magic Institute. There were so many of them he had to create a small portal to his house and feed the records and other items through it. By the time he was done, the sky was beginning to lighten with the dawn.

Kron took a deep breath. "Pagli and everyone else who once lived and worked in this place, I grieve for your deaths. I do not know what all of you wanted or expected after death, so I hope your souls have a safe journey to whatever awaits you. As for me, I will do my best to make sure Salth never does anything else like this again."

He enchanted the courtyard walls to contain fire, then set the magic-saturated wool alight and used it to cremate Pagli. The fire would spread to the building and consume everything that could burn before dying.

As he returned to the portal, the fire's heat burned away all unwanted tears falling down his face.

CHAPTER ELEVEN

The Crystal House

"Kron? Why did you sleep in so late? Are you ill?" Bella felt his forehead. "You don't have a fever. Do you want me to fetch Galia, or Tylan the healer?"

Kron reluctantly opened his eyes. Judging from the light in the room, it was mid-morning. He'd had only a few hours of sleep since returning home. He'd been exhausted enough to fall asleep as soon as he fell into bed, but now the images of the aged bodies and the undead Pagli returned. Kron groaned and shook his head.

Bella leaned closer to him and sniffed. "Why do I smell smoke on you?"

How could he inflict the horrors he'd seen on such a sweet soul? Even though she'd only been to the Magic Institute once, she'd grieve almost as much as he did. Kron wanted to reassure her, but he couldn't force a smile this morning.

"It's...it's nothing, dear one." *Only my second home destroyed.* "You don't need to worry about me when you'll be swearing yourself to the goddess of animals soon."

"She's properly referred to as the Goddess of Fall, or simply Fall." Bella tilted her head and studied him, an unexpected shrewdness in her flecked eyes. "The smoke—is it related to the investigation Spring and Winter asked you to perform? Have you learned more about—" she lowered her voice—"Salth, or Time, or whoever it is who turned your friend into a nightmare?"

"His nightmare is over." Kron pushed himself out of bed. "Is there more beer?" Wine, or something stronger, would be better and help him forget that last attack by Pagli. But Kron couldn't afford to get drunk now, not when he had to create more protective artifacts.

"What do you mean, his nightmare is over?"

Kron splashed cold water on his face.

"Kron, answer me." Bella tugged on his arm. "What don't you want to tell me about last night?"

"You don't want to hear—"

"But if it's that bad, I need to hear about it." She led him to a chair. "And perhaps, you need to talk about it."

Kron stared at her for a few more heartbeats, then gave in and told her everything that had happened last night. As he'd expected, her face grew pale with horror, and her eyes glistened with tears. Part of him hoped she would reconsider pledging herself to the child goddess so she would be safe. Except she wasn't safe now, was she? Perhaps it would be better for her to be under the goddess's protection. The goddess could take care of her in ways his golden sundials couldn't.

"So...the Magic Institute is completely gone?" Bella asked when he finished. "No one else is left?"

"A few wandering magicians like myself, but I doubt they will want to start another school." Kron wondered for a moment how young magicians would learn their craft now. But they had more immediate concerns. "There's nothing else I can do at the Magic Institute. The next thing for me to do is visit Salth's old house and see what I can learn there."

Bella's eyes widened. "But if she knows you're there, she'll try to destroy you!"

Kron fought back a yawn. "Then I think today I'll skip going to the marketplace and prepare artifacts that will hide me from her. I'll prepare more golden sundials and leave them with you to make sure you're safe."

Bella nodded. "But eat something first before you head to your workshop." She set the flatcakes near the fireplace to warm them up. "You need strength."

Kron had no appetite, but he washed down the flatcakes with beer, then set to work. Magically manipulating the gold into the right shape, then enchanting each sundial, was difficult work, and focusing on his task allowed him to forget about Pagli and the Magic Institute for a while. By the time he was finished, the sun had set. Bella had been busy preparing fresh bread and fish stew, but she'd managed to obtain figs and dates—his favorite fruits—for dessert. The gesture made him smile for the first time that day, and he lingered by Bella's side as they stared at the fire for a while, not speaking.

When the evening had turned to night, he said, "I should go," without moving.

"Yes, you should," she said, her voice so low he had trouble hearing her.

They could have remained in those positions for the rest of the night. However, an owl hooted repeatedly outside of the window, making Bella smile as if she understood what the bird was saying.

She rose, came over to him, and put her hand on his shoulder. "Don't worry, Kron, I'll be fine." She bit her lip. "You're the one putting yourself at risk. I don't know how I'll sleep tonight."

He stroked her cheek. "Try, for me. It'll make my task easier."

"And when you return—"

Yes, better to think about the joy of reunion, not the fear of parting. "Yes, when I return." He kissed her, making it a promise of what they would share in the morning.

Bella embraced him and returned the kiss with enthusiasm, but then she tore herself away. "If you're leaving, you'd better do it, before I wrap myself around you and refuse to let you go."

"With such a sweet chain, why would I ever want to break free?" Why did she make it so hard to leave her? If they kept this up, he'd let the rest of the world outside their house rot as long as the two of them could remain suspended in their own private bubble of time. But Salth would never permit that.

With a sigh, Kron tore himself away from Bella long enough to present her with one of the golden sundials he'd created that afternoon. "I know your patron goddess is watching over you, but I'd feel better knowing you have this too."

She wrapped her fingers around it. "I'll keep it under my pillow. Or does it need light to work?"

"Not for protection."

"Then go, and may the Four Gods and Goddesses protect you too." She sketched a compass rose in the air in front of Kron before retreating to the corner of the house where their bed was curtained off for privacy.

Kron let himself out of the house. Owls perched on the roof, watching him with round eyes. A pair of wild cats, larger than tamed ones but smaller than wolves, slunk around the corner. While Kron wasn't sure how useful animals would be against another undead magician like Pagli, they did prove the Goddess of Fall was watching, ready to intervene if necessary. Kron hoped that with Pagli's body burned, Salth would be unable to use him against Bella.

Kron slipped into his workshop and stuffed his pouch with golden sundials and as many raw materials and defensive items as he could carry. He renewed the protective spells on his clothing. An idea came to him, and he enchanted the workshop to hold any magical creature without letting it escape. That way, he could create his portal in the workshop and keep innocent Vistichians from walking through it—or any of Salth's warped constructs from wreaking havoc on the city.

Kron brought branches inside to create a portal, so all he needed was the right image. He recalled the river as it had been, with lush grasses and flowers, but the portal didn't open. Then he remembered the difference in seasons. He needed to use permanent landmarks, not ones that changed over time. Salth probably hadn't been any kinder to her land than she had been to the Magic Institute.

This time, when he focused on the curves and bulges of the riverbank, the portal formed. The land on the other side looked dead. All the plants were gray-brown and wilted, and no animals stirred. Salth's home was farther north than Vistichia, so it made sense that the fall season would be more advanced there. But the area beyond the portal seemed too still, as if a trap lay ahead just out of sight.

I wonder what Sal-thaath would think to see his playground devastated like this. Knowing him, he might think it doesn't matter. If he didn't care about people who lacked magic, why would he worry about a barren land?

Kron shaped a handful of small rocks into flying arrowheads. They wouldn't do more than distract Salth, but that might be enough. Magicfinder in one hand and flying arrowheads in the other, Kron passed through the portal.

The land here wasn't as dead as it had initially appeared to be, but the area was certainly dying. All of the plants, from the grass and rushes to the trees, had turned yellow-green and smelled like spoiled grain. Some trees sported leaves of every size, from bud to full-grown to red or brown, ready to fall. Kron wondered what the gods who named themselves after seasons would think of that. The air was chill and too silent. Why was the area so dead? The magical battle between Salth and Kron couldn't have caused this—their magic had been too focused and contained to have side effects like these. Perhaps the magic that had fallen from the sky had corrupted the land, though that didn't fit with the way it had felt during Kron's brief encounter. Kron had seen nothing like this near Vistichia, though he wasn't certain how much of the star magic had appeared there.

How much magic was left in this spot? Kron brought out his magicfinder to check. It still glowed brightly, and the glow increased as he swung it toward Salth's former house. Had she put new wards up since the last visit? How close could he get without risking his life? It was hard to trust in his own artifacts in the presence of so much devastation.

What he needed was either a way to disguise himself or a way to extend his own senses. His clothes already bore enough protective enhancements; he didn't want to burden them with another spell. That left some sort of magical spying device, such as the far-seer Salth had. Kron grinned. Since he'd created it, he might be able to reaffirm the magic he'd laid into the device and make it work for him. The only thing he needed was something to link to the far-seer, something that could show him what it saw. But he didn't have a lens or anything made of the same material as the far-seer.

Kron ventured closer to Salth's house, pausing every few steps to look around for materials or any sign of life. After the fourth or fifth stop, he heard a faint whirring sound coming toward him? A bird? No, a dark dot flew toward him at rapid speed. It was bigger than he remembered, and now blood red, but Kron still recognized it.

Sal-thaath's ball. I thought it was destroyed. Where did it come from, and why is it moving?

The ball bore a human face, complete with heavy eyebrows and a thick, bent nose. The features weren't drawn on but seemed to emanate from inside the ball. The eyes didn't blink, but the mouth opened and wailed, "Kroooonnn! Leeeeave this plaaaace!" Then, so quietly Kron almost couldn't hear it, "Help me. Help me, please."

That's definitely not my enchantment. Kron stared more closely at it. The face seemed real enough, and very lifelike. *Is someone's spirit trapped in there? How did Salth manage that—and why?*

The pleading expression in the ball spirit's eyes vanished, and he bared his teeth and growled at Kron like a dog. Even if the soul inside needed help, perhaps it was being compelled by Salth to attack him.

Kron pulled on his tunic, and the smooth fabric became stiff as armor. He flicked a couple of his arrowheads at the flying ball. The arrowheads scattered, then dove at the ball from different directions. But the ball swallowed them both and continued its flight toward Kron.

Since Kron didn't have another weapon at hand, he attempted to remove the magic he'd woven into the ball. Maybe that would free the spirit. His original spell came apart easily—perhaps too easily—but the ball didn't come apart. Still, Kron could rip artifacts into their tiniest components if he had to. If only he could focus...

The ball clamped onto his arm like a leech. His enchanted clothing saved him from being bitten, but the ball's jaws chewed back and forth. Even if they couldn't pierce the cloth, his arm underneath was going to be bruised later. Kron shook his arm, trying to dislodge the ball, while he unhooked his pouch and dumped the contents out. Short pieces of wood that could be grown into spears, copper nails that could be transformed into daggers—weapons would be useful right now, but they could backfire. Instead. Kron enlarged the pouch, then placed a spell of attraction on it. The pouch opened wide and engulfed the ball, stopping short of claiming Kron's arm too. The ball ground its mouth against his muscles, but between shaking his arm and the magic in his pouch, the ball finally released him. The bag sealed itself but bounced as the ball inside struggled to escape. Kron hastily reinforced the bag so it couldn't break, then pinned it down with the copper nails. Now he could disenchant or destroy the ball at his leisure, but he wasn't sure that was still a wise idea. What if that harmed the spirit inside, or what if the spirit was still vicious? Perhaps he could find out.

"Spirit," he asked. "Does Salth know I'm here? Did she send you after me, or are you on patrol?"

After several heartbeats filled with snapping sounds and curses, the ball replied, "Who is Salth?"

"She might be calling herself Time now."

"I haven't seen a woman, only a child."

Kron's blood froze. "A boy with six fingers?"

"I don't know."

"Well, where is he now?"

"I don't know."

This wasn't helpful. Kron needed to find out what Salth was doing—and if Sal-thaath really was alive. If this spirit wasn't a helpful informant, then Kron should try something else, such as his original plan of tapping into Salth's far-seer from a distance.

"I'll try to help you later," he said to the spirit inside the ball. Kron then plucked a few dry strands of grass and wove them into a rope. He returned to the riverbank and scooped out a shallow hole with his hands, then filled it, handful by handful, with water, the closest thing he could find to glass out here. Finally, he laid the rope around the edge of the hole, giving it a manmade element to bring both the hole and water under his control. He touched the rope with his fingertips. *Show me the view through the far-seer.*

Nothing happened.

Kron pushed harder with his magic, but again nothing happened. Even if Salth had knocked the far-seer out of position, he should be seeing something. Either he hadn't established a strong enough link to the far-seer, or it no longer existed. Had it been damaged during his final confrontation with Salth? Kron hadn't paid attention at the time and couldn't trust his memory now. But perhaps there was a way he could test his idea. Maybe instead of trying to connect directly with his far-seer, he could use his hobbled-together seer to search for the far-seer. That way, he could tell if it still existed. It might also give him some clues about the state of Salth's house—and Salth herself.

Kron closed his eyes as he reached through the grass rope and water again, searching not just for the far-seer, but anything man-made, including Salth's house. He found that easily enough, but it had changed. The walls were no longer wood or marble, but replaced by crystal, pulsing blue and red and yellow and green. Even stranger, he couldn't sense any breaks in the crystal. How did Salth enter or leave the house? Maybe she was trapped inside—no, she was too clever to let that happen. He couldn't sense anything inside the crystal structure; it was impervious to his senses, both magical and mundane. He had to get closer.

He grabbed the braided coil as he stood up. He cracked the rope like a whip, but at the instant it was perfectly straight he hardened it and sharpened the edges. He was no soldier, but he'd watch them train often enough that he could figure out how to use a sword. Salth wouldn't expect him to attack her with a weapon instead of magic.

Kron pressed onward, feeling as if he was walking uphill despite being on level ground. More magic at work. He tried to gauge exactly what the resisting magic felt like. Not a wall, not a go-away-I-don't-want-to-be-bothered impulse that would divert magicless people away, not even a blast of fear. No, this was a draining, a sapping of his strength. If he wasn't wearing spells in his clothing, by now he wouldn't be able to take another step. Kron frowned. What would happen to someone who wandered by unprepared for this trap and got caught in it?

A few more steps forward, and he had his answer. In the bare dirt— even the grass was gone here—lay a wizened body. From the clothes, it appeared to be a goatherd. He'd fallen forward with his arms stretched out in front of him, as if he'd found a new god to worship but had been judged unworthy.

I'm always cleaning up after Salth these days. Kron prodded at the ground, but it was too hard to dig out a grave. Instead, he retreated to pick a few armfuls of grass and strew them over the body before continuing.

The next body, short enough to be a woman's, covered a child's body as if vainly trying to protect it. *Bella would weep if she saw this.* Kron grit his teeth as he eased the bodies over. The woman's arms were so tightly clenched around the child, dressed in a beaded leather tunic similar to her mother's, that he couldn't separate them without damaging the bodies. He hadn't been able to protect these people from Salth, and now he couldn't even give them proper funeral rites. Kron threw the last of his enchanted arrowheads to the ground, but they rose and circled him like a hive of enraged bees ready to kill.

"What are you doing, Salth?" he screamed into the sky. "Why are you killing these innocent people? They have nothing to do with you! Leave them alone!"

He half-expected her to appear. Instead, the arrowheads grew bigger, losing their sharp edges as they became metal ingots. *Their original state. By the Four, Salth turned back time. If she was as strong as the Four, how much of the world could she reverse?*

The ingots sagged, as if Salth had to carry their combined weight physically. While she struggled with them, Kron willed the tip of his whip to burn hot enough to melt metal. He cracked his whip at an ingot and set it on fire. As it melted, he realized that had been a mistake. Flaming drops of metal were easier for Salth to manage than the heavier ingots. The metal coated him from hair to sandals, burning him wherever they directly touched skin. Hastily he wiped his face with the sleeve of his robe. The enchantments woven into it quenched the heat, but his face still felt stiff and raw.

Kron had no choice but to retreat, but the thought of another defeat where so many had perished lit anger inside of him. Yes, Salth had always been more powerful than him, but he supposedly had the gift of star magic too. Salth had unexpectedly done him a favor by transforming the arrowheads into another manmade shape. He could manipulate them too, and he had more experience with this type of magic than she did.

The rest of the ingots drifted toward him. Kron dropped his whip and reached out for them with both hands. They came to his call the way Bella's birds obeyed her. As he caught each one, he infused it with power and redirected the target back to Salth's crystal house. If he could shatter it, perhaps he could handicap her magic. However, the first two bounced off of the crystal and flew toward him with murderous intent. He flung the rest—with similar results—then raced toward the portal. If he had more time, he could try re-enchanting the ingots, but for now he poured the rest of his energy into his sandals so they would carry him at the fastest speed flesh could bear.

As soon as he reached the portal, he hurried through it, remembering to collapse it an instant before he passed out.

CHAPTER TWELVE

A House for Thirteen

"Thank the Four Gods and Goddesses you didn't get yourself killed." Galia poured more beer on his wounds. It stung as if she was trying to kill him herself. "No one would have known where you were, let alone be able to fetch you." She clicked her tongue. "Magic doorways indeed."

"They do work, Galia," Bella said as she wrung out her washcloth. "I've traveled through them myself."

Kron eased himself into a sitting position. He hadn't expected his trip to Salth's realm the night before to have taken so much out of him. *If I'm somewhere between humans and gods now, shouldn't I have more stamina, or heal faster? Then Bella wouldn't have had to fetch the midwife to mend me.* He had planned to share his news only with Bella, but once his wife told him Galia was also going to be an Avatar and would know everything she knew, he couldn't come up with a graceful excuse to keep silent. Given how much Galia had questioned him between treating his wounds, he wouldn't have been allowed to hide what he'd been doing anyway.

"The portals are not the problem," Kron told the women. "It's Salth—and maybe Sal-thaath. I couldn't confirm that she is Time, but she's doing something. And I have a witness who saw a boy in the area."

Bella let her rag splash into a bowl of water. Her face grew pale, and she leaned against the wall. "Are you sure, Kron? You didn't see either of them."

"But what I saw—the sterile land, the dead people—fits with what she originally planned, as well as what I saw at the Magic Institute."

"That's a place where people go to learn magic?" Galia asked.

"Not anymore."

"Then I guess we'll need to practice our new magic on our own," she said.

Kron suppressed a cringe. Beginning magicians could make the worst mistakes. He knew that from experience. Someone would have to tutor these new Avatars, and he had a feeling it would be him. But he'd deal with that later, once they actually had magic. If they were going to get magic. He hadn't seen one of the so-called gods lately. Had They been real?

"I'm sure Kron will help us after the ceremony tomorrow," Bella said. "Won't you, dearest?"

Trapped, he could only nod.

"Does this mean the gods are still around?" he asked.

Both women stared at him as if he'd asked a question a child could answer.

"Of course They're around," Galia said. "They've been appearing all over Vistichia, performing miracles. Haven't you seen Them?"

"I've been busy making artifacts. And traveling."

"I guess Fall visits Bella when you're gone, then."

Kron looked at his wife. "Is that true?"

She tilted her chin. "There's nothing wrong with it. She's teaching me some of what I need to know to be Her Avatar."

"But She seems so…young!"

Bella's smile faded. "She's much older inside, poor girl."

"I don't think She's the one I need to talk to anyway. When I met the Four of Them, Winter and Spring did most of the talking. Where would I find Them?"

Spring manifested in the center of the room. She didn't use a portal, and no other magical effects accompanied Her arrival. Bella didn't even notice Her at first; she only turned around after Galia did. Both women curtseyed as if meeting a queen. Kron could have managed a bow if he exerted himself, but he wasn't sure yet if Spring was worthy of one.

"Actually, it's always easier for Us to find you," Spring said, "especially when you're in the company of Our Avatars." She brushed Her fingers over Galia and Bella. "So, what did you find?" Wisps of golden hair fell over Her eyes as She gazed at Kron, but there was still enough mystery there to make him uneasy—and irritated.

He pushed himself into a sitting position. "Don't You already know?"

"I'd like to know what you think is going on."

"Something…evil. And deadly. But I'm still not sure Salth is Time."

"Then what would convince you?"

A direct confrontation with Salth, without any dead bodies or spirit-inhabited objects interfering. What did those things have to do with Time anyway?

"We think there is more to Salth than manipulating time," Spring agreed with his thoughts. "But though We have seen her crystal house and the ... energy it contains, We are not sure what she intends to do with it. She has managed to shield part of her domain from Our observation, and that worries Us."

Bella bit her lip. "Does Kron have to go back there? It sounds like a horrible place. What if she attacks him again?"

"We do not think Kron should go alone next time," Spring replied. "You two and the rest of the Avatars will accompany him."

Both women gasped. Anger gave Kron the energy he needed to rise from the bed. He wavered on his feet, but his voice was steady as he said, "I will not lead helpless innocents into danger, Spring!"

"You won't be." She sounded amused, which infuriated him. She held up a hand before he could protest. "After tomorrow, Our Avatars will wield a portion of Our magic. They will assist you in shattering that crystal house of Salth's."

Kron's first impulse was to claim he didn't need anyone's help, least of all that of a dozen novice magicians. Instead, he asked in a carefully neutral tone, "What will they be able to do that I can't?"

"Your magic is linked to artifacts, or things you create or alter. Their magic will be more in tune with the natural world." Spring gestured toward the window. Her stack of golden bracelets clinked together. "Gaila and My other Avatars will be able to heal people; Summer's Avatars will tend to the plants, Bella and the other Fall Avatars will take care of the animals, and Winter's Avatars will control the weather. In addition, My Avatars will also have the ability to link with the other Avatars so they can share and magnify their magic. We plan for all of them to work together to make Our domain one where mortals can live in peace and prosperity."

"That sounds wonderful," Kron said sourly, "but what good will that do against Salth, or Time, or Sal-thaath?"

This time, Spring didn't answer immediately, but stared into the corner of the roof as if it held more answers than spider webs.

"Salth's domain is severely out of balance," She said softly, "And since you, Kron Evenhanded, had a role in upsetting it, you will be required to set it right."

"And how do I do that?" He stepped toward her. "What kind of artifact should I create?"

She faced him and shook the hair out of Her face. Her exposed eyes were pure black, no whites or irises. Gazing into them was like looking into the night sky and beyond, into something so vast as to make Kron feel insignificant. Who was he to question such a one as Her, Someone who had experience beyond his understanding? How did he dare even breathe in Her presence? His vision narrowed. He needed to escape before he lost himself in the darkness. But then he remembered Bella. He couldn't lose himself; he needed to return to her. He pictured her face, and the darkness retreated.

Kron found himself facing Spring again. Her eyes were veiled, but he could still the weight of Her gaze on him, studying him. She nodded Her head a fraction. "You would have survived Ascension, had you attempted it," She told him.

"I don't think I would have wanted it, whatever this Ascension is."

She laughed, and the room smelled like spring flowers. "I can't answer your question without changing the balance of power. Besides, I'm no artificer. Use the skills you and the Avatars have, and you will find a solution."

"And if we don't?"

"Then try another. Salth may claim she is the mistress of Time, but We Four understand eternity. We see much farther ahead than she does." Spring turned to Galia and Bella. "Farewell until tomorrow, dear Avatars—and you too, Kron."

She vanished as quietly as She'd come.

Kron let out a long breath. He still didn't have any answers about Salth, but at least now he was certain Spring and the rest of the Four were, if not what They claimed to be, more than human. He would be honored to have Them as allies, even if that meant training Their avatars.

"What did you see when you looked at Her eyes?" Galia asked.

"Darkness. Not evil, but something unknowable."

"Ah." She sighed. "She won't let me look into Her eyes."

"None of Them will," Bella said. She slipped closer to Kron. "So, does this mean we will be traveling to Salth's realm after all?"

How could he tell her he would be happier if she stayed safely at home? At least he could delay the trip. "No one will be traveling anywhere until you prove you've mastered your magic." *That could take moons, even years.*

"I hope it won't be by portal," Galia muttered. She packed some medicines in a woven bag. "Since you seem to be recovered, you should come with us to our new quarters and explain to the others who this Salth is and what we're supposed to do."

"New quarters?" It took Kron a few heartbeats to recall that Bella had mentioned they would be expected to live with the other Avatars. He hoped this new house was big enough to allow them some privacy, but he wasn't sure where they could find such a place in Vistichia.

"Yes, near the palace. It used to belong to Judge Tyr."

Kron frowned. Tyr had had a reputation of taking bribes. He'd been found dead a couple of moons ago, with his family and slaves gone. "How is that possible?"

"The Four arranged it for us," Galia replied. She surveyed their house. "Perhaps you could bring some of your belongings over and start moving in. Otherwise, someone else, like Domina, will pick the best room. I'm surprised Bella hasn't packed more."

A flush crept over Bella's cheeks. "Kron's been so busy with his artifacts and travel that I haven't wanted to bother him."

"Well, I see no reason to repeat my trip to Salth's domain any time soon, so now's as good a time as any to see these new quarters and meet the rest of the Avatars." Kron stretched, surprised how full of energy he felt now. A gift from Spring, perhaps? "I'll be in my workshop."

***

Kron hadn't thought he had so many artifacts and raw materials, but it took the rest of the day to pack and transport everything to their new home. It would have been easier to prepare a portal between the two locations, but Bella insisted he should save his strength, no matter how fine he felt now. Fortunately, Carver, one of Summer's Avatars, owned a cart and a pair of oxen he used to haul wood from the forest surrounding Vistichia to the city. He and Kron managed to fit all of Kron's and Bella's goods in the cart, with room for Galia to ride next to Carver.

Bella and Kron walked next to the cart. While she kept an eye on her ducks, Kron observed the changes in the city. Many people wore something colored in addition to their brown or gray tunics or leggings. Women wore bright scarfs over their hair or at their waist, while men wrapped cloths over their wrists. Blue, green, red, and yellow appeared in roughly equal amounts. People smiled and waved at their cart as they passed. Even the air smelled fresher—perhaps because the street seemed cleaner.

"Are the colors meant to honor the Four?" he asked Bella when they halted to let another cart pass.

She nodded. "Everyone wants the favor of their God or Goddess."

"Do you just pick One that you like?"

"No." She smiled. "It depends on what season you were born in."

Kron thought back, trying to remember what he'd been told about his birth. It had been muddy, so the midwife had been delayed. "I think I was born in the spring. Perhaps that's why Spring's the One who talks the most to me."

"Perhaps. But since spring is the first season, I think She leads the rest of the Four." The cart halted in front of a gate. "Here we are. Our new home." Bella smiled with so much pleasure he couldn't help but smile too.

Carver opened the gate and drove the cart through. They entered a courtyard even larger than the one at the Magic Institute. This one displayed statues instead of a central garden, and rows of dirt—probably meant for a garden—alternated with stone pathways. The house beyond stood three stories. It wasn't as grand as the palace, but the exterior boasted enough carvings to keep a host of sculptors employed for a year.

"Isn't it lovely, Kron?" Bella asked.

"Yes, Dearest." He hoisted as many of his supplies as he could carry off of the cart. "Any idea where I can set up a new workshop?"

"Maybe in one of the storerooms." Unencumbered, she darted ahead. "Come, let me show you the place I picked out for us."

The room she'd selected had probably not been living quarters before, more like a receiving area, but it was as big as their old home. Bella explained that since the kitchen was big enough for all of the women to work in it at once, she wouldn't need space for cooking or storing food. "So we have even more room here than we did before." The cradle had been returned to a place of prominence, near the fireplace. Kron wondered if one of the goddesses had promised Bella a child in return for her becoming Fall's Avatar.

Bella gave him precise instructions for how she wanted him to arrange their belongings, then left to help prepare supper. Kron set up everything as quickly as he could, but he couldn't remember all of the details Bella had given him. Finally he placed everything off to the side and looked for a room he could use for his workshop. All of the best ones had already been claimed. Kron climbed up a flight of stairs and finally found a spot at the back of the house. A pair of windows let in the sunset, and the wooden door was sturdy enough to grant him privacy. Many of the rooms downstairs had only a cloth hanging in the doorway. For extra privacy, Kron enchanted the door so that only he or Bella could open it, then set up some of his light-producing artifacts in sconces. A cushion to sit on, a low table for his work, and baskets to hold his supplies, and he would be content.

"Kron! Kron, where are you?" Bella called from below.

It must be dinner time—and time to meet the other Avatars. Kron braced himself before joining his wife.

"Dinner's served in the great hall," she said.

The great hall had clearly been designed to impress others. Apparently the judge who used to live here could dine among paintings of floggings and eye gougings without losing the contents of his stomach. Bella grimaced and put her hand over her mouth, so Kron touched a wall and made all of the paint fleck off. A few Avatars applauded.

Galia brought in several loaves of bread. "I think Kron deserves the prime seat after redecorating for us," she said.

Kron sat down at the head of a long table that had been set up in the center of the room. Bella took the seat on his right and Galia the left. Janno bounded back upstairs, calling for Caye and other Avatars Kron hadn't met. At his shouts, more women appeared carrying jars and cups for beer. Kron sipped at his beverage until everyone had gathered. Then he stood. Twelve people stared at him with varying expressions of curiosity or boredom on their faces.

"Greetings, everyone. I'm Kron Evenhanded, an artificer and the lucky husband of Bella."

"You got lucky all right," Janno said. His mother scowled at him until he turned red and muttered something Kron couldn't hear. He decided to assume it was an apology.

"The Four Gods and Goddesses asked me to investigate something in the Western Mountains. Another magic-user lives there, one whom I have the misfortune to know." The room was as quiet as a grave. "She despises ordinary people who can't use magic, but she always looks for ways to increase her own power. I believe she's found a way to do so, but at great cost to everything around her."

"What does that have to do with us?" asked a richly dressed woman with a pointed nose. "The Western Mountains are a moon's travel from here."

"Not if you're a magician. I can create a doorway that will let you cross from here to there in a heartbeat."

Kron described how he'd portaled to Salth's domain, the ball that had attacked him, her house, and the transformation of his arrowheads into ingots. Since Bella and Galia already knew this story, he watched the others. Some of them faced him, listening intently—or at least appearing to. Some whispered to each other or stared into their cups. At the end of the table, the rich woman who'd spoken earlier scowled at him the entire time. When he finished, she said, "If you know so much about magic, why didn't one of the Four choose you?"

He had no intention of revealing to her how much his exposure to star magic had changed him. "My type of magic isn't compatible with the Four's," Kron said evenly. "But I know how to find magic and identify it, and I've helped other magicians learn how to use their magic. The Four Gods and Goddesses have asked me to help you learn yours after you receive it."

A woman with birds embroidered on her tunic glanced back and forth between the first woman and Kron. She opened her mouth and said something so softly Kron couldn't hear her. "What was that?" he asked.

She looked down at her hands before saying, "You mean we won't know how to use our magic? I thought that the Four would give us the knowledge at the same time."

"Many magicians can use some of their magic instinctively, but in order to make full use of it, you need training." Kron looked around. "Any other questions?"

Galia tugged at his sleeve. "This other magician you knew—is she really a threat to us?"

The only sound in the great hall was the slow drip-drip of the water clock in the corner.

Kron avoided looking at Bella. If the other Avatars knew how much Salth hated him and Bella, would they aid or reject them? Did they know about Salth's meeting with Winter and Spring and the threats the three of them had exchanged? If the Four hadn't shared that with their Avatars, he didn't think he should either.

"I'm the one she has the most grievance against," Kron replied. That was true.

The rich woman frowned. "Does that mean we'll be in danger if you're with us?"

"Or the city of Vistichia?" Galia asked.

How could he answer that? Salth would have no qualms about hurting innocents to get at him—or even just to benefit herself.

The quiet woman with embroidered birds spoke up. "The Four Gods and Goddesses told us we would help Them take care not just of Vistichia, but the land surrounding it. Perhaps this is part of our duties: to protect the city against hostile magicians. Why worry about this Salth then? The Four will give us the power to deal with her."

Galia smiled. "I think you're right, Caye."

With that, the other Avatars started conversations of their own, ignoring Kron. He ate what Bella put in front of him, but he couldn't say a heartbeat later what it was. The Avatars dismissed Salth much too easily. He hoped they wouldn't regret that later, but he feared they would.

CHAPTER THIRTEEN

The Avatars

The next morning, after a restless night, Kron was the last one to enter the great hall for breakfast. Everyone stared at him curiously, as if he was wearing his robe the wrong way. When Bella brought in a big bowl of cooked grains, he whispered to her, "What's wrong? Why are they looking at me strangely? Have I forgotten something?"

She studied him for a heartbeat. "You're not wearing any color."

"Color? What do you mean?"

"Your color to honor one of the Four." She turned her head so he could see the red ribbons she'd braided into her hair. He'd noticed her doing so earlier, but he hadn't realized the significance.

"Red is for Fall, then?" Kron glanced at the other Avatars, noting jewelry, tunics, or other items of green, yellow, and blue. "The question is, what color should I wear?"

Galia wore a yellow overtunic too big for her, so Kron assumed that was Spring's color. He'd been born in spring, and that goddess had spoken to him the most, so maybe he was supposed to wear yellow. But he wasn't binding himself to any of the gods, so the thought of wearing one color didn't seem fitting. Should he wear all four colors instead? Then he might look like the old city-king's jester. Kron grimaced at the image.

"White is best," he said. "Clear crystals can split white light into all colors, so it includes all of them. I'll wear my robe from the Magic Institute."

Domina squinted at him. "Does that mean you don't serve a single god?"

"I've had the most contact with Spring, but I wouldn't say I serve Her."

"Perhaps that's best," Galia said. "Otherwise, She'd have four Avatars while the rest of the Four have only three." She grinned. "Not that She doesn't deserve more..."

The general conversation broke up as each Avatar argued why Summer was superior to Fall or Winter more important than Spring. Kron wanted to tell the others that it didn't matter as long as the Four could overpower Salth. The mood was too festive to allow mention of her, but Kron discreetly checked his magic-finder every chance he could. It didn't change.

After breakfast, Kron donned his white robe, then refilled a spare pouch with beads, wire, and other objects he could enchant if necessary. While he was reviewing his supplies, thunder boomed, and the sky darkened so quickly he had to light candles to finish his task.

Bella stood on tiptoe to look out of the window. "It seems a shame to have rain on our investiture. I thought the God of Winter would have given us good weather."

Kron consulted a magic-finder and found the stone glowing red. "This is no ordinary storm. It's magical."

"Magical?" She crinkled her nose. "Did Winter send it? Maybe He means to make the rain stop right before the ceremony to show His power." She frowned. "I'm not His Avatar, but that doesn't seem like something He would do. And He's already made it rain in very small areas, like a patch of flowers, so why would He do this now?"

Kron didn't respond. Instead, he studied the magic-finder, wishing he'd enchanted it to tell him the source of magic, not just the amount of magic in his surroundings. He had never heard of Salth experimenting with weather magic before, but with her power being altered by the star magic, perhaps she'd gained the ability to control weather too, not just time. That would make defeating her even harder than it was now.

"Wait a heartbeat," Bella said. "It's not just rain. It's snow…and lightning! How can you have those two together?"

"Let me see." Kron rushed over to the window. His magic-finder glowed a shade brighter. He studied the sky. Although snowflakes whirled around in the wind, he didn't see any lightning. It didn't mean Bella had been wrong, but maybe the lightning had only happened once and wasn't important. Then again, with magic, everything was important.

Kron was about to finish getting ready when he glanced down at the courtyard. When they'd arrived yesterday, the garden beds had been lifeless. Now shoots of green poked up, taller than they would in any normal season.

"Bella, do you see what I see?" He pointed at the garden.

As she looked, her eyes widened. "Well, maybe the God of Summer is preparing His own display of magic."

"What about the Goddess of Fall? Do you know anything about Her?"

Bella shook her head.

"Do you think She would tell you about something like this, or would She keep it a surprise?"

"I…I don't know."

Heavy footsteps sounded outside their quarters. "Kron, Bella, what's taking so long?" Janno asked. "The Four are waiting for us! You shouldn't be—"

"We're coming," Kron said before Janno could continue with something crude.

When they arrived in the courtyard, Carver's cart had been hitched to four oxen and decorated with scarves in the Four Gods and Goddess's colors. The ground was dry, although the plant shoots Kron had noticed earlier were still there, sending out leaves and buds. "Did anyone else notice those?" he asked, pointing at the plants.

Janno grinned. "It must be a sign from Summer!"

"What does it mean?" Galia asked.

"You don't know either?" Kron had thought the other Avatars might have a deeper connection to their deities. "Have the Four given you any sign?"

The Avatars searched the courtyard, then shook their heads.

"Maybe Their signs will be in the marketplace," Bella suggested.

"Yes, of course, so more people see." Galia struggled to climb into the wagon. Her son came over to give her a boost. "We should get going. We don't want to be late!"

Everyone else followed her example. Kron found himself in the middle, packed in with elbows thrust into sensitive parts of his body and foul breath in his face. With a giggle, Bella sat in his lap—the best part of the trip, as far as Kron was concerned.

He couldn't see past the cart as they drove to the marketplace, as too many other bodies were in the way. A blast of cold rain pelted them for a few heartbeats once they left their quarters, but then the clouds broke and sunshine poured through instead. Cheering sounded, though he couldn't tell where it was coming from.

"See?" Caye said. "Perhaps the God of Winter planned this all along."

Kron glanced at the sky, wondering if that was true. If so, what else did the Four have in mind?

Sylva finally brought the cart to a halt. Everyone climbed out. They'd stopped in the center of the marketplace, near the fruit sellers. Traders and customers bartered as usual, paying Kron and the Avatars no attention.

"What do we do now?" Janno asked.

"Ask the Four to appear?" Without waiting for a response, Caye knelt and closed her eyes.

"I'm sure that isn't necessary," Domina said.

"Especially since We're already here."

Kron looked around, but he didn't see Spring. Then She and the rest of the Four materialized, forming a line from spring to winter. Even though the day had brightened, a nimbus of light surrounded the Gods and Goddesses. A symphony of varied birdsongs blended together rang in the air—without the birds. At a gesture from Summer, bouquets appeared in the Four's hands. Each carried different plants: daffodils for Spring, wildflowers twined around oak branches for Summer, scarlet flowers Kron didn't recognize for Fall, and pine branches for Winter.

This seems more like something They would do. Why would They cause storms They would have to clear away? They told me They want to help humans, not cause problems.

Before he could ask, Spring stepped forward. "People of Vistichia!" She called. "Come witness the ascent of Our Chosen into Our Avatars. They will bear Our gifts and care for you as We do. Honor them as you do Us!"

Shopkeepers left their wares, shoppers dropped the items they had been haggling over, and passersby stopped to watch. Bella and the other Avatars straightened with pride, but they focused on the Four so intently Kron felt isolated from them. For a few heartbeats, he wished he could pledge himself to the Four too and be a part of that unity. He shook his head, but he couldn't dislodge his feeling of being an outsider. Like his magic, it had been a part of him for so long he couldn't lose it without losing part of himself.

Spring beckoned with Her daffodils. "Galia Midwife, come to Me."

The midwife advanced, then bowed her head and knelt in front of the magical healer.

"Galia, for your dedication to healing and helping others, I choose you to be one of My three Avatars. You will dedicate this life and your future lives to Me, healing on My behalf wherever I am worshipped. As Spring is the first season of the year, Spring Avatars will be first among other Season Avatars, linking them so you may work together to achieve great things. In return, I will share with you some of My healing magic and cause you to be given wealth and honor. Do you accept this bargain, Galia?"

Bound not just in this life, but her future lives? Kron had never heard a god talk about future lives before; even the greatest magicians shied from prying too far into death, lest they be caught and never return. Were future lives a promise—or a chain the poor soul would be bound to forever? How could Bella agree to something like this? But she remained in place between the other two women with red, smiling as joyously as she had at their own wedding. Kron wanted to scream at her, tell her to stop and come back to him, but his voice seized in his throat.

Let her make her own choice, Kron, Spring said in his mind.

Kron raised his eyebrows, but he heeded Spring's advice.

"I accept," Galia said proudly, reaching for the flower.

As soon as she grasped it, it melted—the best way Kron could describe it—then flowed over her skin and disappeared. Galia straightened with a smile. Although her features weren't youthened, she returned to her spot with more vigor than she left it.

Spring repeated the ceremony twice more with the other two Avatars she'd chosen before stepping back. The green-skinned youth, Summer, was next in line, but he didn't call for an Avatar. He curled his bare toes on a patch of grass that hadn't been there a heartbeat before. One of the oak branches he carried lengthened and stretched toward Janno, wrapping around his wrist. Janno's eyes widened. Was this an attack? Kron grabbed a bronze blade in his pouch. Then the branch shrank, dragging Janno. He strutted forward as if he was in charge, not Summer. Janno might have more muscles, but Kron knew Summer could encase Janno in oak if he chose. Kron watched the pair, holding his breath, until Janno glanced down at Summer's face and Summer closed His eyes. He gave Janno an intimate smile without meeting his gaze. As Kron tried to puzzle out what that meant, Janno and Summer exchanged whispers before Janno trotted back into position, a smug smile on his ruddy face.

Several more Avatars for Summer and Fall promised themselves to the God and Goddess. Before Kron realized it, Bella hurried toward Fall. The woman-child watched her, one hand resting on the head of a large feline. Kron knew he had no reason to worry about Bella's safety, as the cat had sniffed at the other Avatars as if to greet them, then left them alone. But he couldn't help pleading mentally with Bella, *Don't do it. You can still turn around and come back to me. What if this puts you at bigger risk from Salth? Or, what if you decide not to come back to me at all? Then what will I do?*

Bella didn't respond, but Spring and Fall stared at him. Although Their hair screened off Their eyes, Their gazes burned like a fire behind a door. Kron could only imagine what it would feel like to have the full heat of Their anger directed at him. He looked away and put on a false smile for Bella when she returned, joy radiating from her beaming face. She came over to him and whispered, "Now we have even more binding us together."

Was that part of the reason she'd wanted this magic, so they had more in common? How could he have doubted her? Kron didn't speak, but he took her hand and squeezed it. He kept tight hold of her as Winter transferred magic to his chosen three. The other Fall Avatars glanced at Kron and Bella but left them alone.

After Winter finished the investiture, He spread his hands, and a rainbow balanced on His palms. Appreciative calls rose from the crowd. Winter smiled, but His eyes remained solemn.

Spring's voice echoed through the marketplace. "Thank you, dear Avatars, for your dedication. And thank you, people of Vistichia, for your love. I know you've been wondering how to worship Us. We don't want to impose burdens on you, Vistichia, or the rest of Our domain, but this is something all of Us—and you too—need for different reasons. We would like you to honor Us at each season change, dedicate children to their birth-season's God or Goddess, honor Our Avatars, and treat everyone as kindly as if they were one of Us in disguise. In return, We, working through the Avatars, will guard this land and make it so fruitful no one need ever starve again."

"How will you ever do that if you can't even keep your own seasons in order?"

Kron's magic-finder, already glowing its strongest, snapped as another figure materialized out of nowhere. *Salth.* Everything about her had changed, from her face, bare of tattoos, to her feet hovering above the ground. Bella let out a faint cry and squeezed Kron's hand. He stepped in front of her to shield her if necessary. But for once, Salth ignored him as she faced the Four. Fall and Summer advanced as if They meant to circle around her, but when she raised her hand, They halted.

"You're not allowed to attack Me, are You?" She smirked.

"We don't want to unleash Our power here, surrounded by all the humans," Spring said.

Next to her, Summer cleared His throat. "But what you don't understand—"

Fall stepped forward, a feral expression on Her face. "Is that you're in Our domain now—"

"And while what We rule is more limited than your domain, We have absolute rule here," Winter finished.

They raised Their hands, but before They could join together, Salth shouted, "And who rules the seasons but Time Herself?"

"If you really ruled time, you could make it run backwards and undo your worst losses," Spring said calmly. "But you don't dare Ascend, do you?"

Salth let out a hiss, then spoke in a language Kron didn't understand. The air grew so cold it was painful to breathe. Bella shivered as she clung to Kron. One of the golden sundials he'd created fell out of his pouch and clattered in the stillness.

Salth turned toward him as if orienting on the sound. But before she could move, she and the Four vanished, leaving a breeze in Their wake.

"What happened?" "Where did They go?" "Did They take her with Them?" "They must have defeated her!" The Avatars spoke over each other, making it hard for Kron to tell who was speaking.

"Do you have any idea what just happened, Kron?" Bella asked.

"No." *Other than Salth was about to attack us. Did the Four really take her away? They seemed reluctant to finish her off. I don't think this is over.* He surveyed the area to determine if Salth and the Four had truly gone elsewhere or relocated away from the humans. No sign of any of Them was visible.

"What should we do?" Galia asked. For the first time since Kron had met her, her voice quavered like the old woman that she was.

What could they do? Kron weighed the options. They could wait here, return to their new home, or search for the Four. The last option he dismissed; the Four could go to places no human, however magically gifted, could access. The Four also seemed able to find the Avatars no matter where they were. Since the ceremony seemed to be over, there was no reason for any of them to be here any longer.

"We may as well go home..."

The gentle breeze turned into a gale that attempted to blow his clothes off of his body. Several bystanders who'd watched the ceremony staggered and fell to their knees. Fruit tumbled off of carefully arranged displays, and a cart full of caged chickens started rolling through the middle of the marketplace, straight for the Avatars.

CHAPTER FOURTEEN

Chaos Season

A few of the common people bolted or screamed. Even some of the Avatars froze. "Get out of the way!" Kron shouted. When Caye didn't respond, he grabbed her arm and dragged her away before the runaway cart could knock her down. It passed them to smash against a warehouse. A few cages burst open, freeing their occupants. Other cages tumbled out, and the birds inside protested with caws loud enough to give Kron a headache.

"Don't you have magic of your own now?" he snapped at the Avatars. "Do something!"

"Do what?" countered Domina.

"Don't you have weather magic? Well, use it! Stop the wind!"

As if the wind wasn't enough, hail as big as Kron's thumb pelted them. The rest of the onlookers dashed for safety. However, a little girl got separated from her mother and was knocked down by people running away. No one stopped to help her.

"Poor child." Galia held out her hand as she approached the now-crying girl. "Let old Galia see. I won't hurt you. I just want to help."

"Mama! I want my Mama!"

"Hush now, we'll find her. Here, let me see that bruise. See, it's nothing."

As Kron watched, a purple mark on the girl's forehead faded away.

Galia really is a magical healer now, he thought with astonishment.

Domina, Caye, and a man named Ocul stood in the center of the marketplace. Kron couldn't hear what they said, but Domina and Ocul waved their arms around as if they were arguing with each other. Caye stood off to the side, her eyes closed. Although the wind tossed market goods around, the trio's clothes and hair lay motionless. They were all devotees of the God of Winter; perhaps He had gifted them with weather magic. Kron pushed his way against the wind to them. Once he entered the wind-free area, it was easy to hear what Domina and Ocul were saying—maybe too easy.

"We should go ahead and tame the weather!" Domina said. "That's what He would want us to do!"

"But what if He comes back and is angry with us? Worse, what if we do something wrong?"

"I think Caye's already trying to tame the weather," Kron said. "And I think you two should stop arguing and help her."

Domina and Ocul turned to stare at him. Caye opened her eyes for a heartbeat, then closed them. "How am I supposed to do this?" she whispered. "I can feel the wind, but I can't grasp it."

"You can't grab the wind, fool," Domina said. "You have to command it, like this." She gestured, and the wind died for a heartbeat. Then it howled and flung gravel at her. Domina coughed and shielded her face. Then she narrowed her eyes, glaring as if that was the key to controlling the weather.

"Magic will try to test you if you let it," Kron said. "Aim for firm, but not too demanding. The more you try to control magic, the more difficult it can be. Let it flow naturally."

The women stared at him as if they had no idea what he was talking about. But he couldn't see Bella anywhere, so he couldn't spare them any more time.

"It'll come to you," he said as he turned away. *That is, if you really are ready for it.*

"Bella?" he called. "Where are you?" Maybe she'd gone to help the chickens. The wind blew against Kron as he fought his way to the warehouse where the cart had turned over. The free chickens huddled under the cart, while the caged ones still squawked. Still no sign of Bella. However, the warehouse door was open. Maybe she'd sought shelter in there. He peeked inside to find his wife dragging two caged chickens inside.

"Bella, what are you doing?" he asked.

"I have to get them out of the storm! Could you help me?"

He automatically fetched two cages before he realized that he didn't know who owned these birds or the warehouse. Furthermore, this wasn't solving the bigger problem, that of the storm. Bella was supposed to have animal magic now, not weather magic like Domina, Caye, and Ocul. Still, there had to be something else she could do–and he.

"We should go back to the other Avatars," he told her as he dropped the cages. The birds squawked at his rough handling.

"Why? Have the Four returned?" Bella glanced around before whispering, "What about Salth?"

"I haven't seen any of Them." It seemed right to rejoin the rest of the group, even though he'd always worked alone before and didn't know the Avatars very well. At least Bella would be safer with the other Avatars.

"What do you think happened to them?"

"Who, the Avatars? I know the Winter Avatars are trying to calm the storm—"

"No, not them, the Four." Bella's eyes glowed in the dim light. "How long would it take them to defeat Salth? I thought They would be more powerful than her, especially since there are four of Them and only one of her."

"They told me once They couldn't fight Salth directly because They are so powerful. Others around them would get hurt."

"But what if giving us magic weakened Them? What if something happens to Fall?" Bella smiled painfully, the expression not matching the fear in her eyes. "I know I shouldn't worry about someone far wiser and more ancient and powerful than me, but I can't help it. She's so much like a real little girl, Kron."

Maybe she was a real girl, once. Was it possible for a human to become divine if given enough magic? Kron struggled to remember if the Four had told him that, but he wasn't sure.

He shook his head. "We can't help the Four, but we can help the people of Vistichia—"

"And their animals."

"And their animals too. Come, Bella." He offered her his arm. "Let's go see what else we can do to help." *And see if you have magic now too, and what you can do with it.*

Kron could tell as soon as they'd left the warehouse that someone had done something about the weather. The wind had ebbed to a stiff breeze, and the clouds overhead were slowly breaking up. Perhaps one or more of the Winter Avatars was doing it. Winter Himself would have restored good weather in a heartbeat. He glanced over to where Caye and Domina had been standing, but he didn't see them. Ocul, however, stared up at the sky. Was he using magic? Kron didn't want to interrupt him if he was, but he did want to know what had happened to the women.

Bella closed her eyes for a few heartbeats. When she opened them, she said, "Caye and Domina are with Galia and some of the other Season Avatars. They took shelter in one of the marketplace booths. I think it sells spices; there are a lot of strange scents."

Kron looked around, but he didn't see a spice merchant. "Strange smells? I can't smell anything with the wind blowing so hard."

"There's a cat close to the Avatars," Bella said. "I'm getting the scents from her."

Kron gaped. He'd never heard of a magician who could manage that. "How?

"I ... I don't know. If I try, I can see what she sees, hear what she hears, and even smell what she smells." Bella wrinkled her nose. "But I don't think cats and humans enjoy the same types of smells."

"Never mind that. Can you take us there?"

Bella spun around in a circle, then led him to a section of the market he seldom visited. He followed her, watching to see if she displayed any other animal traits. He hoped the Four would return so They could explain exactly what type of magic They'd blessed—or maybe cursed—the Avatars with.

Caye, Domina, Galia, and the other Avatars weren't actually in a spice stall, but they were next door to one. They sat in the middle of a vegetable stall. Caye and Domina devoured carrots and beans, shoveling them into their mouths as if they hadn't eaten in a moon.

Galia smiled apologetically when she caught sight of Kron. "We were all so hungry," she said, "and I don't know where the stall owner is. Maybe we can barter our magic later to pay for the food."

"I'd say we earned it already, getting rid of the wind," Domina said.

"You did it, and not the Four?"

Caye nodded, looking away before he could encourage her to speak.

Domina reached for a dirt-covered turnip, scowled at it, and bit into it anyway, dirt and all. "Caye and I struggled with the wind on our own. We couldn't feel anyone else interfering with the weather."

Kron frowned. "No one? No one at all?" Too many people already occupied the stall, so he paced in front of it. "But it didn't seem like a natural storm."

Caye glanced up. "Maybe someone set it in motion, then stepped back."

"That might be possible," Kron said. "Could you feel any magic in the storm?"

"How would we know what magic feels like when this is the first time we've experienced it?" Domina asked crossly.

Kron had to acknowledge she had a point. He wasn't sure if their magic worked differently from his, but he had to attempt to teach her anyway. He grabbed a potato to illustrate.

"For me at least, when I try to tell if an object has already been enchanted, I can learn a lot by touching it. Sometimes it seems to quiver under my hands." He shook the potato back and forth. "But touching an enchanted object can be dangerous. If the enchantment is really strong, I can feel the energy coming off the object before I touch it. I can also test it with a magic-finder."

"But we can't make magic-finders, Kron," Domina said. "And I can't touch the wind."

"Really? Then how did you make it die just now?"

She furrowed her forehead. "I...felt it. In my head. It was...loud. And angry."

He'd never experienced magic like that. But angry? Maybe Salth had been behind the wind after all.

Carver, Janno, and a few other Avatars leaned forward, listening to Domina. "Was it alive?" Carver asked.

"How can the wind be alive?" Janno asked. "It doesn't grow."

"What else did you feel?" Kron asked Domina. "Did it seem like another person was controlling the weather?"

"I don't know. All I know is that the wind didn't want to die down."

Caye hadn't spoken during their exchange, and even when Kron looked at her, she looked away. Bella slid next to her and asked, "Did you feel the same thing Domina did?"

Caye fiddled with the fronds of a half-eaten carrot. "Well, I know I definitely didn't feel Winter behind this weather. He has strength behind Him, a certain presence." She gestured with the carrot. "It wasn't there."

"Then where is He? Where are Spring and the others? When will They return?" Galia asked.

The others looked fearful. They needed a distraction. Kron clapped his hands to get their attention. "How about while we wait for Them, you show me your new magic and help restore the marketplace?"

Bright smiles all around showed their support for his idea.

As they fanned out, stall owners returned to collect scattered goods and set them up again. A barrel-chested man hurried over to the chicken cart, complaining about a broken wheel and axle. Kron headed over to him. "I can help you with that," he said.

The man chuckled as he looked at him. "How? Are you going to help me pull it? You don't look strong enough."

"You may not believe it, but I work with my hands. Just help me hold the pieces together."

Kron carefully joined the wheel spokes and rim, then repaired the axle. By the time he was done, the man nodded as if he'd known all along what Kron was capable of.

"Now I recognize you," he said. "You're Kron Evenhanded, the magician who fixes things. What are the other people doing? Are they magicians too?"

The Avatars flitted from stall to stall as a group, looking for things to do. The Winter Avatars hung back, though they studied the sky as if expecting the wind – or some other type of foul weather – to return. The Spring and Fall Avatars seemed the busiest, while the Summer ones eventually broke away to descend on the produce stalls. A few of the stall owners watched with open mouths as the Avatars tried to heal what could be healed. However, the worst damage was to nonliving things that only Kron could mend.

"They're magicians, but not like me. Some of your chickens are in the warehouse," he told the cart owner. "I need to see what else I can repair."

Once word spread that Kron, and only Kron, could repair things, he found himself the center of attention. Local sellers and foreign merchants alike pulled on his sleeves, demanding his immediate attention or offering him so many goods to offer for his services that he didn't know what to accept or where to go first. By the time he was done, it was mid-afternoon. Kron gratefully accepted a flatcake filled with beef and onions and devoured it as he searched for the other Avatars. However, he didn't see them. Their cart was gone too.

Did they leave without me? Even Bella? Kron had worked more magic in a short period of time than he was used to and would have appreciated a ride home. Fortunately, one of the farmers he'd helped gave him a ride.

Kron entered the courtyard to find the Avatars gathered around Janno as he knelt by a garden bed, touched the sprouts, and made them grow to full height. Bella broke away and ran to Kron. "I was wondering when you'd be done," she said. "You had more to fix than the rest of us put together."

"Then why didn't you wait for me?"

"We were hoping the Four would return here." Although Galia hadn't lost any of her years, she walked more easily than she had that morning. She didn't squint as she looked at him. "Did you see Them?"

Kron shook his head.

"Then, what do we do? Are They coming back?"

"I can't answer that," he said, "but since you're all still new to magic, I think you should keep testing what you can and can't do. Maybe start with small tasks and try harder things as you gain confidence." *I hope you don't make any mistakes you can't fix, especially since your magic works on living things, and mine doesn't.*

As the rest of the Avatars scattered to practice on plants and birds and puddles, Galia drew Kron aside. "Spring said yesterday we are supposed to go with you the next time you visit Salth. Is she the magician who challenged the Four?"

Kron didn't answer. Instead, he watched Bella summon finches and other small birds to perch on her head and arms. She laughed, making her seem even more lovely than usual.

"Kron, did Salth challenge the Four earlier?" Galia asked again.

He sighed. "Yes."

"But how could she, when she's just a magician like you, not a god-dess?"

Because I'm supposedly not just a human magician anymore either. "She's more powerful than anyone realizes."

"But she can't be more powerful than the Four." Although Galia's voice started out strong, it wavered at the end. "She's not on Their level. No one can be."

Kron tore his gaze away from Bella and stared northwest. Some-where far away past the courtyard wall stood Salth's crystal castle. Thinking of it made the air feel colder. "Galia, it doesn't matter what exactly Salth is now. We have to find a way to destroy her crystal house." He stomped his feet, trying to gain warmth. "It lets her steal magic she shouldn't have."

"So, if we destroy her house, it will help the Four defeat her?"

"Something like that."

Galia straightened herself to her full height. She still didn't reach Kron's shoulder. "Then, how soon do you think we'll be ready to travel?"

Shouting broke out in the corner where the Winter Avatars stood. Ice coated the walkway, and the plants there had turned a sickly brown.

"It's your fault!" Domina shouted. "I told you I was going to make it rain! Why did you make it so cold?"

Caye balled her fists as she breathed heavily. Then she raised her gaze to meet Domina's. "I started first. You should wait your turn."

"I don't need to wait for you! I'm a councilman's daughter! I out-rank you!"

The third Winter Avatar stepped forward. "You're an Avatar now, Domina. Your old rank doesn't mat—"

He slipped and fell, taking Caye down with him. Domina smirked.

Kron glanced at Galia. "The Avatars have had magic for less than a day. How well do you think they'll fare against someone who was born with her magic and has access to a power reserve?"

Galia's dismayed expression spoke for her.

CHAPTER FIFTEEN

Spring Returns

Three days later, Kron paced up and down in the courtyard as the Avatars watched him. "Before you're ready to face Salth, you need to know how to defend yourselves with magic," he said. "There are too many dead bodies by her crystal house to be a coincidence."

Several of the Avatars widened their eyes or turned pale. However, none of them, even Domina, fled. Perhaps the Four had chosen them not just for their natural talents and interests, but for bravery—or stubbornness.

Kron continued, "So you need to find ways to use your new magical talents for both attack and defense. Go ahead and start." He deliberately stared at Domina. "And try not to freeze the other Avatars."

Galia opened her mouth to say something, but he quickly added, "Galia, you'll be supervising the others while Bella and I discuss strategy."

He hadn't intended to say that, but once he did, it made sense. Bella had met Salth before and knew what she was capable of. Perhaps, since they were both women, Bella might have some insights into Salth that Kron lacked.

He took Bella by the arm and drew her away. For a moment they stood together and stared at the trees, which had put out buds and baby leaves despite the chill in the air.

"Any idea who did that?" Kron asked.

"I don't think it was one of the Summer Avatars. They all worked on flowers and weeds." Bella crinkled her nose. "Except Janno. But he tried to make a tree grow taller and straighten out, not bud. And he was working in another corner anyway."

"Then either his reach is longer than we realized, or else this is Salth's work again, mixing up the seasons."

"An insult to the Four," Bella said. She looked around as if hoping for Fall to reappear and tell them all was well. At this point, Kron would have been happy to see Her too, even if She hated him for being a man. All of the Avatars were dispirited from the Four's continued absence. No matter how often he told the Avatars that the Four were too powerful to work with mortals and that was why They needed the Avatars, the new magicians wanted to work with the Four, not Kron. He was a poor substitute.

Kron sighed. "Bella, unless the Four assist us, I don't believe this plan of Theirs is going to work. It doesn't matter how much magic They gave you or how many Avatars They make, Salth is one of the strongest magicians I've ever known—and that was before she turned her house into a crystal trap. I don't see how taming animals and killing weeds will stop her."

"It must, Kron." She looked up to him with such hope in her eyes he was loath to contradict her. "We don't even know yet how much we can do, but when we all join together, our magic will be stronger than Salth's."

He didn't speak, but he raised an eyebrow.

"Well, maybe not that strong. But definitely strong enough to take down that crystal house." Bella shivered. "I hope she's not sacrificing more people in there."

No, because they're dying before they get there. Kron brushed her hair away from her eyes. "Don't be in such a rush to face Salth, especially if you don't feel ready. You need years of practice and study to master magic."

"But what about the changing seasons?" Bella pointed to the blooming tree. "What if more than one tree blooms or ripens at the wrong time? What if they all do? People will starve!"

"Then maybe you and the other Avatars should focus on keeping the Fours' seasons straight instead of destroying Salth," Kron said. The Avatars would be safer in Vistichia than in Salth's domain. "If you can't counteract her magic here, how do you expect to face Salth on her own territory, when her power's not stretched thin?"

"What do the Four want us to do?" Galia asked as she came over to them. "That's what we need to ask ourselves."

Couldn't she give them a few heartbeats to themselves? He should have led Bella back into their quarters and let the others think they were making love in the middle of the day. Maybe then they would have had some privacy—and a lot more pleasure than discussing Salth.

Caye wandered over, her hands clasped together as if she held a spark. "Maybe if we pray to the Four, They'll return and tell us if we should stay in Vistichia or destroy Salth's crystal palace."

"I wish there was a way we could do both," Bella said.

Galia perked up. "What if we split the group? Half of us could stay here and guard the city, while half of us travel with Kron to tear down Salth's house."

"Because six of you won't be enough," a familiar voice said from behind Kron. "All of you will be needed to defeat Salth."

"Spring!" the Avatars shouted at once. The ones who were still practicing their magic halted and raced toward the Goddess. Kron turned around with less enthusiasm. When he saw Spring, his eyes widened in surprise. Normally She bubbled over with energy and magic, but now She seemed diminished. Her hair lacked luster, and Her face, while still unlined like a maiden's, showed signs of strain under Her eyes. Kron couldn't smell the spring flowers the Goddess used as perfume. But Her smile was as warm as ever as She greeted each Avatar by name. She saved him for last.

"And thank you, Kron Evenhanded, for leading the Avatars during Our absence."

"What happened?" Janno asked. "Why didn't You return to us sooner?"

Galia raised her hand as if she meant to chastise her son, but he slipped away before she could strike him.

"He means no harm, Galia," Spring said. "I know you're all wondering the same thing, even if you don't voice it out loud."

Galia's cheeks reddened.

Spring's smile faded. "I cannot tell you much, dear Avatars, since what delayed Our appearance was a matter not for mortals." She avoided looking anywhere near Kron.

Salth? He thought as hard as he could at Her. *Is she gone for good? Please say so....*

"Strangely enough, there are some things mortals can resolve better than gods and goddesses," Spring continued. "And one of them is Our most unpleasant neighbor. If you destroy her, the consequences would be less severe than if We do it."

The Avatars stared at her for a few heartbeats. "But Spring, how can we kill a goddess?" Janno asked.

"You must destroy her crystal house. Salth is not a goddess the way Fall and I are. She needs the crystal house for power to appear close to Our level. Without it, she will still be strong, but not impossibly strong." Spring lowered her voice. "But you will need to take great care, dear Avatars. If she looks into the future, then she will discover your plans before you can conceive them. Fortunately for Us, she prefers to beat a door to the past. No matter how clever or powerful she is, she will not be able to answer that riddle."

Spring obviously didn't know Salth very well if She believed that.

"How do we hide our plans from her then, Spring?" Galia asked.

"The less magic you use in her domain, the less likely she is to notice you. So you shouldn't portal to her house. You will have to sail up the Chikasi instead." Spring smiled, and some color returned to her cheeks.

"You should do so anyway to see more of Our domain. We selected Avatars from Vistichia so you would all be able to assemble together, but eventually We plan to have you take care of a much bigger area."

Several of the Avatars murmured to each other. Maybe they were excited by the notion of travel. Kron would have been happier to remain in the city. There was nothing of interest on the river besides several scattered villages, all of which had looked at him and his artifacts with suspicion. His trip from Montedge at the origin of the Chikasi to Vistichia had been relatively quick because he'd sailed with the current in the middle of summer. No matter what season they traveled now, it would be against the current and would take twice as long—plenty of time for Salth to spy on them and figure out their true destination.

If only there was an artifact I could make that would hide us from her. But there's no way to hide from time. The only way I could manage it would be to disguise the entire group as non-magical people.

Kron mulled over possible designs and materials while the Goddess of Spring gave more instructions to the Avatars. He could start with the gold hourglasses to protect them from the effects of time, but then he needed something to conceal the Avatars' true natures. Perhaps a mirror of polished metal? Dirt, or something else so ordinary Salth would ignore it?

Bella poked him in the ribs, and he realized the courtyard was silent. All of the other Avatars stared at him. Spring watched him too with a wry smile on Her face.

You must be able to focus extremely well if you can tune out My voice. But pay attention now, as I don't know when I will return.

"What?"

She raised an eyebrow. Her gaze was still obscured even though no hair fell over Her face. *Think what you want to say, Kron, and I'll hear you. This conversation is best kept between ourselves, so don't tell the Avatars, not even Bella.*

A pit formed in his stomach. *Is the news that bad?*

When We chose the seasons as Our theme, We didn't expect a demigoddess of time would be able to tap into Our power. Spring scowled. Even though he knew it wasn't directed at him, Kron still flinched. *Every time We appear in the mortal realm, it gives Salth an opportunity to steal more power from Us, power she will twist for her own ends, against Our own domain. The only way Time will leave Us alone is if We take Our protections from you and your wife. This We will not do.*

Kron shifted his feet. Bella needed and deserved such protection, but him too? *You don't need to protect me. I can take care of myself.*

You're more important than you realize, Kron. We'd planned to spend more time with the Avatars, but We must not. Their training is all on your shoulders.

His shoulders already felt weighed down with this burden. *Then tell me what I should teach them. How I can teach them when their magic is so different from my own?*

Encourage them to practice as much as they can. The more they learn, the more they'll remember later.

Well, what about Salth? Can you tell me anything that will help us defeat her?

Your artifact magic will be useful, but you'll need to find some way to have all twelve Avatars present when you attempt to break her house.

Kron eyed the Avatars doubtfully. How could he manage that if some needed to stay behind in Vistichia? Was their combined strength really that important? All of them put together still couldn't equal Salth.

"All of you must be present in some way when you attempt to break into Salth's house," Spring said out loud. Her gaze swept across the group. "Remember it, dear Avatars. Remember it well. Even if you don't see Us, We will always look after you and Our domain. Farewell."

She vanished slowly, as if She knew the sight of Her would have to keep the Avatars inspired for a long time to come. Some of the Avatars, especially the ones bound to Her, watched closely, while others searched the courtyard as if wondering when the rest of the Four would appear. Kron observed them instead. Galia seemed to have been given

Head Avatar status by the others, perhaps because of her age. But if she let herself become downcast by the disappearance of the Four, then he might have to encourage her privately. That would be better than leading this group himself. They would always view him as someone different, someone who didn't belong and was only tolerated for the sake of his wife.

He clapped his hands to get the Avatars' attention. "Spring and the rest of the Four wouldn't want you to stop working just because They're no longer here in the flesh." He waited for someone to comment, but amazingly, no one did. "Let's continue testing what you can do and not do with your magic. Then we'll figure out how to face Salth."

CHAPTER SIXTEEN

The Summer Avatars

Kron crouched and spread out his hands. In front of him he held an unglazed dinner plate. "Try it again."

Domina frowned and curled her fingers. A bolt of lightning shot out, but it fizzled before Kron had to worry about deflecting it. Magstrom, one of the Spring Avatars, put his hand on her cheek. With his other hand, he held on to Sylva, who was connected to one of the Summer Avatars. The three of them became still. Domina straightened and released more lightning. The bolt struck the plate with enough force to send Kron back a step. The plate glowed as it absorbed the lightning.

"Better," Kron said, "but still weak."

"Weak!" Domina shook her hair away from her face. "I knocked you backward, old man!"

"Kron's not old!" Bella said from the corner of the courtyard, where she gathered loose feathers from her new flock of geese.

"If you think I'm so feeble," Kron said to Domina, "then you'll have no problem handling this."

He threw the glowing plate back at Domina. She flung up her hands again, trying to direct it away with the wind. Although the breeze she summoned blew Bella's feathers out of her hand, it couldn't stop the plate. As it flew toward her chest, Kron wondered if he should summon it back. It wouldn't do to kill one of the Avatars during training, even

Domina. Then she stopped flailing and held out her hands, guiding the plate to her. Once it landed, its glow disappeared.

Galia came over to inspect Domina's hands. "You should be more careful, Domina. I could feel the sparks in that thing back there." She gestured at the spot where she had been standing.

"I had it under control," Domina said, rolling her eyes.

"Not at the beginning."

"Well, I still managed it."

"Enough, both of you." Kron had earned his name "Evenhanded" for his sense of fairness, not just his ability to use both of his hands with equal skill. But living with twelve other strong-minded magicians was enough to fray any temper. "I sent that plate to you at a snail's pace. How quickly can you react in a fight?"

Without waiting for Domina to answer, Kron enchanted a pebble and hurled it at her. She spread her hands to catch it, but it bounced off her fingers and headed straight for Bella. *She can't handle that type of magic!* Kron ran toward her, even though he knew he couldn't outrace the pebble. Then a goose fluttered up to intercept it. The bird honked in surprise and pain as the pebble scorched its wings. As the goose fell, Bella ran to catch it, murmuring soothingly and stroking the foul-smelling feathers. Had the goose willingly sacrificed itself for Bella, or had she commanded it to do so? Kron found it hard to believe his tender-hearted wife would do such a thing, though he'd rather let ten thousand geese perish than her. But all the geese in the world wouldn't be of use against Salth.

"I think we've settled it, then," he said. "The Winters are the ones with the best magic to face Salth. The rest of you will simply be extra sources of power for the Springs to feed into the Winters."

Domina smirked, as if she expected that this declaration made her a hero. Caye stared at her hands as if she feared seeing lightning burst out of her fingertips. Ocul, the only male Winter, didn't even look up from a puddle he was freezing and thawing over and over. The Four might as well have picked field mice to face an eagle.

Janno stepped forward with an oak staff. "That's all we are, just an extra source of magic? Cattle dung!"

Galia released Domina. "Janno...."

"But I have this. See how tough this staff is?" He smashed the end of the staff several times on the stone paving. No bark or splinters chipped off. "All I have to do is get close enough to Salth, and I can bash her skull in!"

"Janno...."

"What would you do, Mother? Make her sick? Age her?"

Galia glared at her son until he dropped his gaze and shuffled back to the courtyard wall. Then she addressed Kron. "What do you think? Are we ready for our trip?"

"After only a moon of training? Of course not. You haven't even managed a complete link among all twelve of you. You'll need that to face Salth."

As they formed friendships, alliances, and even animosities with each other, the Avatars had sorted themselves into three groups of four. Each group had one Avatar representing one of the Four. The Spring Avatars could link with the others in their group but not with each other, and Kron couldn't figure out how to help them manage that.

He glanced up as the sun broke through the clouds and the air grew as warm as summertime in a few heartbeats. A week of hard rain had ruined the last of the harvest and flooded the homes closest to the Chikasi River. Ordinary people in the marketplace had grumbled that the Avatars weren't as good as the Four at managing the weather or regrowing crops after a storm. To Kron, that was more evidence the Avatars should focus on clearing up the chaotic seasons here. But if the magical storm was widespread, banishing it here wouldn't be enough. Perhaps that was another reason why they had to travel over land instead of portaling....

Kron suddenly straightened. "That's it!"

"That's it? What do you mean?" Bella asked.

He gestured at the entire group of twelve. "The Four want you to travel up the Chikasi River. But if we all go at once, the city of Vistichia will be left unprotected, right?"

They nodded.

"So, what if we leave one group of four behind, and the rest travel with me? I can create a portal right before we enter Salth's territory so she doesn't detect it. That way I can fetch the final group."

The Avatars gathered in their groups, exchanging glances with each other as if each eyebrow lift or slight frown was a word in a language Kron couldn't hear. Occasionally the Springs looked at each other, but most of their attention was for their group members. What did that entail for the Avatars' confrontation with Salth? Would all of them be able to work together, or would their union fall apart?

Galia seemed to be their spokesperson to Kron. She was the only one who seemed able to read everyone else, and she was the one to face him and say, "That doesn't seem to be what the Four intended for us to do."

"They didn't specify all twelve of you had to journey up the river," Kron said. "Besides, it would be much easier for you to portal to Salth's territory than traveling on the river, especially in winter."

By now, he should know better than to point out any weakness to an Avatar. Galia straightened to her full height, though she still had to tilt her head to glare at him. "I may be old, but I'm not frail. What about your wife? Would you ask her to stay behind too?"

To keep her safe, I'd do that and a thousand other things. Kron could feel non-magical heat in Bella's stare and chose not to argue with her in front of the other Avatars. Instead, he pressed his attack on Galia. "Does that mean you agree to my plan?"

"I said nothing of the sort!"

Janno grinned. "Mother, if this plan means we can leave now, I say we should do it."

"By the Four, Janno, you're not ready to face Salth." Kron feigned tossing another pebble at the Summer Avatar, and Janno flinched. "The overland journey will give you more time to develop your magic."

"How much more do I need to develop?" Janno flexed an arm. "I'm plenty developed in all ways that matter."

His mother turned her head away from him and made a disgusted face. Kron wondered if Janno was married, and if so, how his wife put up with him. Then he worried if Bella found him so difficult.

Janno smirked at Kron. "I bet I can beat you in a fight, old man."

All of the Avatars' attention was on him again. Kron shook his head as he stared at Janno. The woodsman was half a head taller than him and nearly twice as broad, but Kron felt no fear, only annoyance.

"How many times do I have to tell you this fight won't be physical?" he asked.

"If I can stop you from using magic, you're nothing."

"Nothing? Really?" Kron choked down memories of the magic-users who had seen him as just a handy tool. "Did nothing stop Salth and her son from trying to sacrifice Bella? Would the Four have asked me to mentor you if I was nothing?"

Janno snorted. "My mother would be a better mentor! If she was the leader, we'd be halfway to Salth's by now."

She shook her head and said softly, "Janno, that's not true." But he didn't seem to hear her. Instead, he took a deliberate step toward Kron, as if trying to flush game from its hiding place.

If he thinks I'm going to run away, he's very much mistaken. That never worked with my cousin. Only standing up to him made him leave me alone, even if we both wound up with bloody faces.

Kron squared his shoulders, smiled, and stepped forward. Overhead, a bolt of lightning fractured the sky and disappeared. "Since you're so confident, Janno, I'll let you throw the first punch."

That made him widen his eyes, but Janno took the opening and stepped forward, his fist seeming to come at Kron with the speed of a snail. Kron dodged and countered by grabbing Janno's arm and throwing him to the pavement. His defense teacher at the Magic Institute would be pleased that he'd remembered that move.

Janno grunted as he rose, his tunic ripped. Then he rushed Kron again. This time, Kron let him collide with him. The force knocked him back a couple of paces, but his tunic and outer robe absorbed most of the blow and turned it back on Janno. He staggered backwards. While he scrambled for balance, Kron stepped forward to tap him with the second pebble, allowing only a little bit of magic to escape. Even so, the jolt made Janno yelp and his mother hurry to his side.

"Are you hurt? How badly?" She glared at Kron and said to him, "That last bit wasn't necessary."

"Better from me than from Salth. She won't hold back."

Galia turned away and touched Janno's shoulder, intent on healing minor scrapes and burns. Kron noted wryly the other two Spring Avatars didn't come forward to check him. Bella took a couple of steps toward him, concern shining in her eyes, but he waved her away. "I'm not hurt, dear. My clothes are enchanted to protect me."

Galia glanced in his direction. "Then you should do the same for us before we set out on our journey."

"You still believe you're ready to face Salth?"

She sighed. "Maybe not. But we have to do something, and I think we've learned all we can in Vistichia. Maybe your portal idea is a good one, Kron."

Pride that she agreed with him warred with his worry for Bella. He didn't want her exposed to the dangers of the trip, but he hated the thought of leaving her behind—especially if Janno stayed with her.

"Who's going to stay behind?" Bella asked, her eyes dark.

"Not me," Janno said as he stood up. "You might need me out there on the river."

"Your talent is for wood, not water," his mother reminded him.

"At least you know the boat won't leak."

Galia and a few other Avatars smiled at that.

"Are you still planning to stay in your quartets?" Kron asked. "Galia might prefer to travel by portal. It'll be easier on her."

"Nonsense. I feel at least ten years younger now, maybe even twenty." Galia straightened, but she still appeared hunched over.

"And if there are two of us Springs, we can take turns healing each other if need be," Magstrom said.

And two to take care of Bella if she needs it. Kron sighed as rain clouds formed above the courtyard. They still had a lot of preparation to do before they could leave Vistichia, and Salth wasn't going to make it any easier for them.

* * *

Now that they'd decided it was time to go, it turned out that there were no boats available in Vistichia that could sail upriver in the middle of winter. After more discussion, Carver suggested they hire a boat builder to make them a boat. "If we help him, it won't take long," he said. "We can shape and harden the wood."

"Are we going to collect it ourselves?" Janno asked. "It'll take a lot of trees for a boat big enough for all of us—and supplies."

A couple of people laughed at that, as all of them had larger appetites now. Kron, however, took the matter seriously. Normally they would be able to barter for food along the way, but during the winter, supplies would be more precious and people less willing to part with them. Foraging would also be more difficult, though perhaps the Summers and Falls would be able to help with that, just as the Winters would have to make sure the Chikasi wasn't impassable with ice.

"Let's start with the boat first," he said. "We'll need a lot of wood, so let's collect it."

Carver and Janno, along with the other Summer, a woman named Flilya, led Kron into the forest near Vistichia. The Avatars had been lax about tending this area, and it showed in the snowdrifts high enough to swallow Kron. Cold ate away at the protections on Kron's clothing, leaving him with a dripping nose and chunks of snow inside his boots. Animal tracks showed them the best path, but breaking through the snow slowed them down. Kron's ox struggled through the deeper drifts and almost got stuck. Too bad they hadn't thought to bring a Fall with them to make the animal more cooperative.

"How far are we going in?" Kron asked. "And how are we going to bring the wood back? Our ox won't be able to haul it all in a single trip."

"We're almost there," Carver said.

It felt more like a season had passed by the time Carver halted in the middle of a grove. It must have been impressive at one point, with trees taller than the city-king's palace. Now several of the giants lay toppled, some having taken their neighbors with them.

Carver turned to Kron. "How many trees do you need again, and how big do they have to be?"

Kron paced off twenty strides. "They should be this long. Are we using oars or sail?"

"Sail, of course, since the Winters can summon the wind," Janno said. "Or are you going to enchant the oars so they work without us?"

"I'd rather not rely on magic when Salth's storms could interrupt it."

Janno narrowed his eyes. "You mean, Salth's storms could prove stronger than three Winters?"

"Only two Winters. And yes, they could. Better gather wood for oars too."

Janno and Carver grumbled as they conferred with Flilya. She protested that she knew more about herbs and healing plants than trees. However, the three of them went to the fallen trees and put their hands on the trunks. Most of the trees were still sound, but the Summer Avatars judged a few of them to be too rotten to use. They decided to harvest some of the standing trees too.

"Do we cut and shape the trees now, or do we just bring them to the boat makers?" Janno asked.

"They'll probably want to cut the planks themselves." Kron rubbed his hands together, trying to coax warmth back into them. The sooner they could return to the city, the better. "I say hitch them up to Brownie so we can go."

Flilya busied herself with weaving fallen branches into a makeshift sled. Janno and Carver downed the selected trees, secured them with ropes they'd brought along, and dragged the trees over to Brownie. Flilya came over with her sled and tried to tell Janno that it would make hauling the wood easier, but he refused to listen to her.

The pouch at Kron's waist grew warm. The only artifact in there that would react like that was a magic-finder, but he'd fine-tuned it to exclude the Avatars. "Magic's coming," he announced. "Be prepared—"

A portal opened in the middle of the clearing, big enough for a person to step through. Salth, dressed in white, pointed a finger at him. A bolt of red energy writhed toward him but bounced off the portal. She grunted and stepped forward, only to halt before passing through the portal.

Kron couldn't help but grin as he reached into his pouch for a protective artifact. Maybe Salth's power was limited after all, or maybe the Four had managed to prevent her from traveling to Vistichia again.

"What do you want, Salth?" he asked.

"Besides your head? Or your wife's?"

It took all his effort not to flinch at the threat to Bella. "Our deaths won't bring Sal-thaath back to life, Salth."

"If you hadn't interfered, your death would be unnecessary." As if noticing the Avatars for the first time, Salth glanced at Janno. "You jumped-up Nils should be careful of Kron. They call him Evenhanded, but he causes more problems than he solves."

Janno snorted, but Flilya, who hadn't spent as much time with Kron, glanced back at him as if she was seeing him through a broken far-seer. She wouldn't believe Salth over him, would she? Salth was a stranger, and someone who'd confronted the Avatars' gods. But Flilya asked, "Is that true, Kron?"

The familiar feel of rejection strung for a moment until he reminded himself that Bella loved him, Galia asked for his advice, and even the Four respected him.

"I never wanted Sal-thaath hurt. I just wanted him—and his mother—to leave everyone else alone." Anger surged through Kron as he spoke. Why let Salth stir up further trouble? She had no right to open a portal to Vistichia, even if she remained on her side of it. He turned to her. "Close this at once, before I do it for you."

"Then go ahead and try, if you're able." Her mouth twisted in a smirk.

Kron ignored her to focus on the portal. No matter how powerful Salth was, she needed something physical to anchor her portal. Would he be able to reach it on his side? Crossing over would be suicidal, but if he could break one of the items Salth was using for the portal, the entire opening would collapse. Using a magic-finder as an aid, he tried to identify the portal anchors, but he couldn't sense them.

"Something wrong, master of artifacts?" Salth asked in a tone that made him want to slap her. She must have done something to stop him from closing her portal, but what? Even if the anchors were invisible, he should still be able to sense them. No matter what magic she used, he ought to be able to sense it. Could she have moved the portal so that it wasn't on its anchors? Kron didn't think that was possible, and his reach into Salth's domain was limited. Unless...Salth supposedly had the magic of time now. But how could she use time magic to make a portal?

Kron frowned and let his shoulders droop. "What did you do, mistress of time?" Hopefully the flattery would distract her so that she'd actually tell him.

Her grin widened. "Ah, you can't figure it out?"

A pity she had to be too clever to fall for his trick. The Summer Avatars didn't speak, but disappointment showed in their eyes. If word got back to the rest of the Avatars that he wasn't as intelligent as Salth, they wouldn't accept him as their leader, no matter what the Four said.

Besides, what if Salth figured out a way to send her magic through the portal? She had to be stopped here and now.

Kron brought out one of his sundials and ran it up and down the edges of the portal. When he reached the apex, the entire portal wavered for a few heartbeats. Salth stretched her arm over her head as if to touch something Kron couldn't see.

He stepped away from the portal so Salth wouldn't overhear him. "The three of you can make plants grow, yes?" he asked. "What about making something decay?"

The Summer Avatars exchanged glances. "We can try it," Janno said. "What do you want us to work on?"

"I think Salth's concealing the physical supports of the portal by moving them in time."

"In time?" Flilya creased her forehead. "How is that possible?"

"She's an expert in time now," Kron said bitterly.

"But, time's what we measure with a water clock or a sundial, or the moon. What is it that you can move in it?"

"I don't know. All I can tell you is that she's using time on that portal, and the only way we can destroy it is by using time against her. So if there's any wood in that portal, you can break it down and break the portal as well."

Janno crossed his arms. "And if it's not wood, or anything we can work with?"

"Then it'll have to be an artifact, and I can handle that." Kron sketched a triangle in the dirt. "Portals are normally made with two or three sticks. See if you can magically contact them without crossing into Salth's territory." *Only the Four can save you then.* "I'll keep her distracted."

He broke away from the Avatars and charged toward the portal, brandishing one of his protective devices. As he advanced, it glowed. Had Salth managed to send some of her magic through the portal? If so, it might prove dangerous to the Avatars, since none of them were protected.

"You won't get away with this, Salth!" He willed the device to pull in Salth's magic.

"And who's going to stop me, gods under my control?" Salth casually extended her hand toward the portal. It didn't pass through, but the surface rippled as if something had. The Avatars halted. Flilya bore an expression of fear on her face, as if she expected to be struck down by Salth any heartbeat.

"The Four are not under your control, stupid woman!" Janno yelled.

Kron winced. Salth would make Janno pay for that comment. However, he used the distraction to check if any of Salth's magic had indeed escaped into Vistichia. There was just a trickle winding its way around a tree. Perhaps she intended to make it fall on them. Kron nudged Flilya and pointed at the affected tree. She blinked a few times before staggering forward to check it. Meanwhile, Salth had sent more magic through, this time directed at Janno. Kron stepped in front of the Avatar and intercepted the magic with his artifact. The sundial burned in his hand until he was forced to drop it. Kron shook his damaged hand about and twisted to take another artifact out of his pouch with his good hand.

A sudden cry from Salth startled him. During the confusion, Carver had managed to grab the portal—Kron would have to remind him later about the risks of grabbing magical objects with bare hands – and had broken it. The window through which they could see Salth shrank, then disappeared. Kron stood on guard for several more heartbeats in case she decided to return. Perhaps she'd decided she'd given them enough trouble for one day, for nothing happened except for his hand throbbing hard enough to make him long to cut it off.

"The Four didn't come," Flilya said sadly, hugging the tree Salth had enchanted. At least no traces of her magic remained.

"They didn't need to come because They knew we could handle her," Janno said. "That's why They shared Their magic with us."

"But is it true what she said about Them being under her control now?" Carver asked.

"They can do things Salth can't—or won't." Kron scooped up snow with his burned hand. The snow provided some relief until it melted and ran through his fingers. "She's just trying to trick us."

Flilya came forward and peered at his hand. "I think I can find some leaves that will soothe your hand until a Spring Avatar can heal you."

"Thank you, Flilya. Carver, Janno, can you hitch up my ox without my help? I need to let Galia and the others know what happened." *And make sure Salth isn't attacking them.*

"Of course, Kron," the men answered.

While the Avatars busied themselves, Kron nudged fallen tree branches into a portal. Unfortunately, he couldn't make it large enough for the ox and his burden, but it would allow him to return home and check on the other Avatars. Too impatient to wait for Flilya, Kron dashed through the portal as soon as it was active. He arrived in the courtyard. "Bella? Galia? Anyone?"

Bella hurried out of the kitchen a few heartbeats later, cornmeal sticking to her skirt. "Kron? Where are the others?" She gasped. "Your hand! What happened? Galia, come quickly! You're needed!" she called over her shoulder.

"Is there any cold water? I can use that to soothe my hand."

"Don't be silly, husband. Why suffer when we have three Spring Avatars here?" Bella ushered him into the kitchen. It was so hot in there from baking that his hand burned again in sympathy.

Galia bustled in from a storeroom with a pot. She scowled as she peered at Kron. "What did you do now? Is my son all right? Where is he?"

"On the way back with the wood, I hope. After what we went through to collect it, it would be a shame to waste the trees."

Galia grasped his wrist and shut her eyes. His own skin tingled as the redness faded. A few heartbeats later, his hand itched as old skin flaked off to reveal shiny tender skin beneath.

"Well done," Kron said as he inspected his hand.

"Now, tell us what happened," she said. "And Bella, get me some of that grain mush from breakfast. A little honey would be good with it too. Magic gives me such an appetite. I haven't eaten like this in over twenty years!"

Kron related what had happened, pausing occasionally to sip a hearty beer Bella prepared for him. The women Avatars who were busy cooking and baking drew closer to listen. To spare them worry, Kron omitted the lies Salth had told about the Four being under her control.

"There's been no sign of Salth trying to portal anywhere close to here, has there?" he asked when he was done with his tale—and his beer.

Bella closed her eyes for a moment. "The birds and cats and rats all say they've noticed nothing like magic – or at least, nothing like our magic."

"Are the animals to become Avatars next?"

She gave him a look that was worth a thousand tongue lashings.

"As long as Janno and the other Avatars weren't hurt." Galia helped herself to the last of the beer. "When do you think they'll return?"

"Is anyone home?" Janno called from the courtyard. "Who'll help us unload? We're short a man."

Kron rubbed his palms together. His skin still tingled, but he supposed he ought to assist the Summer Avatars. He should make sure Salth hadn't returned to harass them after he'd left. The ox had only been able to haul two logs back to the Avatar's house, so unloading them and moving them to a storage area didn't take long.

"Can you make a portal to the grove so we can finish fetching the logs before dark?" Janno asked. "The sooner we finish, the less likely Salth finds us again."

"She can't hurt you here," Galia said. The way she drew closer to her son suggested she thought otherwise. "The Four will protect us."

Flilya shuddered. "But she said she controls the Four, since They're aspects of time."

All of the Avatars who'd come out to the courtyard turned to look at Kron as if they expected him to know for certain.

"Salth did claim she controls the Four," he spoke carefully, weighing every word, "but I'm sure she doesn't. They are eternal in a way she's not, or can ever be. As much as she would like to claim the Four's power, that's beyond her reach."

Most of the Avatars sighed and relaxed at his words. However, Flilya still didn't look convinced. "Then what happened when we became Avatars?" she asked. "Why haven't the Four returned to us?"

"Spring did return," Galia told her. "And They haven't returned because we're supposed to take over now." She scowled at Flilya. "Unless you admit you're not fit for the task Summer gave you…"

"Enough of that, Galia," said Tylan, the third Spring Avatar. He stepped to Flilya's side. "If you want to insult a member of my group, you insult me too."

Galia flushed, but Kron wasn't sure if it was in anger or shame. Either way, he couldn't let these emotions run rampant and split this group even further.

"If you think you work best in groups of four, I won't tell you otherwise—"

Domina sniffed. "You don't fit into any of our groups, Kron."

Bella stepped closer to him and said, "He's my husband, so he belongs in my group." She glanced at Galia, Janno, and Caye as she spoke, as if she sought their agreement. Galia and Caye nodded immediately, but Janno hesitated, nodding only after his mother glared at him.

Kron ground his teeth. He'd meant to establish himself as belonging to no group, an outsider who could offer them impartial advice. Bella meant well, but she'd inadvertently done the one thing he'd wanted to avoid: force him to take sides. Admittedly, he did seem to speak the most with Galia and Bella, but Galia had acted as an overall leader for the Avatars until now. This divide disturbed him more than he'd expected.

"All of you shouldn't be so quick to divide yourselves up." He glared at all of them—except Bella. He didn't have the heart to do that. "The Four have told you over and over again you have to work together to defeat Salth. Have you forgotten so soon?"

A few of the Avatars blushed and lowered their heads. Domina, however, had to be defiant. "But we do work better together in the smaller groups."

"Have you been practicing as a full group, or in smaller ones?"

Silence answered him.

Kron shook his head. "You'd better start working as twelve, not three groups of four. Otherwise, Salth will drain the magic out of all of us before we reach her house."

Suddenly fed up with all of them, Kron pushed through the group to enter the house. He headed straight to his workshop and shut the door. Once alone, he sat on a stool and rubbed his temples. What would it take for the Avatars to realize how dangerous Salth was? Perhaps the Four would protect the Avatars while they were in Vistichia, but that wouldn't last when they journeyed upriver. Bella knew from experience what Salth was capable of. Perhaps he should ask his dearer half to tell the rest of the Avatars how close she'd come to losing her life. If they knew about that and still insisted on rushing into a battle they couldn't win, then he'd have to try to persuade Bella to stay behind, even if that doomed the rest of the Avatars.

* * *

Nearly two moons passed while Janno, Carver, and Flilya worked with the shipbuilders. In the meantime, Kron experimented with artifacts to protect him and the Avatars from Salth's soul-trap. He wandered around his workshop, touching items—hard, soft, smooth, woolly, and cold—and trusting his training and instinct to lead him to the proper materials. To protect himself from a magical draining, he chose a scrap of wool for blanketing and warmth, a nail to channel magic away from him, a firestone as a symbol of renewal, and a four-leaf clover for the blessing of the Four Gods and Goddesses Who had trusted him with this mission. He used magic to fuse the rock and nail, then pressed the clover against the rock and wrapped them all in the wool. Finally, he fused the wool with a leather cord so he could wear the anti-draining device around his neck.

There. That will work for me, but I don't have enough four-leaf clovers for the Avatars. I'll have to think of a substitute. He sighed as he remembered his last trip to Salth's territory. It was hard enough protecting a few people, but who knew how many others lived west of the mountains, past the Four's protection? If only Kron knew how to counter Salth's soul-trap with an artifact of his own. He needed to start working on an artifact now, while he could still obtain supplies. But what should he bring with him, and what type of design should he use?

I should start with what I know. Kron sketched a drawing of Salth's crystal house, adding estimates as to how long and wide it was. *Is it actually crystal, or diamond?* If it were the latter, it would be impossible to shatter. A pity Kron didn't have a sample to experiment on. If Bella could persuade an animal to bring back a piece of the house—that is, if it survived the journey--Kron would be able to learn what he faced.

He left the workshop to search for Bella and was surprised by how much time had passed. He'd entered the workshop after breakfast, but from the angle of the sun, he'd missed lunch. His stomach immediately reminded him of the fact, so Kron headed for the kitchen. If Bella wasn't helping to prepare the evening meal, one of the other women would be able to tell him where she'd gone.

He heard her voice before he saw her. Bella sat in front of the fire, peeling root vegetables and singing. Flilya and Caye ground corn for flatcakes, and Sylva cleaned fish. All of the women looked at him as he entered, and Bella fell silent.

"Sorry to interrupt," he said. "Bella, would it be possible for you to persuade an animal—any kind—to travel to Salth's crystal house, take a piece of it, and bring it back here? I'd like to study it."

She closed her eyes and stopped moving for a few heartbeats, but then she shook her head. "Sorry, Kron, all the animals strong enough to try attacking Salth's house are terrified of the area. I don't have the power to force a creature to suppress its fear for so long and over such a distance." She raised an eyebrow. "Not that I would want to."

"Even if it would protect us?"

"But I'm supposed to protect the animals!"

"We also need to use animals, Bella." Kron pointed to the fish Sylva was cleaning. "Otherwise, what would we eat? How would we plow fields and obtain wool? This is the same thing."

Bella didn't respond, but she looked away from him, studying Sylva. "What do you think Fall would say?" she asked.

Before the other Fall Avatar could reply, Domina entered the cooking area, dressed up in a silk robe and wearing a crystal pendant. Obviously she wasn't there to help with dinner. However, she carried a large glass bottle of a design Kron knew well.

"Is that...is that..." Kron intercepted Domina so he could examine the bottle up close. "Wine from Delns? Wherever did you find it?"

"In the marketplace, of course." She smirked. "Or didn't you know that a ship from your country arrived yesterday?"

"It did?" For a moment, Kron wondered how much it would cost to book passage for himself and Bella back to Delns. That had to be far enough away from Salth for her to leave them alone. Then he glanced at the other Avatars. Bella wouldn't want to leave them, and they wouldn't leave Vistichia except to fight Salth. He touched the bottle with great care. This would be the closest he ever came to returning home. He gave Domina a warm smile—but not too warm with Bella watching both of them. "Thank you for thinking of me."

Her eyes opened wide, making her look younger and more innocent than she really was. Then her mouth set in a calculated expression. "It's my pleasure to make our teacher as ... comfortable as possible."

Bella sang a couple of lines from a song about an unfaithful husband who lost all the women he slept with. Kron didn't need the warning. He stepped backward and said loudly, "We'll have to share the Delns wine with everyone."

"Or it could be a reward for the most skilled Avatar," Domina suggested.

"I'd be hard pressed to judge." Kron retreated to Bella's side. "And I do have a favorite, of course."

He leaned over and kissed her. It was only on her cheek, but it was enough to make her blush. Flilya and Caye grinned. Domina narrowed her eyes.

Bella returned to her work and shifted to singing a lullaby. Just as she began an ascending refrain, her notes became a shriek. She dropped her knife and put her hand on her skirt. An ember had jumped from the fire and burned a hole through the cloth.

"Are you all right, dear heart?" Kron asked. Now he wished he knew how to make healing artifacts.

"I'll fetch Galia," Flilya said, abandoning her corn. She grabbed the wine from Domina before leaving.

"It's not so bad." Bella spoke with indrawn breath that gave the lie to her brave words. Kron put an arm over her shoulders for reassurance, but she stared first at Domina, then Caye. Caye nodded slightly. She and Bella were part of the same quartet, but Kron knew they couldn't exchange thoughts without linking through Galia. So when Bella sang again, continuing her interrupted song, Kron wasn't sure what to expect.

Bella reached the highest note she could sing and held it. At the same time, the air suddenly grew warmer. With a faint pop, the crystal pendant Domina was wearing split and fell off of its chain.

She stared at it in confusion for a couple of heartbeats before whirling upon Caye. "What did you just do? You clumsy fool! Winter should have never picked you!"

Caye drooped, but Kron hurried over to pick up the crystal pieces. Bella and Caye had somehow conspired to damage Domina's necklace, but how? And could it work on a larger crystal, like Salth's house?

"Can you fix it, Kron?" Domina asked.

"Perhaps," he replied, "but I'd rather leave it as is for a while so I can study it." He turned over the fragments displayed on his palm. "This shattered crystal may be the key to bringing down Salth's house."

Crystal, Gold, and a Shell

"Do you honestly think Bella's singing could be the key to defeating Salth?" Galia asked that evening after dinner. Bella had the place of honor closest to the fire, with everyone gathered around her. Domina was the exception; she sat at the table with the empty wine bottle in her hands, staring at it. The glass sweated or beaded over with frost, changing at her whim.

"If singing's the key, why didn't the Four choose more musicians?" Bella said. "There were plenty of them at the old city-king's palace."

Kron had to agree that the rest of the Avatars lacked Bella's talent. Janno's baritone wasn't half bad, though his taste in songs must have been acquired while drunk. But Caye was too timid to speak above a whisper, let alone sing, and Carver made donkeys sound musical.

"Perhaps one singer is enough." Kron paced back and forth, examining every object in the room as a potential part of an artifact. "That, and an artifact." All he had to do was figure out what the artifact was supposed to accomplish.

"Bella couldn't have done it without Caye's help." If Domina still resented the loss of her pendant, she hid it well. "Caye made the crystal grow warmer. I felt it a heartbeat before it shattered. Watch this."

She placed the bottle in the center of the table and backed away, hands extended toward it. The frost on the jug melted, then turned to steam. The bottle burst with a larger pop, sending shards everywhere.

A couple of Avatars grumbled and brushed themselves off, while Galia and Magstrom healed minor cuts.

"Glass and crystal aren't the same," Kron said. "They feel different when I work with them."

"But it's still the same idea, isn't it? Maybe what you need are more Winter Avatars."

"Then why didn't Winter choose more of you?" Galia asked.

Domina's pleased expression slipped a little. "We were the best He could find?"

"One for each moon of a season," Caye said quietly.

"I think the Four wanted balance," Galia continued, speaking over Caye. "There are supposed to be equal numbers of us. Adding more Winters would throw that off."

Domina scowled. "But there's nothing wrong with saying Springs should be first and giving them extra magic?"

"Peace, all of you." Kron presented an open palm to each woman, but they glared at each other instead of listening to him. He raised his voice. "There's a simple way to solve this problem."

Bella gazed at him with a wry expression on her face, as if she already knew what he was going to say.

"I'll create an artifact that will multiply my wife's singing and the Winters' magic for creating heat to the strongest levels possible. That should bring down Salth's house."

Now all I have to do is figure out how.

* * *

The next day, Kron brought a sack full of artifacts to the marketplace. They sold faster than he'd expected, since he hadn't realized being married to an Avatar would bring him so much attention. Customers stopped to ask him to ask Bella for a favor and ended up bartering for one of his items as well. Others simply wanted to talk about the Four or ask if the chaotic storms would return. Kron reassured them as best as he could. By the time his sack was empty, his mind was full of questions—but still no ideas for the crystal-shattering artifact. Kron yielded his market space to a spice trader and roamed the market, seeking inspiration.

Let's see...making it warm while singing a loud note will do the trick. What items would help me with that? Lutes? Drums? Pipes? Bella's a singer, not an instrumentalist. What about heat? What would be useful for the Winters? Why just the Winters? The Four said all twelve Avatars need to journey to Salth's house, and I think that must be true even if I don't think they all need to travel upriver. Are they only needed for their linking power, or something more? What? What?

Kron didn't think the food section of the market held the answers, so he worked his way around the square. There were booths with spun wool, both natural and dyed; pots, cups, and plates, each one uniquely decorated; bronze mirrors; perfumes; jewelry; tools; weapons; games; and more. He stopped occasionally to feel rough yarn or cool clay, but nothing kindled his internal magical sense that always led him to what he needed. By the time the sunlight took on the clearness of pre-dusk, Kron had completed his circuit but still had no answer. Even though he was hungry, he pushed himself to head down to the docks. If Domina could find a bottle of wine from his homeland, surely he could figure out what he needed for his artifact.

Most of the ships had already finished unloading by the time Kron made his way past the taverns and brothels catering to the sailors. A couple of ships too large for the dock stood anchored in the harbor. Teams of oxen pulled barges loaded with barrels and pots up the Chikaski to the center of Vistichia, where they could be taken directly to the marketplace Kron had left. Kron watched the barges but felt no pull to investigate their wares. He doubted the crews would let him paw through their goods in search of something he couldn't identify yet.

He sighed. His instincts must be failing him. He should return home, even though he had no answers for Bella or the other Avatars. Instead, grim determination set him walking toward the water. Low tide had left a variety of natural treasures exposed on the beach. Seaweed didn't seem like it would be suitable for his needs, but Kron made his way to a patch of it anyway. Flotsam or jetsam always produced special effects in his artifacts.

He turned the seaweed over with his foot, watching for any crabs. They might be good to eat, but they would try to bite him in return. To his disappointment, no shiny coins or jewels appeared. Not even a piece of salt-stained wood from a wreck. All he could find were a few clam shells—and a type of shell he didn't recognize.

Kron dug the strange shell out of the sand. It was larger than his hand and heavier. Instead of being hinged at one end like the clam shells, this shell was a single piece, open in the middle and closed and twisted at the ends. The most intriguing feature of this shell was despite its rough exterior, the lip of the opening was smooth and pink.

Bella would love this. Even before she'd become a Fall Avatar, she'd enjoyed examining unusual things, like his artifacts. He doubted she'd ever seen a shell like this one before. However, the inside of the shell smelled rotten, despite the saltwater. Kron took the shell down to the edge of the beach and scooped out the decayed flesh with a piece of driftwood. He rinsed the shell thoroughly in the water. As he held the shell up to dry, a breeze picked up. At the same time, Kron thought he heard something humming. He glanced around the beach, but no one was close by, and gulls screeching, waves lapping at the sand, and sailors yelling to their mates would have covered up such a quiet sound.

Where is that coming from? He lowered the shell as he examined the water, and the humming stopped. *Strange. I don't think there's any magic already in this shell...*

Kron angled the shell until it caught the breeze, and the humming resumed. It was as if this shell could catch sounds in the air....

Suddenly seeing the possibilities this shell offered him, Kron sprinted back to the dock. As much as he wanted to show this to Bella, he needed to make some modifications first.

* * *

"Kron?" Bella called from the hallway. "Are you in your workroom again? Are you going to eat dinner tonight, or should we put the leftovers away and go to bed?"

Kron rolled his head from side to side, trying to ease the ache in his neck and shoulders, and glanced at the water clock. The level was lower than he'd expected. With only a single shell, he couldn't afford to experiment, so he'd had to create an artifact to help him figure out how to modify the shell for best results before he could begin his work. All he'd managed to do so far was drill a couple of holes in the shell and apply gold around them. Still, perhaps he should have Bella test it before he continued.

"Come here, dear," he replied. "I have something for you."

She opened the door. "It's late, Kron. Why don't we wait until morning?"

"Just come in. All I need you to do is sing into this."

She wove around the piles of supplies he hadn't had a chance to reorganize or move somewhere else. When he held the modified shell out to her, her eyebrows rose, and some of the sleepiness left her expression. "What is this?"

"A shell."

"Yes, I can see that. What did you do to it? It's too large to wear as a pendant."

"Just sing a couple of notes into itd." He pointed to the gold funnel on one end.

She gave him an odd look, but she complied with his request. Her voice was as soft as if she was singing a baby to sleep, but the notes resounded in the shell until they sounded like shouts.

"Kron! By All Four Gods and Goddesses, what was that?" Janno shouted from the room below.

Kron grinned. "It worked!"

"It did? You wanted a noisemaker?" Bella stared at the shell for a few heartbeats before her expression cleared. "Oh! You think if I sing into this, I can break Salth's house like I did Domina's pendant?" She shook her head. "I don't think this will be enough."

"It's not done yet," Kron said. He didn't tell her he hadn't figured out the next part of the artifact. He had a vague idea of stretching a chain or thread all the way around Salth's house, but he wasn't sure what material was most suitable.

"Will I need to sing a special song when I use this?" Bella asked. "My magic isn't related to singing."

"But it's related to animals, and this came from an animal. Maybe that will help."

She ran her fingers over the shell, even reaching inside, before nodding and tucking it under her arm. "Maybe you'd think better on a full stomach. Come eat something before we go to bed."

Kron drew her against him. "Ah, but my appetite's not for food."

She flushed and looked away. "I asked Galia if we'll ever be able to have children."

Then take my suggestion, dear.

"What did she say?" he asked when silence indicated Bella wanted him to respond.

"She says I should have no issues getting a child and carrying one, so she wants to check you next."

Kron clenched Bella more tightly. "She doesn't know about the star magic I carry, does she? Or that time flows a little more slowly for me?"

"She might sense it if she examines you closely enough. Does it matter?" Bella swallowed. "I mean, not just for a child."

"I don't know what the other Avatars will say when they find out. They might fear me, or think I'm more like Salth than them."

Bella shook her head. "You might be more like Salth in magic, but not in heart." She turned her face upward to meet his. "And that's what's important."

"Actually, I don't want to think about the other Avatars right now." Kron lowered his head until his lips were a kiss away from hers. "Just you."

And for a while, that's what he did.

* * *

Bella was still on Kron's mind the next morning as he returned to the marketplace, trying to figure out what else he needed for his artifact. A light snow fell, but none of the vendors or customers complained about the weather. Kron wondered if the recent storms had made the citizens of Vistichia more appreciative of normal weather, even if it wasn't sunny or warm. Then, as he approached the corner of the market where the goldsmiths display their wares, he heard a ship captain lean over and whisper to one of the merchants, "You'd best sell all your jewelry, or hide it somewhere no one can find it. Rumor has it there's a new type magician like your Avatars, but less helpful to ordinary people. He claims he's an Avatar for the God of War."

Kron halted. "What's this about a God of War?"

The captain straightened up and stared down at Kron past a long, thin nose that Kron impulsively wanted to pull. "Who are you?"

"An artificer, and husband of one of Vistichia's Avatars."

The goldsmith nodded. "Aye, Captain. I know him; we've done business before. He should hear what you told me."

The captain studied Kron for a moment before continuing, "I came from the east."

"Northeast, near Delns?"

"No, south of there. I normally sail between Halwiz and Vistichia."

Kron nodded. Halwiz was one of the coastal city-kingdoms across the Salt Waters. He'd never been there—it was farther south than Delns—but he'd heard it was a good trading port for spices, cotton, and copper.

"Anyway," the captain continued, "All the copper I'd been scheduled to bring here was gone. So were all iron and coal supplies. They'd been sent inland."

"Inland? Where to?"

The captain glanced around, as if suspecting a spy from one of the eastern city-kingdoms had disguised himself as an ordinary Vistichian. "The rumors aren't certain. Some say it's Fip, others say it's Kallentin."

Kron vaguely remembered touring Fip with his would-be-mentor-turned-slave-driver. Like Vistichia, it was situated on a river, but in Fip's case, it was at the conjunction of two rivers, an ideal spot for trade. Kron hadn't been allowed to see the famous animal collection at the palace, or anywhere past the smelly inn where his master had made him stay and create artifacts that he sold at great profit. He didn't know anything about Kallentin. Maybe it was his own bad memories of Fip that made him want to portal over there and investigate who was buying all the metal—and why.

He rubbed the back of his head. "You said something about an Avatar for a God of War. What sort of magic does he perform?"

"I don't know. Some say the God and His Avatar will create a new type of weapon, one that causes death and destruction worse than the last war."

"I hope that's not true," Kron said.

"I hope so too." The captain nodded at the goldsmith. "Think over my advice and let me know if you're ready to leave this city. We sail in four days."

The captain left, so Kron studied the goldsmith's work. He specialized in chains and finely spun strands of gold.

"Gold's easy to work," the goldsmith said, "and there's no other metal that stretches out as finely as gold does. And it never rusts or turns dark. It lasts longer than a marriage bond. Are you looking for a gift for your wife?" He winked. "Or another fine lady, perhaps?"

"Yes. I mean, no. I mean, I am married, but I need gold for another project." Kron studied a necklace with equal amounts of yellow, green, red and blue beads, partly to recover his composure and partly to study the craftsmanship. "How fine can you stretch gold until it breaks?"

"Finer than a hair on your head, good artificer."

The comparison reminded Kron there was less hair on his head than there used to be. A pity the star magic hadn't restored it. However, the goldsmith's chains, if enhanced for strength, might be useful for Kron's artifact. Unfortunately, they weren't long enough to wrap around Salth's house, but they might be useful for directing the energy of Bella's singing to weak points in the structure.

Although Kron had decided to purchase as many chains as he could barter for, he couldn't help but look at the four-colored necklace again. "Is that a tribute to the Four Gods and Goddesses?"

"How clever of you to notice," the goldsmith replied. "Yes, I made that after watching the Four in the square when They picked Their priests and priestesses. One of them came by last moon-phase and tried to heal my hands." He held one out so Kron could see how it trembled. He resumed working on his current project—twisting strands of metal together—as if his tremor was no hindrance. "I think she was more up-set than I was when she failed to make the shaking go away."

Kron hadn't known there were limits to the Spring Avatars' healing gifts. "And you still honor the Four?"

"No one else has even tried to help me, young man. And the midwife did do me some good. My vision's clearer than it's been in years."

"Galia is a good healer." Kron brushed a finger over the necklace, spinning the beads. "Are you planning to flee Vistichia, as the sea cap-tain advises?"

The goldsmith snorted. "By the Four, no. I've spent my whole life in this city. I'm too old to travel now, no matter who flatters me."

Or fails to give you back your youth. "Then perhaps you could help me with an artifact I must make for the Four."

Kron explained a little what he had to do, but he didn't tell the man the nature of Salth's soul-trap or how deadly it was. "I'll need as much gold wire as you can create," he said when he was done. "Long, but not too thin. I don't want it snapping at a critical time."

"Let me see your wares first," the goldsmith countered.

"I'm sold out today, but I can make something special for you if you want." Kron studied the man for a few heartbeats. "I could adapt a far-seer for you to help you with close work."

"A far-seer to see things close? I had no idea you could make such jokes." The man's fingers trembled as he reached for a topaz.

"It's no joke. Or..." Kron studied the man's hands. "Give me a pair of your thinnest gloves, and I'll enhance them so your hands don't shake so much."

The goldsmith's fingers halted in the air. "Now I know you're joking."

"I'm not. If I fail, I'll ask one of the Avatars to make you a new pair." Caye had been a seamstress and weaver before the God of Winter had chosen her.

"Stop by here tomorrow then, and I'll have the gloves."

"Good. You won't regret it."

As Kron walked off, he couldn't help but smile at the thought of how outraged Galia would become when he helped an old man deal with his infirmities in a way she couldn't.

* * *

Kron picked up the gloves the next morning, spent most of the day trying various materials to steady them, then finally returned to the marketplace to make final adjustments after the goldsmith tried them on. It was nearly dinner by the time the goldsmith pronounced himself satisfied. Not just satisfied, but amazed.

"Such magic as yours is as powerful as any of the Avatars," he told Kron. "Perhaps even stronger."

Kron couldn't help preening for a couple of heartbeats before he thought of Salth's pride in her magic. The praise went down like poison, but he put on a smile for the goldsmith's benefit.

"And how many chains are the gloves worth?" he asked.

"Four, one for each of the Avatars."

Disappointment left a sour aftertaste in Kron's mouth after the praise. Still, he could always barter other artifacts if necessary.

Maybe they won't be necessary. Four is a fitting number. I could put one on each corner, or link them together to string along one wall. Kron felt one of the chains between his fingers. It wasn't as fine as one of Bella's hairs, but he could spin it out and strengthen it with his magic.

"Very well," he said. "I'll take them."

He secured them in his pouch.

"Will they be safe in there?" the goldsmith asked.

"It's enhanced with protections against pickpockets."

The goldsmith rubbed his chin. "How useful. Could you protect my wares the same way?"

"My pouch is attuned to me. That wouldn't work for items you want to sell. But I could enhance some bells to act as alarms. We'll save that for another barter if I need more gold." Portaling would allow him to travel back and forth between Salth's domain and here if he needed to.

Kron turned to go, then casually glanced back as if he'd forgotten something. "Oh, and the necklace? What would you trade for that?"

The goldsmith smiled. "Which Avatar are you married to again?"

"Bella. The Fall Avatar who works with Galia."

"For her, nothing then." He extended the necklace to Kron as if giving him a great gift.

Kron thanked him and hurried home. He was very close to completing the artifact he needed to shatter Salth's crystal house. Once the boat was ready, he would be too. The thought filled him with more dread than pleasure. With no more reasons to postpone their trip, he had to lead his wife and the rest of the Avatars into the lair of a warped and divinely powerful magician.

CHAPTER EIGHTEEN

Departure

Kron wanted a moment alone with his wife before he addressed the entire group of Avatars, but before he could steal Bella away from dinner preparations, Janno bounded into the common room with a gleam in his eye.

"We did it!" he announced. "The boat is ready!" He grabbed each woman in turn and swung her around in a wild dance.

Kron stepped forward to snatch Bella away from him. "Ready? Are you sure?"

"We took the *Avatar*—that's what we named the boat—out in the river right around sunset. She sailed like a charm."

"I doubt we'll have charmed sailing once Salth finds out we're going to visit her."

Janno's eyes narrowed. "How would she find out?"

If she's watching me specifically, she'll find out as soon as we leave Vistichia. Perhaps all the portaling I plan to do will confuse her. Out loud, Kron said, "She has ways of tracking us. I'm sure magicians like us will attract her attention."

Galia stepped forward. "Can you hide us from her with one of your artifacts?"

"I could try, though if she detects the artifact, that would also give us away."

"What about the protections the Four put around the city?" Caye shuddered. "Will we be facing more weather storms again?"

"I think the protections are farther out, not just around the city." Kron looked around at each of the Avatars. "Speaking of protection, which group will wait here to protect Vistichia?" His head throbbed.

Galia and Magstrom stared at each other fiercely, while the third Spring Avatar, Tylan, watched them. Although nearly as old as Galia and considered a great surgeon, he had a stiff manner that reminded Kron of a couple of his teachers at the Magic Institute. He also tended to ignore Kron whenever he offered the Avatar advice, as if Kron's relative youth made him ignorant. Kron privately thought he was the least adept of the three Spring Avatars and would have chosen him to stay behind, were it not that meant he have to expose Bella to danger.

"The fairest way to do this is to draw a lot and leave this decision in the hands of the Four," Tylan said.

Did chance fall into the realm of any of the Four? If it didn't, would They find some way to influence the outcome? More importantly, should he make his own effort to rig the lot? Perhaps the Four would consider that blasphemy, but Kron had to put Bella's safety first, no matter how painful it was for both of them to be separated. Surely the Four would forgive his meddling for Bella's sake—even if she didn't.

Kron's headache dissolved. He examined the common room for something they could use for the lot. A few wooden spoons lay scattered on the table. They would do nicely. "Who's going to draw, the Spring Avatars?" he asked as he reached for them.

"Yes." Galia positioned herself between him and the table with unfortunate speed. "But you'd better not touch the spoons, Kron Evenhanded. You'd use your artifact magic on them faster than a father running from a screaming woman in labor."

Kron's hand trembled. Magstrom seized the spoons and carried them to the far corner of the room.

"What if he can still contaminate the drawing by his presence?" Tylan said. "He should leave the house and wait in the yard."

Bella put her fists on her hips. "He's my husband and our staunchest ally. That's no way to treat him."

Kron claimed the chair at the end of the table and crossed his arms. If they tried carrying him out, he'd make his robe adhere to the seat and the chair legs to the floor. "I would rather not lead any of you into danger, especially my dear Bella." Despite his words, he was afraid to meet her eyes, in case she thought he was insulting her with his protection. "But I am the one your own Gods and Goddesses asked to take you on this journey. So you'll suffer my presence now—or suffer my absence later."

His words rang in the room for several heartbeats. Finally, Galia said, "Will you give us your word not to interfere with the drawing?"

He bit back a sigh. "I promise."

"Then, let us move forward." She spoke with authority, as if she were the Avatar to lead all other Avatars. Kron couldn't help feeling proud that she respected his wife enough to include her in her group, even though a sick feeling in his stomach warned him Galia and the rest of her quartet were likely to face danger with him.

"How shall we mark the spoons?" Galia continued.

Her son came forward eagerly. "Let me color the wood."

Janno took the spoons away from Magstrom and clutched the handles. He squeezed his eyes shut, as if this task required extreme effort. When he opened his hand to display the spoons, one of them had turned dark brown, almost black.

"Thank you, dear," his mother said, making his cheeks turn scarlet. "Now, who will hold the spoons while the Spring Avatars choose their fates?"

All of the Avatars glanced around the room, but no one seemed willing to volunteer.

"Admit it, Kron said, "All of you will be affected by this lot, so all of you have as much reason to influence the decision as I do."

The lines around Galia's mouth deepened. "Then place them on the table, blindfold us, and let us all choose at once."

Everyone nodded at that. Carver and Ocul pulled the chairs away from the table, while Sylva, Caye, and Hala tied scarves around the

Spring Avatars' faces. With nervous giggling, they led the Spring Avatars to one side of the table, while Janno shuffled the spoons. The dark one ended up on the right. Kron tensed.

"The Springs can link with someone in their quartet and learn about the spoons that way," he pointed out. "Turn around and don't touch anyone while Janno mixes up the lots again."

Some of the tension left his stomach when everyone obeyed. The trip would be a long one if they refused to let him lead.

When the dark spoon was between the other two, Kron said, "All right. Spring Avatars, on the count of four, turn around, walk to the table, and take the first spoon you touch. Ready? One, two, three, four!"

Galia, Magstrom, and Tylan spun around and hurried to the table. Magstrom bumped Tylan, causing him to misstep and Galia to surge forward before both of them. Had that been intentional? Kron had no way to know. He clenched his fists as he watched Galia grab a light-colored spoon. The other Avatars watching didn't speak, but some of them let out breaths that they'd been holding. *Will Magstrom and Tylan learn anything from that?* They reached the table before Kron could decide if he should halt the lot. After fumbling for a couple of heartbeats, Magstrom held the light spoon and Tylan the dark one.

"You can look now," Kron said, even as murmuring among the other Avatars gave away who would go and who would stay behind.

The three Spring Avatars opened their eyes in unison. All three of them smiled as they checked their spoons. *How fortunate; they all seem to have gotten what they wanted. Perhaps the Four still listen to their Avatars even if They no longer appear to us.* Envy twisted inside of Kron for a heartbeat before he reminded himself he didn't owe his magic to anyone.

"It's decided, then." Tylan raised his spoon above his head so everyone could see it. "Ocul, Flilya, Hala, and I will remain behind for the first part of the trip in case Salth attacks again. The rest of you can leave civilization for a while and portal us to you when you need us."

"Wonderful." Janno slapped the table. "When can we leave?"

"We'll need food, plenty of it, and warm clothes," Domina replied. "Prices may be high in the market this time of year, but I'm sure I can haggle the merchants down. It should take no more than two to three days to gather everything we need."

But what about my artifacts? The shell is done, but I need some time to test the best placement of the gold chains on a crystal model. And what about protection from Salth's magic? I've barely done anything about that! Kron wanted to protest, but the words stuck in his dry throat. The Avatars surged forward, gathering about Galia and Magstrom, all exchanging ideas and arguments faster than he could follow. Even Bella was caught up in the excitement. She and Sylva went off to the side, discussing the types of wild animals they might encounter and how useful they could be. Ocul passed a scroll to Magstrom, who unrolled it and weighed three of the corners with the fateful spoons. The scroll showed a map of the Chikasi River, with settlements marked by simple figures. Kron had no idea the Avatars possessed such knowledge of the river. His travel experience would be less important now.

Kron backed out of the room, but no one came after him, not even Bella. "If anyone wants me, I'll be in my workroom," he said. This time, he didn't bother pitching his voice to gain attention, and not surprisingly, no one turned or responded.

It doesn't matter what I do. They come to me only when they want something, otherwise I'm as welcome as Salth's storms.

As he entered his workroom, the thought came to him that no matter how others treated him, he always had his magic as a constant companion, always responding. Was that why Salth loved magic so much?

He stared at his tools and materials for a long time contemplating the answer.

***

Kron let the other Avatars gather the mundane supplies while he frantically tested and reassembled artifacts, packed and unpacked supplies, and wore himself out with little sleep and less food. When he finally came up with a workable protective artifact, suitable for protecting a single person, Bella and a few other Avatars dragged him away from the workroom before he could make twelve more artifacts.

"I'm not done yet," he said as Janno pressed him into the room Kron shared with Bella.

His wife glared at him. "Well, you're not returning to your workroom until you finish this bowl of soup."

He slurped the noodles, broth, and greens down quickly, burning his tongue in his haste. As soon as he laid down his spoon, weariness overtook him, and he didn't resist when Bella led him to bed and covered him with a blanket.

The next thing Kron knew, the room was dark, with gray light coming through the window. "Get up, dear." Bella shook him. "It's time to go."

He rubbed his eyes, trying to reach an ache behind them. "I think I slept longer than I planned."

"You needed the rest. Go wash your face. We have to get ready."

"Yes, I must finish the artifacts—"

"By all Four, I think that sleeping potion Janno made was too strong. You're not going to your workroom today, Kron. Today's the day we leave Vistichia."

Her words jolted him awake. "We are? But how? We can't be ready!" *I'm not ready.*

Bella smiled. "It's all right, Kron. We knew you were busy, so we handled the arrangements ourselves."

"But my equipment and supplies—" Kron put his feet on the floor, intending to rush to his workroom and gather everything he could carry. The floor was cold, and he couldn't find his indoor sandals.

"We already packed them, or at least what would fit in the boat." Bella held out a pair of fur-lined boots. "Here. You'll need these when we leave."

Kron pulled them on quickly, then hurried toward his workroom. "Who chose what to take and what to leave behind?" He asked as Bella struggled to keep up with him. "If it was Janno, he probably ignored my successful artifacts and took the ones that didn't work."

"Don't worry. I'm the one who told them what you'd need. I can tell while piles of things are something you're working on and which ones are trash."

Kron refrained from commenting for fear of upsetting her. But when he inspected his workroom, he had to admit she'd done a good job. She hadn't known about the gold chains, since he'd hidden them in a gourd, but she'd collected everything else he needed, especially the shell. He picked up the gourd, along with more rope and a bar of metal. One could never have enough of either of them.

"What do you need the gourd for?" Bella asked. "It doesn't seem like something you would normally use."

"Neither was the shell," he reminded her.

After a quick breakfast, all of them, even the Avatars who would remain behind, proceeded to the river docks. They were located in a wide bend of the river and looked as if they'd been washed away and rebuilt a couple of times. Janno proudly led them to the center dock. "Welcome to the *Avatar.*"

The boat was as long as a royal barge, with tapered ends at the bow and the stern. A cabin occupied most of the center, and a sail sprouted from it like a lily. Kron couldn't have made a finer boat himself. Perhaps he should have made his own and sailed away to Delns before he'd gotten tangled up with Salth and the Four. But then he wouldn't have met Bella...

He stepped onto the dock and said, "May this be the last time I have to return to Salth's house."

Bella, Galia, Janno, and all the other Avatars followed him to the boat. Each of them carried some last-minute necessity. Tylan led the final three Avatars down to the dock, but they didn't step on to it.

"When will we see you next, Kron?" Tylan asked.

Normally it would take them at least two weeks to travel all the way to the Western Mountains via the Chikasi, but that was in summer. Kron wasn't sure yet if Caye and Domina would be able to keep the river clear of ice and provide a steady wind to push them, despite their assurances they could do it. Perhaps they would fail to leave the city, or even the dock. He wouldn't be upset if this voyage came to an early end, as long as everyone was safe. Especially Bella.

"I'll return once we're ready to leave the boat," Kron replied. He extended a hand to help Galia and Bella on board. Janno leaped in, then took Caye's baskets from her. Despite being short, she managed to climb aboard the ship without assistance.

Kron moved away from the side to give the rest of the Avatars space to board. He poked his head into the cabin. Hammocks were stacked one above another above yet another, and there were two more sets of hammocks beyond the column by the door. By the Four, were they really all going to share the same quarters? How was he supposed to get private time with his wife? She'd be upset if they couldn't attempt to conceive a child. The only good thing about this arrangement was that Kron could poke Janno without leaving his bed whenever the Avatar snored.

"I hope this will turn out to be a short trip," he told Galia as he returned to the deck.

"I don't." She softened her tart voice with a smile as she gazed around her. "I've never left Vistichia before and can't wait to see what it's like outside the city. You've traveled this way before, haven't you? Are there any more cities along the river?"

"Nothing as big as Vistichia." He leaned against the railing, watching Ocul and Tylan struggle with the knots on the lines. None of the Avatars coming on this journey knew anything about sailing. The Four would have to work a miracle for them to make it out past the city walls without tipping over.

"But you said there were trading villages where we could pick up fresh supplies, right?"

"During the normal travel season, yes. Now, I don't know if anyone will be willing to empty out their larders for us in the middle of winter."

"Don't worry so much, Kron," Galia said. "The gifts we Avatars have will stop a lot of unnecessary deaths this season."

"I hope you're right. But if we're going to save lives, we should do it by stopping Salth."

Flilya finally took pity on her fellow Avatars and unraveled the ropes with a touch. The ends slithered into the water. The *Avatar* listed to one side for a heartbeat, but before Kron could add his weight to the other side, Caye took up position behind the sail and raised her hand. The cloth billowed above Kron, but not a breeze stirred his hair. Not enough force in the wind, he guessed. Caye kept their speed slow as she maneuvered them away from the dock and the last four Avatars waving and shouting advice.

Galia sighed. "At this speed, I'll die of old age before we reach Salth."

"Give her time to learn this, Galia. If she's ready, she's ready. If not—"

The boat came to a halt as they reached a part of the river that was more frozen than free.

"I'd better see if she needs me," Kron said before going back to check on Caye. Domina raced past him to the front of the boat, grinning as she directed her magic against the ice. For all of her faults, she handled her weather magic as if she'd been doing it all her life, not just a couple of moons. She would be very useful in the battle against Salth— if they made it there in one piece.

* * *

The Four Gods and Goddesses must have been watching out for the Avatars. Despite their lack of sailing or navigation experience, Caye and Domina managed to keep the wind constant and the river clear. They came dangerously close to the river's edge a few times, but Domina called up an opposing wind each time, loudly calling to Caye each time that she would take care of it. By sunset, both Winters trembled with exhaustion, but Caye seemed more drained than Domina.

"Bring the boat in over there." Kron directed them to a small bend in the river not far from where he'd shared a lunch with Sal-thaath. "We'd better tie up for the night so the Winters can rest." Perhaps he and Bella could find a private spot to sleep. Surely the two of them could keep warm enough if they shared a single blanket.

"Are you going to sleep on shore?" Galia peered at the bushes as if already picking her spot.

While Kron searched for a way to gently discourage her from joining them, Caye, looking even more pale than normal, said, "Please, I want off. The boat..."

She sagged. Janno caught her before she hit the deck.

Galia and Magstrom pushed through the staring Avatars in a struggle to be the first to reach her. Galia, accompanied by Bella, won. She laid a hand on Caye's forehead.

"Is she all right?" Bella asked.

"She's exhausted from using her magic all day. She needs meat and a chance to rest."

Bella nodded and entered the cabin. A few heartbeats later, thumping sounds emerged. Kron guessed she was searching for a basket of dried meat.

The Avatars' magic seems to be especially draining. It had been a long time since Kron had had to push himself as much as Caye had done today, so perhaps it wasn't fair to think of the Avatars as being weaker than him. But they hadn't traveled as far today as he'd hoped they would. What if Caye didn't recover overnight but required extra rest? Then their trip would take even longer.

Maybe she and Domina can take turns with the wind. Or is melting ice just as draining? Kron glanced around for Domina. Fear rose in him when she wasn't immediately visible, but he finally found her curled up by the stern, her head touching her knees.

"Domina?" He shook her arm. "We're stopping for the night. Come rest and eat something. You'll feel better."

She raised her head to glare at him, but the weariness in her gaze muted her ferocity.

"Magstrom!" Kron called. "Domina needs you!"

The Spring Avatar detached himself from the group surrounding Caye and hurried over. "Domina! Did you faint?"

"I don't faint." Her words came out under her breath.

"Here, take my hand." Magstrom smiled tenderly at her as he sent more energy into the Winter Avatar. A blush returned to her cheeks, but Kron suspected that had more to do with Magstrom's attention than his magic.

"I hate to interrupt a private moment," he said, "But By All Four of your Gods and Goddesses, Magstrom, why didn't you do that sooner? The Winters are going to need all the energy you can give them if we're going to reach Salth's domain before the summer solstice."

Magstrom rounded his shoulders. "I thought she could handle it. She said she could handle it."

"But did you check?"

Instead of answering, he gave Kron a dark look, as if questioning his right to doubt an Avatar.

"See that you do so tomorrow. If we need to halt to let the Winters rest, we'll do so."

Kron left them so he could instruct Galia to do the same thing. She, at least, nodded and looked rueful for not having thought of it herself. "It's the excitement of being out of Vistichia," she said. "I'll keep a close eye on Caye tomorrow."

"Do you think she'll be ready to travel tomorrow?" Kron asked.

Caye looked up from the bowl of dried meat Bella had prepared for her. It didn't look appetizing, but she'd already eaten most of it and seemed to have more energy. "I'll do my best, Kron. I don't want to disappoint the Four."

The Avatars may have been united in their devotion to the Four, but they seemed divided in their feelings for Kron. When Galia and Caye decided they would sleep on shore with Kron and Bella, Janno followed suit, leaving Magstrom and the rest of his quartet in the ship's cabin.

"Maybe we should return to the boat," Bella said as she glanced at the snow-covered riverbank. "The cabin will be warmer than this."

"Not to worry, dear. Our blanket will keep us warm." Kron examined the campsite, then laid out their bed near a small hill that would shield them from the others. Not as much privacy as he'd hoped for, but still better than what they could find on board.

"But what about Galia? And Janno and Caye?"

"I can enchant their blankets as well."

While he did so, Janno lit a fire and hauled water from the Chikasi. Galia and Bella cooked a stew, waving aside Caye's offer to help. The other quartet of Avatars didn't join them for dinner, taking some of the flavor away. Carver came out once to wave to them, but he didn't speak.

"Magstrom needs to learn who's leading this frozen trip," Kron grumbled.

"You may be leading this trip, but we Springs lead the Avatars, Kron." Galia drew herself up straight. "Let him worry about managing Domina's magic. I have to focus on Caye, and I can't link directly with Domina anyway."

"I'm sure by morning things will be better between you and Magstrom," Bella said.

He ran his hand down her back and murmured into her ear, "And how shall we make the time pass until then?"

The other three Avatars grinned when Kron and Bella retired to their bed as soon as they'd eaten, but even Janno refrained from crude comments.

After making love to Bella—and struggling to keep it quiet—Kron said to her, "Close your eyes. I bought you something." He sent protective magic into the necklace before draping it over her head.

Bella didn't wait for permission before examining it. She smiled. "It's beautiful."

"Not as much as you." He pulled her closer to him, enjoying the feel of her plump breasts against his chest. "Bella, I know you're an important part of our plan to destroy Salth's house of death, but please, protect yourself. Don't hesitate to flee if she attacks, even if I or the other Avatars are in trouble."

"How can you ask that of me? Do you think I could live with myself afterward, knowing I was too much of a coward to save my friends or my husband?"

"Do you think I like knowing the person I love most is also the one Salth is most likely to hurt?" He touched the necklace. "I've put as much protective magic into this necklace as I can manage, but against Salth's power, that may not be enough."

"Salth may be powerful, but she's not half as clever as you." She brushed her fingers against his chin. "You saved me once from her. I have faith you're as important to this task of stopping her as I am, maybe more. Let's forget about her for a while and enjoy being together."

Kron pleasured her again, and afterward, she fell asleep in his arms. Her drowsy warmth and the hushed murmur of the river nearly lulled him to sleep too, but first he hauled himself out of the blanket—a tricky thing to do without waking his wife—and set wards around the campsite. Then he boarded the *Avatar* and set a ward there too. Magstrom might be angry at him, but they couldn't afford to be enemies when they ventured close to Salth's territory.

* * *

Kron started awake, unsure at first what had startled him. Then a spark flashed by the river. One of his wards had gone off. He raised his head, searching for whatever triggered the ward. Nothing moved, not even tree branches laden with snow. The ward winked again, as if it was trying to trick him. The boat creaked, and something splashed in the water. Maybe an animal was wandering around in the night, but it shouldn't have triggered his ward, especially twice. With a sigh, Kron pried himself out of Bella's embrace and left their bed, tucking the blanket around her to keep her warm.

Unwilling to use a light and scare off whatever had triggered the ward, Kron waited until his eyes had adjusted to the darkness before heading toward the ward by the boat. They'd tramped around enough while setting up camp to make trails in the snow. He followed one now, letting his feet find the path while he scanned the campsite. None of his other wards had gone off. Maybe this was a mistake. Maybe he hadn't been as careful in setting up the wards as he'd thought, and this one had gone off accidentally. But he knew he wouldn't be able to sleep unless he checked first.

When he reached the boat without further signs of activated wards, Kron took a stone from his pouch and tapped it. The stone glowed with enough light for him to see two or three paces in front of him. Kron examined the ward he'd set on the boat's hull near the bow, as high as he could stretch. He'd made this ward using a strand of hair from Bella's head, a magic-finder, and a hunk of misshapen copper. The copper had melted and the hair had snapped, both signs that the ward had been triggered by magic and not accident. Could it have been one of the Avatars? Kron thought he'd set the ward to recognize the four types of magic the Avatars used, just as the ward would recognize his own magic and not react to it. But even if he'd omitted that step, Magstrom's quartet had been inside the cabin since dusk. They shouldn't be close enough to the ward to set it off.

If magic happened around here, then what did it do? Frowning, Kron reached for the ward again, but his fingers didn't touch it. He swung the glowstone around to make sure the ward hadn't fallen into the water. No, there it was, just above him. But he didn't have to extend his arm so far to touch it.

By All Four, what's going on?

He touched the ward again to confirm that was indeed closer to him now, then brought the glowstone closer to examine it. As he did so, he noticed the wood planks no longer ran parallel to the river, but tilted at an angle.

The *Avatar* was sinking.

CHAPTER NINETEEN

A Sinking Boat

Kron tilted his head back and roared as loud as he could, "Magstrom! Domina! Carver and Sylva! Wake up! The boat is sinking!"

He took the glow stone between his teeth and placed both hands on the hull. Now that he searched for it, he could tell that magic had been used to breach the hull on the bottom. The hole was smaller than his hand, but it resisted his first attempt to seal it.

I need to get as close to it as possible. Since he wasn't going to wade into the icy river, Kron needed to get onto the *Avatar*. But when he sprinted for the ladder, it had been drawn back onto the boat.

He spit out the glow stone and called again, "Magstrom! Domina! Wake up and get off the boat before you drown!"

"Kron? What's going on?" Janno yawned as he approached him.

"The boat—there's a hole in the bottom. Can you fix it with your magic?"

"A hole? Now? Which one of the Winters did it?"

"It wasn't them! It must have been Salth!" Kron grabbed Janno's arm and dragged him to the *Avatar*. "Can you feel it? Better yet, can you get the ladder? It's on deck, and I need to get on board."

"Only you would be crazy enough to board a sinking boat," Janno muttered. But he laid his hands on the wood.

"Can you feel it?" Kron asked.

"What, the ladder? No. But I can feel the hole." He grimaced, his face looking monstrous in the low light. "It's like the wood rotted away. But I cut that tree myself. I know the wood was good."

"Never mind that now. We need to board the ship and get the other Avatars off."

Janno grinned. "I should be able to get their attention."

"No, I'll do it," Bella said behind them.

Kron turned to face her. "What are you doing here?"

"Your shouting woke us up."

Sure enough, Galia and Caye plodded toward them. Kron felt guilty he'd disturbed them, since they needed rest. But they might still be able to help him.

"What's wrong with the boat?" Bella asked. "Why is it tilting like that?"

While they'd been distracted, the boat had sunk another handspan. Why weren't the other Avatars awake yet? Were they really stubborn enough to shut themselves in the cabin while their ship sank, or had they been spelled by the magic that had broken through the ward?

"The boat's been sabotaged," Kron said. "We need to wake the other Avatars and get them off."

"Oh, that's easy enough. A few flea bites in sensitive areas should get them going."

One of the advantages of having a wife with a gift for animal magic was that she'd discovered how to repel lice and fleas from their clothes and bed. Kron would have expected Sylva to know that trick too, but if she was sleeping, then she wasn't actively protecting herself or the other Avatars. Kron couldn't help but grin at the thought of Magstrom's nose—and other areas—getting bit. Then he looked at the boat again. This situation was too serious for jokes.

"Janno, can you do anything about that rotten wood around the hole?" he asked again.

"I...I don't know. The wood's not alive anymore, Kron. It was easier to work with when it was fresher. Isn't this boat like one of your artifacts now?"

"Yes, but I need to move closer to the damaged area. Can you get the ladder, or maybe make one?"

"Let me see what I can find."

Janno retreated to the bushes at the same time as Magstrom finally bolted out of the cabin, followed by the other Avatars.

"Kron!" Magstrom shook a fist at him. "By All Four, what are you doing?"

"Trying to save you and the boat! You get off and let me get on!"

When he stood there, glaring at Kron as if he'd wrecked the boat, Sylva grabbed his arm. "Do as he says, fool! Can't you feel we're taking on water?"

"I'm sure he did this," Magstrom said. However, Carver grabbed the ladder and lowered it.

About time. Kron stuffed the glow stone back in his pouch and climbed by feel, not sight. The ladder tilted for a heartbeat, and he gripped it tightly, trying to brace himself against the side of the boat so he wouldn't fall over. Then the ladder steadied, and he hurried up as quickly as he could.

As soon as Kron landed on the deck, he reactivated the glow stone. Magstrom stepped in front of him before he could start searching for the hole. "What did you do to the boat? You know the Four wanted us to sail the Chikasi, not use your portals. Are you trying to force us to do things your way?"

Kron sighed. He didn't have time for explanations, especially when he'd already given one and been ignored.

"Ask Janno what happened. Better yet, find me something waterproof I can use as a patch. Carver, I might need your help with the wood."

Galia's voice drifted up to them. "Janno, let me climb up there."

"Mother, the boat's sinking!"

"It won't with Kron here to fix it."

At least one of the Springs believed in him. Kron let the conversation fade into the background, like the water rippling under the ice, and headed for the bow of the boat. Janno and the boat builder had laid a deck over the hull of the boat instead of simply building the cabin right on the hull. Kron had first thought the design extravagant and wasteful, even though the boat builder had assured him the trapped air would help keep the boat afloat. Now he appreciated their expertise. Without the deck, the boat would be sinking even more rapidly than it was. However, the deck also blocked the hole in the hull. He might have to remove part of the deck to fix the hole.

"Someone fetch my pouch and tools, please." Kron paced back and forth, narrowing down the area where the hole was. He was very close; if he strained his ears, he could hear water bubbling up into the air space between the deck and the hull.

"What else should we do?" Sylva asked as she handed him this pouch.

"Leave the boat, of course." Kron knelt and listened. Yes, the hole was right below him.

"Isn't there anything we can do to help?" Domina asked. "Do you want me to freeze the water so it stops coming in?"

"Freeze all of the water? That could break the boat!"

"That's not what I meant. I could create an ice cap over the hole."

Kron glanced at Domina. "Do you really have that much control?"

"Of course!" She'd draped herself in a blanket, and her hair was loose of its normal elaborate style, but she still seemed not just determined, but fully restored.

"Then do it." If she could manage the ice cap, it would give Kron more time to seal the hole. He still hadn't found anything that could work as a patch.

Domina knelt next to him. Kron ran his fingers along the planks, searching for the pegs that held them together. When he found one, he summoned it out of the plank with his magic and set it aside. Three more pegs followed rapidly, but the plank was so well shaped it fit in snugly next to the other ones, as if all the boards had grown like this in the tree trunk. He pressed against one end, but the board remained stuck. Kron pulled a knife out of his pouch and outlined the board with the tip, sending thoughts of separation through the blade. This time, he was able to pop the board out of the deck. Cautiously holding the glow stone over the opening, Kron peered into the air space.

A stench both magical and mundane assaulted him. Part rotten fish, part spoiled egg, and part blood and death, the odor presented a barrier almost as strong as the planks of the boat. Kron wished Galia was here to block his sense of smell; it would need healing after he was done. For now, he gripped his robe in his teeth and drew it up over part of his face. The protections he'd placed on the cloth didn't remove the bad smell completely, but it did filter out part of the odor, confirming Kron's guess that Salth's magic had contributed to it. If only he could fix the hole as easily.

He had to get down on his stomach and press his head against the deck to see the hole—or rather, Domina's ice cap. It glinted against the dark water like silver in a pile of rocks. He maneuvered so he could stick his hand into the air space. Only by moving to the edge of the plank and stretching his arm until he nearly dislocated his shoulder was he able to touch the hole. He found the ice first. As Domina had promised, she hadn't frozen all of the water, but it still stole warmth and flexibility from his fingers. The cap was slightly smaller than his hand. When Kron touched the edge of the wood, he could feel what Janno had described. The wood crumbled under his touch like cheese. Underneath the physical damage he could feel the oily magic of Salth. Or was it hers? Something about it felt different. But Kron had no time to ponder the difference. The ice plug Domina had created slipped out of the hole. The cursed wood wouldn't be able to accept a patch until he removed Salth's magic.

Domina's eyes were shut, a sign she was probably still trying to make another ice plug for the hole. Was anyone else on the boat?

"Can someone bring me my bag from the cabin?" he called.

When no one answered, he grumbled and extracted his arm from the hole, then struggled to his feet. He might not be as old as Galia, but he felt like it tonight. There was a noticeable tilt in the deck as he made his way to the cabin. Even with a glow stone, it took him longer than he wanted to find something that would contain Salth's magic. He settled for an empty perfume bottle with a clay stopper. He rolled the bottle in his hands, enhancing its strength, as he returned to the boat's bow.

Domina's eyes were open. "I lost the ice cap, and I can't make another one." she told him, hugging her knees to her chest.

"Let me disenchant the wood first before you try it again. Do you think you could remove the water?"

"My magic isn't about water; it's about...weather." She gestured at the sky. "I need more space, or sunlight, to do anything with it."

"Then find some buckets. We'll need to bail out some water after I'm done."

This time when he plunged his arm into the gap, water reached halfway up to his elbow. The bottle resisted his efforts to force it next to the hole, but since the bottle was only as long as his forefinger, he had enough strength to overcome the repelling spell Salth had woven into her curse. As soon as the bottle's lip sank into the soft wood, Kron exerted his own magic and pulled Salth's curse into the bottle. Her magic had no mass or form, but even so, the bottle felt heavier. When Kron judged he'd captured the entire spell, he pulled the bottle away, capping it as quickly as he could. Part of him wanted to hurl the bottle into the river, but who knew how long the curse would have power? The bottle could break, or the stopper come loose, leaving the curse free to damage something else. For now, he'd label the bottle and keep it until Salth was neutralized. Maybe then her magic would be harmless.

With effort, he worked his arm out of the gap in the deck. "Try sealing the gap now," he told Domina. "Janno was right; the wood around the hole is rotten. He'll have to replace it, and then the rest of you need to bail out the water before we can continue our journey."

"Us? What about you?" she asked.

Kron sighed. "I need to sleep."

CHAPTER TWENTY

An Encounter

The group was able to resume travel by noon the next day. Kron wasn't sure if the Four had secretly intervened on their behalf, or if Salth was reserving further attacks for when they approached her realm. Either way, the challenges he and the Avatars had to cope with were easier to deal with. Caye and Domina still squabbled about who should sail the boat and who should break the ice, but they shared tips about each task. Every day, the number of furlongs they sailed increased. This was even more impressive because the land sloped gently upward, toward the mountains. They passed fewer farms and villages as they drew closer to the Western Mountains.

When Kron wasn't needed, he claimed a space next to the cabin and prepared more protective artifacts. With the boat rocking back and forth—not to mention the sudden starts and stops—it was difficult to keep his materials in place, let alone concentrate on assembling and enchanting them. At least the Winter Avatars kept the ship warm. Bella sat with Kron, keeping him company, fetching supplies when they scattered across the deck, and occasionally scouting ahead with birds.

"There's a group of people traveling next to the river," she announced one afternoon. "They're heading toward us."

Kron carefully coiled his gold wire before he snapped it. "How many of them do you see? What do they look like, and how are they travelling?"

Bella closed her eyes for a few heartbeats. "It's a large group, at least fifty people, with a few horses and cattle. The animals are pulling wagons, with women and a few children riding."

A group of families would be less likely to fight than merchants or soldiers. Kron instructed Caye to steer them closer to the opposite shore, just in case.

The first few wagons appeared a short while later. From the way the animals strained to pull them, the wagons had to be filled with everything these people owned. Perhaps they were fleeing from Salth's destruction. Kron wondered if it might be worth speaking with these people after all.

Bella clenched his arm. "Do you see how the driver is whipping that team of horses? Can't he tell they're straining themselves already? I should do something!"

"But what, Dearest? Tell them to lighten their wagon?" Kron stroked his chin. Some stubble poked through his skin, but he wouldn't need to shave until the moon was full. "Actually, that's not a bad idea. Perhaps I could barter with them for more supplies. We can't take anything too big with us, but I might find something useful for an artifact anyway." He called to Caye, "I've changed my mind. We should sail closer to them."

"Now you tell me." The boat leaned sharply as she turned it. "We might overshoot them."

Galia clutched the cabin door as she peeked out. "What's going on?"

Kron pointed at the shore. "Travelers. A chance to trade and learn more about what's ahead."

They were close enough to make out people's faces. The group had come to a halt, with a few wagons decorated with red-and-white triangles catching up with them.

"I wonder if they have fresh food," Galia said thoughtfully. "Even a few herbs to season dinner would be welcome."

A stout man waddled forward. He appeared to be only a few years older than Kron. His robe of finely spun wool with stripes of scarlet and black stood out in the crowd of people dressed in brown. He carried a staff decorated with fringe and bells. Kron studied it intently but couldn't detect any magic in it.

"You there, on the boat!" The man pointed his staff at Kron. "Are you the leader?"

Galia mumbled something Kron couldn't make out. He gestured at her to remain silent and keep the other Avatars in the cabin. Until they knew if the strangers were friendly or hostile, it was wise to keep their numbers—and their talents—hidden.

He put on a smile. "I'm Kron Evenhanded, lately from Vistichia. Who are you, and where are you from?"

"Lammar Marstud, father of the Mount Clan." Lammar didn't match Kron's friendly expression. "How does your boat sail so swiftly in the middle of winter, especially when there is no wind?"

"I might ask why you and your clan wander during this dangerous season."

"Only because death has spread into our land. If you're fleeing death as well, then all of us are doomed."

"Fear not, Lammar. This land still thrives." Although the boat was too far away for Lammar to board, Kron beckoned him forward, hoping the gesture would encourage him to talk. "What sort of death stalks your land? Another plague? Famine?"

"Both and neither," Lammar answered. "This plague kills all life. Everything ages and dies out of time."

Kron fought to keep his expression still. This was definitely more of Salth's work, except for the fact that these people had somehow managed to escape her. How had they done that when everything else in her domain was dead or dying?

"I'd love to learn more about this dying land, and how you got away before suffering a similar fate," he said. "If you've time to spare, we could come ashore and barter both goods and information."

Lammar glanced up at the sky before answering. "Perhaps for a level of the water clock. We need to find a suitable place to spend the night."

Kron directed Caye to bring them over to the bank. They had to sail on a little farther until they found a tiny beach where they could disembark. Kron searched through his materials for something he could part with but still valuable enough to offer in barter.

"Food is always a good bartering tool," Galia said. She sat in one of the lower bunks, swaying as she watched him. "But is this a good idea, Kron? We don't know anything about these people."

"I know they were exposed to Salth's time magic but didn't die." He hauled a jar of beer closer to the entrance. "If I can learn how they managed that, I could get some new ideas how to protect us—and others."

"Are you sure they don't have magic of their own?"

"I'll know for certain once I go on shore. The magic finder isn't reacting to them, but I might have to get closer if their magic is weak." He frowned as he thought about what he'd said. How could weak magic survive an encounter with Salth's strength? It couldn't. Perhaps they had some way to counter or neutralize magic. If so, he—and the Avatars—would have to be even warier than they were now.

Galia tapped her fingers on the cabin wall. "I wonder if I should go with you. Perhaps if I offer my magic healing for barter, we could obtain more supplies. We'll need lots of food before we face Salth, and it sounds like we won't be able to find anything when we get close to her home. Besides, what if these people have been affected by Salth's magic but don't know it yet?" She pushed herself off of the hammock. "It's my duty to make sure they're healthy before letting them get too close to Vistichia."

A few moments ago, Kron would have welcomed her assistance with the Mount Clan. Now, he wondered if it would be safer for her to remain behind. But how could he convince her of that?

He checked his pouch for defensive objects. Yarn would work, even though it was short. "Galia, Salth's curse isn't subtle. If she was draining these people of their remaining time, they'd already be dead."

Her forehead furrowed. "I suppose the Four wouldn't permit Salth's curse to extend too close to Vistichia. But these people could still carry a plague. I'd best check."

Kron bit back a sigh. If she wouldn't stay behind, they should bring another Avatar with them to help defend themselves. Should it be Janno or Caye? He refused to consider Bella. Maybe he wanted to protect her too much, but unless there were more wild animals about than was normal in winter, Bella wouldn't be able to do much else than make the draft horses run off. Janno could damage any wooden weapons or the wagons, while Caye's magic was the most flexible. But when Kron approached her seat and found her slumped over, sleeping, he decided it was more important to let her rest. He beckoned Janno over and explained the situation to him in a whisper so Galia wouldn't overhear them. Janno stared at his mother with so much worry in his expression Kron feared Galia would suspect something.

"Here. Take this." Kron piled magic-finders and a few semiprecious gems into a basket, then handed it to Janno. "Don't tell the strangers that you're an Avatar, not until we know what their intentions are."

Janno scowled. "So, I'm just there to be a porter?"

"Well, you can show off your strength and flirt with the women too. Maybe you'll learn something useful from them."

Janno's expression lightened at the idea.

Kron descended first from the *Avatar* so he could hold the rope ladder steady for Galia and then catch the basket that Janno lowered. Janno brought down a second basket full of fish by strapping the basket to his back. Lammar strode forward to welcome them. "What have you brought to trade? Fish?" He laughed. "That's the last thing we need so close to a river!"

"Ah, but these are saltwater fish, not from the river," Galia told him. "We brought these from Vistichia, but they're smoked so well they'll last for moons. Go on, try a sample."

While she distracted Lammar, Kron tucked a magic-finder into his pouch and wandered around. Some of the other travelers had started fires for cooking, while others tended to their beasts. He didn't recognize the tools they used, but his magic-finder didn't glow or grow warm.

He stopped by one of the men. "What is that artifact you're using to start the fire? I've never seen anything like it."

"It's not an *artifact*." The man spat out the word. "And it's not something I can share with an outsider."

Maybe not, but I can make some guesses. The device appeared to be metal, but although it was silver-colored, it didn't gleam. Kron's fingers twitched, aching to touch the object and decipher its secrets. He needed another distraction. Could Janno provide one?

Kron circled back to where Janno was attempting to flirt with a young woman who didn't know their language. "Could you come with me?"

"Can't you see I'm busy?" Janno countered, stepping closer to the woman. She retreated.

"I need your help to investigate something."

"You want my help? Well, in that case...."

Janno set his baskets down, grunting as if they were heavier than they actually were, and followed Kron back to where he'd seen the man with the metal tool. The man was coaxing kindling to catch fire, but the metal tool he'd used before wasn't visible.

"What do you want me to do?" Janno asked.

Kron winced. "Whisper so they don't hear you," he said, suiting the action to the word.

"Is that it?"

"No. There's a special tool I want to examine. I need you to cause a distraction so I can find it."

"Humm..." Janno stared at the wood, and a flame roared up so high it nearly scorched off the eyebrows off the man who was feeding the fire. He rocked backward on his heels, swearing.

"Actually, it would be better if the fire went out," Kron murmured. "Maybe he'll use his metal tool again."

"Now you tell me."

The fire died as abruptly as if Janno had dumped a bucket of water on it.

The stranger shook his head. "First too much fire, now none...this isn't right. Wood doesn't behave like this." He swiveled his head to stare at Kron and Janno. "At least, it never did—until you two came to our caravan."

Kron bowed, hoping to hide any telltale changes in his expression. "We are but strangers passing through." He stepped back a couple of paces as if to give the man more space to work. He could still study an artifact from this distance, hopefully without being obvious.

The man rose, took a few steps toward one of the wagons, then turned his head to glare at Kron. "Why are you still here? Shouldn't you be bargaining with Lammar?"

"Galia can handle bargaining for the fish." What would make this man willing to share his knowledge with him? "I'd rather bargain with secrets."

The man halted. After a couple of heartbeats, he said, "Some secrets are meant to be kept that way."

"Why?"

"Because they don't belong to just a single person, but a clan."

Did he mean this whole clan was made up of artificers? Kron hadn't encountered so many tinkerers since his days in Delns. He studied the man more closely. The patterns embroidered on his tunic did remind him a little of clothes from his homeland, but they would have been worked in different materials. His accent was harsher than Delns's language too. Still, maybe there was a link here Kron could exploit.

He switched to his native language. "Can you still understand me?"

Several long heartbeats passed before the man reluctantly nodded. "You speak like my grandfather did when I was a youth. I haven't heard such words in a long time. Where did you learn them?"

"In my home country of Delns, east of here and across the sea. Have you heard of it?"

The man shook his head.

Kron tried another tactic. "Have your people always lived in the mountains?"

"You'd have to ask Lammar, or one of the elders. If they'll well enough to talk." The man spat on the ground. "The curse on the land affected them more than the rest of us. Only two are left who've known more than seventy winters, and their minds wander."

"A pity." Why would Salth target the elders? They had little time left in this life. Did that make their few heartbeats more precious, or did they know something that might be useful when facing Salth? Kron hoped it was the latter.

Inspiration drove him to bargain, "I think I may know where your ancestors came from. If I tell you about my home country of Delns, would you show me the metal artifact that makes fire?"

Interest flickered in the man's eyes for a couple of heartbeats, but he concealed it under a sneer. "You're still an outsider."

"Even if we once hailed from the same land?"

"You can't prove that."

"What about the link between our languages?"

The man shrugged, then turned away and entered the covered wagon. As soon as he disappeared, Janno sidled up to Kron. "Here," he whispered, pressing a cold object into Kron's hand.

Kron raised his eyebrows as he studied the fire-starter. "How did you get this?"

"I just...borrowed it."

"Borrowed?" Even Kron winced when his voice sounded too loud in the clearing. "Janno, I can't believe you would do something like this. Have you done this before?"

"Isn't that what you wanted, though? I thought you kept talking to that man to keep him busy."

Kron sighed. "Well, see if you can distract him some more."

He headed toward the pile of kindling to examine the fire starter. This metal was harder than anything he'd ever seen before. No bronze or rock could scratch it. However, the magic-finder didn't react to it.

Kron turned his own magic onto the artifact, but he still didn't recognize the metal or figure out what made it so hard. However, he did identify a piece of flint that had been bonded to the metal. The metal was joined with a screw so that the flint could be scraped against the metal. Kron tried it a couple of times. He thought he saw a spark. As he struck it again, he heard the man from the caravan arguing with Janno. His first impulse was to drop the fire starter near the pile of kindling and walk away as if it had been there all along. But how could he leave this new artifact behind without figuring out its mystery? If it wasn't magical, it was still a material he'd never seen before—and that meant Salth hadn't either.

The man's face grew red as he approached Kron. "You had it all along! Thief!"

"I'm no thief. You can have it back." Kron extended the fire starter toward the man. "But I do want to barter for it. Will your clan allow that?"

A sly look came into the man's eyes. "Maybe for its weight in gold."

Kron's heart clenched. Did these people know how much gold he'd brought from Vistichia? But he needed it all for his artifacts. He couldn't afford to give away a single speck.

"I can't offer you gold, but I might have a gem."

"What kind of gem?"

Kron showed the man turquoise, quartz, and citrine, but he refused them all. "I'll have to fetch more trade goods from our boat. Do you want to come with me while I get it?"

"No." The man called out using words Kron didn't understand. Three more men approached, all wearing swords made from the same material as the fire starter. "But I want your friend here—" the armed men surrounded Janno–"to wait with us. Don't tarry." The man grinned. "Your friend is annoying, and we get bored easily."

Kron exchanged glances with Janno. Janno scowled, but for once he didn't speak. Instead, he studied the trees around him as if wondering how he could persuade them to drop branches on the clansmen.

Trusting Janno to figure out a way to defend himself—or attack—with magic, Kron nodded. But before the men could demand their fire starter back, he sprinted for the boat, calling behind him, "If you want a hostage, then I'm claiming this!"

Galia was still bargaining with Lammar by the riverbank. They stopped talking as Kron passed them to ascend the ladder.

"What are you doing, Kron?" Galia asked. "Do you need something else to trade? Where's Janno?"

He didn't answer.

Bella met him as he climbed back on deck. "What's wrong?"

"No time to explain. Take this and hide it somewhere." He passed the fire starter to her, then kissed her cheek. "Can you control their animals from here?"

"I think so. Why, what do you want me to do?"

As he darted into the cabin, he said, "Wait until I return to their camp, then have their draft animals stampede."

She frowned. "But what if they get hurt? What if people get hurt?"

Kron opened a wooden box, enchanted to respond only to him or Bella. Several gems lay inside. Which one could he part with but was still valuable enough to appease the travelers?

"What happens if Janno gets hurt?" he countered. "Or Galia? These people have swords made of the hardest metal I've ever encountered."

He shook the box until he found a couple of pearls. They were slightly misshapen, which limited their usefulness in artifacts. Kron hoped the clansmen wouldn't object to the pearls' imperfection, but in case they did, he selected a topaz and an opal as well. They wouldn't be useful for the artifact he intended to construct around Salth's house.

Shouts rose from outside. Bella followed Kron as he ran to the ladder. "Let me come with you so I can link with Galia. I'll have more control over my magic."

"They already have Janno surrounded by swords. Galia's down there too." Kron put his hand over hers. "I don't want you to become another hostage."

Her mouth hardened. "I won't be."

He took a couple of steps down the ladder, and despite everything he'd said, she followed him. Although Galia's furious voice urged him onward, he halted, blocking his wife. Why wouldn't she listen to him? Didn't she know what the other men might do to her if they caught her? Not that he would let that happen—they'd have to kill him first—but didn't all women want to hide from strange armed men?

"Kron, hurry!" Galia screamed.

The panic coming from a normally level-headed woman spurred him into action. He scrambled down, dropping past the last two rungs to land in the dirty snow. He turned around to check the situation.

Galia knelt next to Lammar, sprawled on the ground as if he were asleep—or worse. Surrounding her were Lammar's people, displaying fear, grief, and anger. Janno's guards had brought him to the riverbank. One of them held his sword so close to Janno's throat Kron thought he saw a thin line of blood trickling down.

"What happened?" he asked. He chided himself for just grabbing gems, not an artifact he could make into a weapon. He should have guessed the confrontation might go beyond threats to actual violence.

"It's their fault!" "It's her fault!" Galia and the man with the fire starter shouted at the same time.

It's my fault for being so obsessed with a fire starter. I'm as bad as Salth. Maybe I should give it back. But the travelers were too worked up to calm down now, even if he returned the fire starter.

"Kron Evenhanded, why didn't you tell me about Janno?" Galia said. "How could you abandon him like that?"

"That's no call for killing our leader!" one of the guards retorted.

"I told you before, he's not dead, just stunned. See, he breathes." Galia drew herself to her full height and spread out her hands. "And my son better keep breathing, or no one else will."

As the crowd murmured, Bella plopped into the snow next to Kron. He glanced at her to tell her to climb back up, but she kept a grip on the ladder. He stepped partly in front of her to shield her.

"This was all a misunderstanding." Kron projected his voice to carry to the edge of the crowd by the treeline. "I have several gems to give to Lammar, more than enough to trade for the fire starter. Let my companion go—"

"He admits it! He took a fire starter! Seize them all!"

We're doomed, Kron thought. He grasped the pearls, but they were too natural to be affected by his artifacts. Perhaps one of the shaped gems would hold a spell, though Kron wasn't sure how to target only the travelers and not Janno and Galia.

The swordsmen lunged for Janno, only to trip and fall as grass and weeks snaked around their legs. The rest of the clan abruptly shrieked, contorting and slapping at themselves as if the Four had driven them insane. Galia huffed as she trotted as fast as she could toward her son. Janno swayed as she reached him. Silently, she touched her hand to his throat. Then she drew back and smacked his face. He gave her a hard look and rubbed his red cheek, but otherwise he didn't protest.

Bemused by how rapidly and effectively the travelers had been disarmed, Kron hurried over to Galia and Janno to offer his assistance. Galia, pale and out of breath, leaned on his arm as he escorted her back to the ship.

"What did you do to them?" he whispered. "How long will it last?" A couple of the swordsmen shouted and strained to pursue them, but the plants gripped them securely.

"I only put Lammar to sleep," she replied. "I didn't do anything to the rest of them."

"Then what—"

A fierce cry from behind them made Kron turn around. One of the swordsmen was clever enough to slash the weeds holding him with his swords. He had to twist and bend at impossible angles to do it without injuring himself, but although more grass clutched at him, he mowed it down easily. He paused for a moment to grimace and slap at something, then he took a couple of steps toward them, sword pointed at one of Janno's kidneys.

At last, here was Kron's chance to use his own magic. The sword was the same strong metal that had baffled him earlier, but the hilt was weaker. A couple of magical pushes in the right spots, and the sword fell off the hilt. The swordsman stopped to stare at it. Kron couldn't understand the language he used, but the words had to be foul.

Bella scurried up the ladder to give them space to climb. Galia and Janno went next, followed by Kron. Domina posed at the side of the *Avatar* as if she meant to hurl lightning at the strangers. As soon as everyone was aboard, Caye sent a burst of wind to drive them away from the bank. The boat lurched, sending everyone sprawling. Kron barely had time to throw the pearls and gems at Lammar before they sailed out of range.

With a groan, he sat down on the deck as his energy faded away. The rest of the Avatars copied him. Galia stared at Domina for several minutes before the Winter Avatar finally brought them beer and bread.

They ate in silence for a few heartbeats before Janno asked, "What made them twist and stomp around like that? That wasn't my doing."

"It was mine," Bella announced with a smug smile. "All the fleas in their furs suddenly woke and bit them."

Kron bit back a laugh, then toasted his wife.

* * *

Bella used birds to watch the travelers in case they decided to pursue the *Avatar*, and Caye and Domina pushed themselves to melt the ice and sail upriver even faster than they'd already been traveling. A few travelers did pursue them on horseback, but by the time both of the Winter Avatars collapsed from exhaustion, the *Avatar* had outpaced them. The Western Mountains were visible in the distance, a sterile landscape made all the more astonishing by the number of animals fleeing from it. Herds of wild goats and deer trotted past as if unconcerned by the wolves and mountain lions trailing them. Flocks of birds—Bella reported they contained everything from songbirds to seabirds to birds of prey—darkened the sky overhead. Bella clung to the side of the boat and stared at all the creatures as if she meant to gather them with her gaze.

Kron came over to join her. "It seems as if our friends from this afternoon had reason to leave."

After a few heartbeats, Bella nodded.

"Are they still following us?"

She shook herself. "Who, the travelers? They could be. The last I noticed them, two horses were still traveling upstream." She smiled, and her eyes shone with light. "Forgive me, Kron. All these animals, unlike anything I've seen before…they're beautiful."

He couldn't scold her when she was this excited. He hadn't seen her like this since the first moons of their marriage. "Never mind about the travelers. I'm sure they'll give up and return to their caravan when they realize we're so far ahead."

Some of the joy left Bella's face. "So, what did you take from them? Was it worth the trouble?"

His face grew warm. "It's a fire starter made of a metal I've never seen before. It might be useful against Salth."

"But why did you take it?"

Kron sighed. "It's hard to explain." He did his best to describe what had happened, not sparing either Janno or himself in the details. "I'm not sure why they're so protective of something non-magical, though. It wasn't even their only sample of the metal. The swords were made of it too."

"Could it be sacred to them?" Bella asked. "Or something that's important to their tribe?"

"Perhaps." Kron leaned forward, studying the living landscape in front of them. "It was well done with the distraction you created this afternoon." There was more he longed to tell her, how he'd worried about her having magic at first but now couldn't imagine her without it, that he'd still feel the need to protect her no matter how powerful she was, that he wished they could stay in this peaceful moment forever, without worrying about Salth or Sal-thaath or the caravan. He even wished he could be a better husband to her and give her the children she craved. But no words could show her everything in his heart. Even a kiss seemed inadequate, but he swept her into one anyway. The taste of her sweet mouth made him pull her closer to him. She wrapped her arms around him, and their kiss deepened….

"If you two keep that up, you're going to be making a child right in front of us all." Galia cackled as she brought out a big bowl of boiled grains and vegetables. "When are you going to show this magical new artifact to us, Kron?"

He glared at her for spoiling the mood, but she ignored him and portioned out their meal. The other Avatars crept over to join them, all except for Domina and Caye. They collapsed at their stations and refused to budge. Galia brought each of them their portions and urged them to eat.

Kron waited until everyone was satisfied before bringing out the fire starter and passing it around. "Notice how hard the material is," he said. "I haven't had a chance to test it yet, but I expect it will be less likely to rust or go soft over time than bronze. That means it will be able to resist Salth's time magic."

"Really?" Galia played with the loose skin on her hands. "I didn't think anything could resist time."

"Well, some things last longer than others. I've made some artifacts that will protect you. Bella, could you fetch them, please? We're close enough to her domain that you should never take them off."

Kron had designed the Avatars' protective artifacts as snug bracelets with miniature sundials and clasps enchanted to stay shut until the wearer pinched it. To invoke the Fours' protection as well, each bracelet bore an oval piece of glass colored to match the God or Goddess the Avatar served. He'd guessed at the sizes, but most of the bracelets fit well. Only Janno's was too small, but Kron was able to coax it to expand. He set aside the last four bracelets for the quartet still in Vistichia. He'd bring them along when he fetched them.

Bella helped the other Avatars figure out how to open and lock the clasps. Domina sat up and spun the bracelet around her wrist. "Do we need to do anything to make this work, Kron?"

"No. The spell is always active."

"You could have added a few more gems to mine," Domina said.

Galia glared at her, but Magstrom chuckled and said, "When we return to Vistichia, I'll give you all the gems you want."

Ah, so the wind blows that way, does it? Better you're with her than me, Magstrom.

Janno and a couple of other Avatars grinned and made sly comments. Kron let it continue for a few heartbeats while he activated another artifact, a wooden eye. He'd scratched out the pupil to keep them hidden from Salth. Although she might guess they were here by the presence of foreign magic, the artifact would make it harder for her to learn what they were discussing or doing. Once he was sure the eye was working properly, he cleared his throat. "If we keep sailing as quickly as we did today, tomorrow will take us so far up the Chikasi that the river will be too shallow for this boat. Although Salth does live close to the river, it'll be another couple of days to journey there on foot. But before we do that, I need to return to Vistichia and collect the rest of the Avatars, as well as any more supplies I can buy." He looked at Bella. "Dearest, is there any animal that can take a message to Vistichia faster than I can portal? A hawk or crow would be less likely to catch Salth's attention than my opening of a portal."

"Maybe a falcon, but they can't fly at night. Even if I summon one at dawn, it wouldn't get there until the following day."

"I should have asked you to send one sooner. I might have, if the travelers hadn't distracted us." Kron glanced down at the artifact in his hand. "I'll use this to disguise the portal. While I'm gone, it would be wise to hide your magic. Don't use it unless you have to, and if you do, try to keep the effects from spreading over a wide area."

"Kron, how big of a portal are you planning to create?" Bella asked. "Will you be able to bring our wagon and ox through? We would get there faster."

He hesitated. It would have been a good idea under other circumstances. However, they would have to bring fodder along for the beast, since it wouldn't be able to find anything to eat in Salth's domain. And while his magic didn't limit the size of the portals he could create, larger ones would attract more attention than one a person could slip through.

He shook his head. "No, I'm afraid that's too risky. We'll all have to walk." He avoided glancing at Galia. Despite the health and vigor Spring had given her, she was most likely to slow them down. That was also a risk, but Kron thought he could manage to conceal a small, slow group better than a larger, fast-moving one.

"Anything else we need to know about Salth or her house?" Galia asked.

"You'll have to prepare yourselves for pitiful corpses and possible monsters." Kron omitted the part about them possibly being the same. "We should set a watch, starting tonight."

Kron and Janno wound up sharing the first watch. Everyone else spent the night in the cabin and hammocks, since this might be their last opportunity to do so. Even the animal migration had stopped at sunset. Now the stars shone down on the ice and snow, with the white expanse broken up by dark mounds where herd beasts huddled together.

"Kron, are you sure we can't use this portal thing to go straight to Salth's house?" Janno asked. "It would be much easier on my mother, and it would give us a chance to sneak up on Salth."

"You expect to sneak up on the world's greatest magician by using magic? That's like scattering gold and jewels behind you and hoping thieves won't trail you home."

"Well, can you use magic as a trap? Set it off in one place while we're somewhere else?"

"Maybe." Kron scratched his chin. "But then she'd definitely know I'm here, if she hasn't sensed us already. We'll see in the morning."

"Then I suppose I should let you rest." Janno winked. "Or not, maybe."

"Maybe would be more of a yes if there weren't so many of you around," Kron said. "Or maybe you should find yourself a wife of your own, so you don't have to poke your nose into my business."

Janno's expression sobered. "I've had two wives. First one died trying to give me a son and a daughter at the same time. I lost the second one during the last plague."

That had taken place a couple of years before Kron had arrived in Vistichia, plenty of time to mourn and move on. "You must have loved her very much," Kron said.

"She was fair, but perhaps too quiet for me." Janno sighed. "Mother tells me all the time how much she'd like a grandchild. I suppose when we're done with Salth and go home, I should find a new wife. That shouldn't be hard now that I'm an Avatar. Hopefully the next one will be a love match, like what you and Bella have."

Kron smiled. "If I was the master of time like Salth, I'd spend it all with her."

With that, Kron focused on creating more protective amulets for the rest of his shift.

* * *

Caye and Domina still looked weary when everyone rose at dawn, but they pushed off without complaint. The morning's sailing brought them a better view of the Western Mountains, grey mounds with tops lost in the clouds. However, Kron couldn't admire the scenery, as smaller streams joined the Chikasi, making the path they should take difficult to determine. Kron placed magic-finders at the front and rear of the boat, then, with Bella's help, used the different glow intensities between the two to figure out the direction to Salth's house.

"We should go this way," he said, pointing to one of the smaller streams.

"We can't," Janno replied. "It's too shallow."

Before Kron could argue, the boat proved Janno right by coming to a halt. Kron staggered for a couple of steps before he regained his balance. Galia bumped into the railing. Bella reached for her, but Galia waved her off. "Just give me a moment to catch my breath and heal my bruises."

Domina collapsed. "We're...not going...anywhere."

"Is anyone hurt?" Magstrom asked, poking his head into the cabin.

No one seemed to be severely injured, so Kron secured the ladder in place and climbed down. He didn't recognize the area, but other than the clump of dead trees by the river, there wasn't much here to distinguish it. At least the trees would provide shelter for the Avatars, as well as materials he could use to portal back to Vistichia. Kron snapped off several dry branches and lashed them into a door frame.

Galia peered over the *Avatar's* side. "What are you doing?"

"I think it's time for me to return to Vistichia and collect the other Avatars. Are the rest of you going to wait in the boat or on land?"

"I think by this point, I prefer being on land," Galia replied. "Hold the ladder steady so I can climb down, please."

Kron went one better by sharpening the ends of two branches to points, hardening the posts so they would penetrate the frozen earth, and finally bonding the ladder to the posts. Now the Avatars would be able to move back and forth between the riverbank and the boat.

"It's time for everyone to pack supplies," he told Galia. "Let me know if you want me to bring back anything from Vistichia. But it has to be something I can find easily, so I can return in time for us to start moving."

Galia shook her head. "I think we should stay here tonight, Kron. We have water and shelter here, and we may not be able to find them on the march. Besides, Caye and Domina could use the rest. They're exhausted."

She probably was too, even if she didn't admit it. But while she made good points, the thought of lingering anywhere in Salth's domain made Kron uneasy. If she found them before they were ready, they would have thrown their lives away for nothing and left Vistichia and the rest of the Four's domain vulnerable.

"Only if I decide it's safe to stay here," Kron said. "I'll return as soon as I can with the others. Guard the portal while I'm gone."

Bella hadn't disembarked, so Kron swiftly returned to the boat to tell her he was leaving. She kissed him and said, "Bring back another set of furs if you can. It's cold."

"I think Caye and Domina don't have the strength to keep the cabin warm anymore. There's wood, so you can make a fire and have a hot meal." He lowered his voice. "And we can share a blanket tonight."

She grinned, and that was enough to keep the cold at bay as Kron descended back to the portal. He attached the blinded eye artifact on top of it, then pictured the courtyard of the Avatars' house and stepped through.

His face broke out with sweat as he changed location. Caye and Domina had spoiled them with warm air during the journey, but the air and light here felt as bright as springtime. An apple tree bore ripe fruit out of season. Kron walked a wide berth around it in case that was Salth's doing. Then he reminded himself that the Four had limited Salth's influence in the city, and she wouldn't set up anything this pleasant. *It could still be a trap. But if it is, why haven't these Avatars taken care of it?*

Kron ventured into the kitchen. "Flilya? Hala? Are you here?"

They weren't, but embers glowed in the hearth, and the scent of rising bread filled the air. *They must expect to be back by dinner. I could wait for them here, but then we won't be able to portal back until dark, and it'll be too late to go anywhere tonight. Where could they have gone?*

Kron retrieved a magic-finder from his abandoned workshop and keyed it to the Avatars. As soon as he left the house, he saw crowds of people everywhere, talking, preparing food, playing music, and eating as if a festival was going on. The spring feel he'd noticed earlier in the courtyard was still here. By the Four, had these Avatars decided to do away with the Season of Winter? Kron wondered what the god Himself would think of that.

A maiden approached him with a ring of flowers. She tried to drape them over his head, but he waved her away. "Could you tell me if the Season Avatars are receiving supplicants today?"

She smiled. "No, not today."

"Then where are they?"

"Why, they're at the temple, of course, getting ready for the ceremony of season change."

"Where's the temple?" How much had Vistichia changed while they were gone?

"In the old city-king's palace, near the center of town."

Kron thanked her, then turned and made his way as fast as he could through the crowd. Unfortunately, no one else seemed to be in a hurry. They strolled along in colorful lightweight clothes, making Kron feel more out of place in his wool and fur garments. Stubbornly, he kept them on. Soon enough he'd drag the other Avatars back to winter.

The crowd thickened as he approached the palace-turned-temple. It had been built on a hill, and stone steps led up to a partly exposed porch. He asked a bald man next to him where the Season Avatars were. The man stared at Kron as if he were a stranger. "They'll come out when they're ready," he said. "About noon, I would say."

Noon? I left close to dawn! At this rate, we won't return to the grove of trees until nightfall. He had to enter the temple and convince the Avatars to cancel this ceremony and come with him. However, the front steps were blocked off, and watchmen with trained dogs paraded back and forth. Kron approached the closest watchman. As the dog came to attention, hair bristling along its spine, he said, "I need to get through, please."

"No one's allowed up here."

"But I'm Kron Evenhanded. I'm married to one of the Fall Avatars."

The watchman laughed. "There's only one Fall Avatar, and you're not her husband." He scowled. "No go away!"

Only one Fall Avatar? How could the people of Vistichia have forgotten us already? The trip hasn't been that long! Kron would have a lot to discuss with the Avatars once he managed to meet them. But first he needed an artifact that would enable him to pass both man and beast. If he made himself invisible, the dogs would still be able to smell and hear him. Could he outrace them or fly over them? Those seemed like a waste of magic. Perhaps a simple distraction would suffice, and he could do it with a piece of metal.

Kron took out the fire starter and twirled it around. The strange metal resisted his magic at first, but after a few heartbeats, it yielded and displayed four other images of himself. The dogs might be able to sniff out which one of him was real, but Kron hoped that if the artifact scattered sound as well as images, the dogs would be confused enough to let him through.

He positioned himself off to the side, between two watchmen, and ran up the stairs. His doubles copied his every move. Shouts of "Look at that!" "Who is he?" and other words Kron couldn't make out rose from behind him. More importantly, the watchmen both cried out, "Halt! This area is off limits!" and ran toward the duplicates. The dogs, still on their leashes, strained against their masters' holds as they pointed unerringly toward the real Kron.

If only I had meat to distract them. Could he conjure it? Meat wasn't something he normally used in his artifacts, and he didn't have any bone pieces in his pouch. Perhaps a carved disk of ivory would be close enough. Kron rubbed it, flung it behind him, and put more effort into climbing the stairs even faster. He couldn't help gasping, conscious of the years he had over the younger guards. But the scent of roasting meat wafted into the air, nearly tempting him to turn around and find the skilled chef preparing the food. A dog whined as its master yelled at it. Kron reached the top of the temple and slipped behind a column to catch his breath. He caught sight of one of his doubles doing the same, so he banished it, since it was no longer needed. Perhaps he'd been too quick to dismiss it, as a set of footsteps pounded on the marble steps. *What a time for someone to do his job properly.* Well, the sooner he found the Avatars, the sooner they could cancel this ceremony so they could join Bella and the others.

Kron squeezed into a narrow opening and checked his magic-finder. It glowed brightly, pointing toward the center of the temple. The corridors here twisted into various storage rooms, making it hard for him to navigate to the center even with the help of his magic-finder. Kron wondered if the watchman would follow him or report immediately to the Avatars. Perhaps he would be better off trying to shadow his pursuer.

After running through dust and spider webs, Kron finally emerged into an open space at the center of the temple. He froze as he saw the Avatars. Although the trip upriver had taken less than half a moon, they seemed as if they'd aged a bit more than that in the meantime. However, they'd compensated by dressing in silks and jewels that Domina would envy. Ocul stared overhead as if studying a cloud pattern on the ceiling—or wondering how his beard had grown so much. Tylan stood with his arms crossed as the watch man gestured. Hala petted the watchdog, and Flilya turned around, faced Kron, and gaped.

"By All Four Gods and Goddesses, what are you doing?" Kron asked as he stepped forward. "We've sailed up the Chikasi as far as we can. Now it's time for your four to portal back with me so we can march to Salth's house."

Everyone turned to stare at him now. The watchman struggled to say something, but Tylan held up his hand for silence.

"Kron Evenhanded, is that you?" he asked. "What happened to the others?"

"They're fine," he replied, puzzled. "They're waiting for you by the boat."

"What took you so long? Was the trip hard?"

He shrugged. "A few things happened on the way, but it wasn't too bad for a winter journey."

"But it's the first day of spring," Tylan said, "We're here to honor the Four with a special ceremony. We call it the soltrans."

"The first day of spring? It can't be. We left during the first moon of winter." The Avatars stared at Kron with pity, and his hands trembled. "I know we did."

"Yes, Kron, you did." Tylan dismissed the watchman with a wave. "But we had no word from you for two moons."

Kron was silent as he replayed the journey in his head. He was sure they'd been traveling for twelve days, not a single heartbeat more. How could the Avatars have gotten the time so wrong? He sucked in his breath. "Salth. That cursed woman...or whatever she is....Come, Avatars, we must hurry! If Salth managed to breach my protective artifacts, the rest of the Avatars are in danger!" *Bella, Bella, beautiful Bella....*

"But the soltrans..." Tylan said.

"Freeze the soltrans!" The others gaped at him, but Kron continued, "The Four asked you to take care of Salth, not create rituals for Them!"

Tylan pointed at Flilya and Hala. "Go ahead to the house and get things ready. We'll be there as soon as possible." Kron glared at him, but he said, "We promised the people a ceremony. If we cancel it, it will cause more problems. I swear, Kron, we'll keep it as quick as possible."

Hala shook out her hair. "And if you don't, Tylan, next time you perform in costume."

Tylan shuddered.

"Costume?" Kron wondered as the women led him to a flight of stairs descending into the temple.

"When Tylan proposed this soltrans," Flilya said, "we said since we were doing this on behalf of the Four, we should each dress up as our God or Goddess. Tylan would have had to dress like the Goddess of Spring."

Hala shook her head. "That would be an insult to Her."

Kron didn't join in their banter. How could Salth have created the time distortion between her land and Vistichia? More importantly, how much time was passing for Bella and the others, and what was happening to them? He reminded himself that he'd given the Avatars protection before he left, so Salth shouldn't know where they were. That was, if they didn't make a big display of their magic, or if she didn't have some way of tracking all living things in her domain. But if she was the mistress of time…

Kron stumbled and had to brace himself against the wall. The Four had said before that Salth wasn't able to pass the final test that had allowed Them to Ascend into godhood. Maybe that meant she didn't have complete mastery of time, despite her extensive talent and experience with magic. He still had a chance to return to Bella before Salth could hurt her. But how? What did he need to do?

"Come on, Kron." Flilya unbarred a door leading to an underground tunnel. The air felt close and damp. "I thought you were in a hurry."

The tunnel was shorter than he expected, but it brought them far enough from the crowd to escape without notice. Food vendors called to them as they ran down the street, but for once the Avatars didn't seems to care about eating. Kron couldn't run as fast or as long as the women, especially after his earlier sprint. A sense of urgency propelled him on without rest. By the time the house was in sight, he wished Galia had come with him to give him a second wind. However, he pointed to the apple tree and gasped. "We must be careful. Salth may have left a trap for us."

"No, I did that," Flilya said. She turned red under Kron's stare and added, "Well, we were out of apples, and it seemed like a good way to practice my magic."

"Never mind." Kron sank down on a bench. "You two go ahead and gather supplies. We may have to stop somewhere overnight, so be sure to bring bedding. Extra food and water would be good. I'll stay here and catch my breath." *And figure out if there's any way my artifacts can counter Salth's talent with time.*

While Kron waited, he studied the garden. No sign of the portal was visible from this side, and he panicked for a heartbeat. He could rebuild the portal, but it shouldn't have closed like that. A new portal would have to be stronger, resistant to time. The trees wouldn't work. The stone wall, however, might. It would only provide one side of the portal; he needed more stone to form the other side and the top. All he could see was a statue of a dancer with her arms overhead. He couldn't lift her, but maybe he could make her move of her own accord.

He'd sat long enough to be able to breathe normally again, so he walked between the prickly bushes surrounding the statue. Then he grasped the statue's buttocks and pushed. The stone resisted his physical efforts, but once his magic poured into it, the dancer extended first one leg, then another. With surprising grace, she leapt off her pedestal and flattened a bush. Kron took her by the arm and guided her into position. She had to bend over to form an arch with her neck and arms. Kron and the other Avatars would have to stoop to pass through the portal, but it was worth it to have something Salth wouldn't be able to tamper with.

Now, is there any way I can use Salth's time magic against her, or at least undo it? A water clock, I need a water clock.

As he hurried into the house, Hala came out with a bulging sack. "Where is the water clock?" he asked.

She closed her eyes. "In the kitchen, opposite the hearth. Why bring that, Kron?"

"I'm not going to bring it. I'm going to destroy it."

"Destroy it?"

"Well, maybe just alter it."

The water clock was where Hala had said it would be, but no one had filled it recently. Kron rolled the jar outside, next to the portal. He paused for a heartbeat, then knelt, touched the jar, and fused all the holes. "Now we can add the water."

Hala shook her head. "We had plenty of other jars in the pantry. You could have used one of those."

"But not for this magic." He glanced around. "How much longer will the other Avatars be?"

"Flilya's still packing. I don't know where Ocul and Tylan are."

"Can you use animals to check on them?"

After a few heartbeats, she replied, "The birds report that the crowd by the temple is breaking up. But they can't tell people apart, so I can't use them to track how close Ocul and Tylan are to us."

At least they shouldn't have to wait much longer for the other Avatars. Kron rested, reserving his power, while Hala filled the water clock-turned-artifact with water from the well. Magic bubbled up inside him. Perhaps power wouldn't be an issue in the upcoming battle with Salth, but knowing how to use it would be.

Ocul and Tylan returned heartbeats before Flilya dragged the last of her supplies—how did she suppose they would carry them all?—out of the kitchen. She wiped her hands with an air of satisfaction. "That's food for everyone," she said, "and I have things for them too." She nodded at the two male Avatars.

Kron stood up and stretched his back. "Then I suppose we can leave immediately."

"Right now?" Tylan asked. "We should—"

Kron didn't care what Tylan was about to propose. "You two should help me push this artifact through the portal."

Despite the resentful expressions on their faces, they assisted him. As soon as the jar was exactly halfway through the portal, Kron turned to Ocul. "Freeze the water in that jar, now!"

"All of the water, or just on the surface?"

"All of it!"

Ocul muttered, "It's the wrong time of year for this," but he did it anyway.

"Perfect!" Kron said. "That should keep Salth from playing with time while we pass through the portal. I'll go through first and make sure no surprises are waiting for us on the other side."

"But I thought the other Avatars were waiting for us." Hala frowned. "Or do you think they could be in trouble?"

"That's what I'm afraid of." Kron distributed the protective bracelets he'd made for the Avatars. Then he brought his magic-finder out again and grasped it in one hand while he scooped some enchanted metal shavings in the other. Prepared for anything, he stepped through the portal.

After the gentle warmth of spring, winter's cold assaulted every exposed part of his body. Snow pelted his face, making it hard to see. Where were Caye and Domina, and why hadn't they bothered to tame this weather? Maybe they still needed to regain energy after all of the magic they'd used on this journey. He called out, "Bella? Galia? Janno? Caye? Anyone here? I'm back with the other Avatars."

Only the wind answered him.

CHAPTER TWENTY-ONE

Two Krons

Kron swept his magic-finder in a circle, trying to use its heat to sense where the Avatars were and what had happened. He bit back a curse as his own portal overwhelmed the readings. If Salth had scrambled time here, the traces of her magic had probably faded by now. What would Salth have done to the Avatars? More importantly, would Bella or Galia had left him a clue as to what had happened? And how could he find anything in this snowstorm?

"Ocul!" Kron called through the portal, "Come here and clear up this weather!"

The Winter Avatar hesitated for a few heartbeats before obeying. He raised his hands and squinted into the storm. "I need a link!" he shouted.

One by one, Tylan, Flilya, and Hala crossed into Salth's domain. As they joined hands, Kron brought over the rest of their supplies and the water clock with frozen time. Maybe he would still be able to use it against Salth.

The snowfall tapered off, leaving their whole world white. Hollows in the snow suggested footprints. From what Kron could make out, a single person about his size had approached the group from the direction of Salth's house, and the Avatars had followed him.

"Where did he come from?" Kron murmured. How could anyone wander around here without protection? More importantly, why had the Avatars followed him?

"I thought you said the other Avatars were here, Kron," Tylan said. "Where are they? Back on the ship?"

Hala shook her head. "I already checked there through the field mice. All of the supplies are gone."

Kron exhaled with relief. If they'd taken supplies, then they'd chosen to leave and hadn't been hurt. But why had they left? He couldn't tell how much time had passed for them.

"Well, we should follow them," he said. "If we're lucky, we can catch up to them. How fast can Galia move anyway?"

"Do we have to walk?" Tylan asked. "Can't we bring the oxen through to pull a wagon?"

"They won't last long enough here. Do all of you have the protections I gave you? Put them on now and let's get moving."

Despite the Avatars' grumbling, they quickly prepared for the march. However, by now it was close to sundown. If the situation hadn't been so desperate, Kron would have allowed them to camp in the dead grove and set off at dawn, but fear for Bella gave him new energy. He used the magic-finder to guide him, holding it high so they could all see its glow. The Avatars stuck right behind him as if they'd all been woven together into one tapestry. Ocul, at the end, rolled the frozen water clock along.

Kron kept his other senses alert for any other signs of a threat. The silence was unnerving. No mice rustled in the meadow, no owls or bats flew overhead. Even the snow seemed muted as he slogged through it. As the moon rose, he realized the snow was giving way to mud, clinging to his boots like a lover pleading for him not to leave. His feet became heavier with each step, but with nowhere to camp, he was forced to keep moving. The Avatars brought out hunks of bread, rinds of cheese, and a small skin of watered wine. The first bite awakened his appetite, and he ate as if his magic depended on it. For a while—he wasn't sure how much time passed in this barren landscape—they all marched with renewed vigor, but then the Avatars' pace slowed.

"Kron, I know you're worried about Bella and the others, but we won't be of any use to them if we collapse before we can reach them," Tylan said. "We need to rest somewhere—anywhere. I don't care where we sleep as long as we do."

Kron studied his magic-finder as he walked, mulling over Tylan's words. Tylan made sense, yet something urged him to keep walking. Bella and the others could be right in front of them. Or Salth could have warped time and put them a heartbeat out of reach. How could he stop until he knew? Maybe he should let the Avatars rest and continue his search without them. But would he be able to find them again?

"Perhaps you could rest here for a bit while I go a little further ahead—"

Hala held up her hand. "Wait! I think I heard something!"

Everyone held still and listened. At first, Kron thought she'd been mistaken. But then he heard it: a female voice, holding a pure note that rang through him. *Bella.* Where was she? Why was she singing? They couldn't possibly be that close to Salth's house!

"Bella?" He called. "Is that you? Where are you?"

The singing cut off. Without the sound, Kron couldn't guess which direction to go. But Bella and the other Avatars didn't speak.

"Bella, it's me." Kron raised the magic-finder over his head. The glow still didn't extend past an arm-length or two. "Where are you?"

A burst of hail answered him.

Kron snapped his robe to strengthen its protections. "Watch out!" he yelled to the others behind him.

Ocul advanced, palms outspread, and the hail melted. But another barrage followed, then another, faster than he could counter.

"What's going on?" Tylan stepped forward to touch Ocul. "Are the other Avatars attacking us? By All Four Gods and Goddesses, why?

It didn't make sense to Kron either. How could Bella not recognize his voice? Maybe it was time to disregard caution and light up the area so they could all see each other. He took a candle stub out of his pouch and lit it. Its glow only extended an arm-length in front of him, so he pushed more power into it, rolling back the darkness.

Domina and Caye stood in front of him, balls of ice in their hands. Magstom and Galia peered out from behind them, their hands on the Winter Avatars' shoulders. Kron couldn't see the others, particularly Bella, but he guessed they brought up the rear. All of them stared ahead towards Kron's group, but their faces were slack, as if they didn't understand what they saw in front of them.

"Why have you stopped?" a very familiar voice called out. "Keep attacking, Avatars!"

Kron's double, identical except for his lighter clothing, positioned himself directly between Caye and Domina, smirking at Kron.

The candle slipped from Kron's fingers, distorting his vision. "Who are you?"

"Can't you guess?"

The taunting tone gave him the answer: Sal-thaath. But how was he still alive, let alone disguised so cleverly to fool his own wife?

"What have you done to the other Avatars, Sal-thaath?" Kron asked. "Domina, Caye, it's us! Stop attacking!"

Together, they threw more hail, aiming not just at Kron, but at Tylan and Ocul.

"What are they doing, Kron?" Tylan asked. "It's like they don't recognize us!"

"Maybe they don't." Kron directed his will to the candle stub, intensifying its light. Then he studied the Avatars. Was Sal-thaath controlling them directly? He didn't think the boy understood people, even magicians, well enough to manage that. An illusion, then. If he could figure out how Sal-thaath was creating this illusion, perhaps he could counter or disrupt it. Could this be related to time? He wasn't sure how, but then again, he wasn't sure if Salth's powers were just limited to time or if she could still use the rest of the magic she'd learned. Even if Salth's magic was specialized, Sal-thaath's might not be.

While Kron considered what to do, Ocul raised an ice barrier between the two groups of Avatars. At first, Domina's and Caye's attacks actually helped him, but then they changed tactics and blew strong winds against the still-fragile wall. It toppled over like a pile of badly-placed jugs.

"If we don't stop them soon, they'll hit us with lightning next!" Tylan said. "Maybe I should try to put them to sleep before they kill us."

"Wait! I have another way to stop them." Kron turned to Hala and Flilya. "Bring me the water clock."

The women rolled it to him through mud, which clung to the jar as though assisting Sal-thaath. Kron pushed it through the remainder of Ocul's ice wall. At least the cold would help keep the water frozen. Kron had planned to let the water clock roll on its own to the other group of Avatars, but when he released it, it simply stood there. He gave it a final push with magic, directing it toward Sal-thaath. If Sal-thaath was as skilled with time as his mother was, the frozen time wouldn't hold him for long. But if it worked, even for a few heartbeats, then the Avatars might break free from Sal-thaath's magic. If they didn't, Kron might be able to help them.

"Forget the enemy!" The false Kron pointed at the water clock. "Destroy the artifact!"

Domina raised her hands, sparks crackling between her fingers. But before she cast them at the clock, Caye spoke. "The artifact?" She spoke slowly, as if still waking from a deep sleep. "But Kron, I thought you were the only magic-user left who could make artifacts."

"I am!" Sal-thaath's voice slipped into a childish register. "I mean, I mean…."

The water clock bumped into him. Kron watched for some sign he'd been affected by it. But Sal-thaath didn't stop moving or breathing. Instead, he reached down to touch the artifact. With a single tap of his fingers—Kron's fingers—the clay shattered, leaving behind a block of ice. Sa-thaath crouched next to it and pulled it toward his chest as if it would give him strength and power.

Well, of course it would, you fool. Salth was obsessed with two things: her magic and her son. She must have used time somehow to bring him back to life...

Kron shuddered as he recalled the drained land and the corpses, both drained and animated, he'd encountered. Perhaps Salth wasn't draining life, but time, time she could transfer to her son. If so, then all he'd done was give this abomination more time he didn't deserve.

"You...you frozen thief!" he shouted. "I've had enough of you and your mother!"

Sal-thaath smirked and crossed his arms. "Too bad you can't do anything, you powerless old man. All of your artifacts put together can't affect me."

Rage built in Kron, wakening depths of untapped power. With a tilt of his head, he saw how to reassemble the broken water clock—and what to do with it. The golden magic he'd absorbed so long ago flowed out of his hands and surrounded the pottery shards. They flew back together, melding smoothly enough to let not a single drop of water escape. But that wasn't what it was meant to hold this time. Kron flexed his fingers, and the pot swung about, its mouth facing Sal-thaath. Time streaming out of the child and into the jar. Sal-thaath backed away from it, his face turning pale and shifting back to his own features. He shrank as well. Domina, Caye, and the other Avatars halted their attack to stare at him.

"Bella? Galia? It's me, Kron," he called. "I've brought the other Avatars. That other Kron was Sal-thaath, Salth's son."

They glanced his way as he spoke, but then turned back to Sal-thaath. What was going on? Maybe there was another spell or time distortion affecting them. His magic-finder fizzled out, as if his most recent effort had been too much for it. He sent more power into the light artifact until he could see all twelve of the Avatars clearly. Then he realized that when he peered at Caye, Domina, and the rest, their images wavered as if a screen of smoke separated them.

Maybe we're looking at each other in different times. The thought terrified him. How much time separated him from Bella? Caye and Domina didn't appear to have aged much, if any. Perhaps he and the final quartet of Avatars had aged. No, he was sure his back and knees would tell him if that had happened. The real question was if he could destroy this temporal curtain.

"Bella?" he called. "Where are you?"

"Kron? Kron?" She peered around as if she couldn't see through the time rift. "Where did you go? You were just here, and now you sound so far away—" She turned and gasped as she stared at Sal-thaath. Kron had trouble recognizing the boy. His skin had turned ash white, and he flickered in and out of view as if he were stuck in the middle of a portal. Yet he didn't seem bothered by it. He smiled at Bella, exposing needle-like teeth. She didn't flinch or scream as Kron had expected. Instead, she scowled at Sal-thaath as if he'd stolen the teeth from one of her favorite animals. Other Avatars were less calm. Domina screeched and hid behind Magstrom, and Janno jumped in front of his mother.

"By All Four, what's going on?" Galia pushed herself in front of Janno but halted when she saw Sal-thaath. "Who are you?"

He pouted and gave her a forlorn look that did nothing to improve his appearance. "I'm lost. Can you help me find my mother?"

Kron hoped Galia wouldn't fall for Sal-thaath's trick. But he also had to figure out why the other Avatars didn't seem to know where he was. If it was a time distortion, how could he correct it? He glanced at the water clock, but it was out of reach. Unless...he crooked his fingers, drawing on his connection with the artifact. It rolled toward him. He slowed it down, testing for resistance. Yes, there was a heartbeat where the water clock had to push against an unseen surface. He forced the water clock to halt, then crack. As the jar released the magic he'd drained from Sal-thaath, the barrier shimmered. More importantly, it disappeared from Kron's magical senses, not just his vision.

He beckoned to the four Avatars he'd brought with him. "Hurry! Follow me!" He ran forward. As he passed the jar, he felt the world beneath him shift. The feeling was similar to crossing through a portal, but less smooth, like running from a well-maintained path onto sand. He managed to keep his footing, but Ocul staggered as he came up to Kron. Ocul nudged Kron to the side, where he had a clear view of Salth's crystal house, now twice as large as it had been last time.

Salth's house? How did we get so close to it? I thought we were a couple of days' march away!

Kron only had a few heartbeats to stare at the structure before Bella ran over and threw her arms around him. "Kron! Is it really you?"

"I'd answer yes whether or not I was trying to trick you, wouldn't I?"

She laughed. "Only my Kron would say something like that."

"What happened after I left?" He found it hard to take his gaze away from Salth's house. "Why did you follow Sal-thaath? Don't you know where he led you?"

"We thought he was you. How did he manage to impersonate you?" She shuddered, then finally glanced in the direction where Kron was looking. Her face turned pale. "By the Four, how—"

"The Four had nothing to do with it!" Sal-thaath jumped in front of them, spreading his arms as if he meant to protect the crystal house. "I did it all by myself!" He faced Kron. "I found a time when you came here and captured that heartbeat. Then I had to learn how to play the heartbeat over and over again so I could live inside of it, inside of your image."

Sal-thaath gazed at him as if expecting praise. All Kron could feel was revulsion. Still, he managed to ask, "And why did you do that?"

Sal-thaath looked down at the ground, drawing a line with his foot and not saying a word.

"Ah, there you are, Kron, just in time." Salth herself, looking as transparent as her crystal house, appeared in front of them. She smiled, exposing teeth as sharp as Salth's. "Thank you for bringing Me these double-strong magicians. They will serve Us well."

"Serve them?" Hala asked, voice squeaky with fright.

"Well, not directly, child. All We need from you is that magic the Foolish Four gave you. It's for my boy." Salth's voice dropped. "It's always been for my boy."

A few of the Avatars pulled away from Kron, muttering and staring at him suspiciously.

"She's lying!" he said. His heart sank. After all the moons they'd spent training together, how could even one of the Avatars believe Salth over him?

Galia raised her head. "Kron's right. Salth's trying to trick us, just the way her son did."

"I can't believe we left the Spring Soltrans for this," Flilya muttered. "I want to go home."

"We can't leave now, Flilya!" Bella said. "Kron needs us."

"Yes, we're all here to work together." Kron faced Salth and her son, drawing on his courage and the anger he felt for all of their victims. "Salth and Sal-thaath, we have you outnumbered."

"Do you really think that matters, when we have many-magic over you?"

Kron flexed his fingers, remembering the star magic he held. "I wouldn't be so sure of that."

Salth didn't answer; instead, she beckoned them. But although the Avatars trembled, none of them stepped forward.

A furrow appeared on Salth's forehead. "Your trinkets are stronger than your far-seer, Kron. But not strong enough."

She and Sal-thaath stepped closer to each other, moving in unison. Kron sensed the magic building in each of them. Magic stretched behind Sal-thaath, tethering him to the crystal house. *That must be what's restored him to life. All the death Salth has caused to feed one thoughtless, cruel boy who refuses to change.* If Salth and Sal-thaath joined their magic, they would be able to overwhelm the protective artifacts he'd given to Avatars, maybe even his own personal protections. Then they would all be helpless, their magic—their lives—drained away to give Sal-thaath a life he didn't deserve.

"Avatars, link!" he snapped at them. He had an idea for cutting Sal-thaath off from the magic in the crystal house, but he needed time – the one thing Salth could deny him – to put it together. Hopefully twelve Avatars could distract the mother-son pair long enough for him to dodge them and reach the house.

At his words, the Avatars snapped out of their trance and linked into three groups of four, with the Winter Avatars facing Salth and Sal-thaath. The temperature dropped, hail poured down on the pair—then stopped in mid-air a handspan above their heads.

Salth and Sal-thaath might not be able to freeze the Avatars directly, but if they could halt time for the weather, would the Avatars be able to do anything against them?

Is there a way I can turn their mastery of time against them? Kron pulled out the two artifacts he'd planned to use, the shell to enhance Bella's voice and the gold wire. The shell seemed like it would be better suited to trapping magic. For an instant, Kron regretted that Bella wouldn't have a chance to sing, but with the house grown so much, he doubted she could have shattered it even with the shell's help. He poured his magic into the shell, strengthening and enlarging it. When it was the size of his head, he pitched it at Salth and Sal-thaath. A gust of wind positioned it perfectly between them. As he'd expected, both of them turned their attention to it. Sal-thaath shot corruptive magic at it, but Salth said, "Wait, son! He might have set a trap in there."

Kron took advantage of the distraction to sprint past both of them toward the house. He braced himself, expecting either an attack from one of them or else a ward or trap. But Salth must have assumed the time-absorbing nature of the house would be enough of a defense. Magic reached out, trying to penetrate his clothing and leach his re-maining years from him. When that failed, the house tried to repel him. Each step became a struggle, as if it took a year to raise and lower each foot. Kron pulled the coil of gold wire from his pouch and held it in front of him. That seemed to help. As he drew closer, he wondered if he would be able to make the gold wire stick to the crystal. Normally fusing two dissimilar materials together was tricky but not impossible, but with this house Kron didn't know what to expect.

A moat of bones, both animal and human, surrounded the house. Kron tried to kick them aside, wincing at the sacrilege, but they stuck in the frozen mud as if planted there. The one that he'd tried to dislodge stirred, and meat and fur grew back over it layer by layer. Other bones started returning to life. Salth hadn't left her house defenseless after all. *Looks like I'm going to have to come up with some way to destroy or neutralize these poor creatures. Actually, maybe I don't.*

He stepped back, turned sideways—it would be foolish to leave himself exposed to the reviving creatures and people—and called, "Bella! Galia! I need you here!"

Salth had drawn closer to the shell and was peering at it, probably trying to figure out how to destroy it when it kept trapping her magic. Sal-thaath pranced around, shooting magic at an ice wall the three Winter Avatars were building around him. Neither side seemed to be able to gain the upper hand. Pulling two Avatars away would upset the balance in favor of Sal-thaath, leaving him free for more mischief, but if Kron could sever his tie to the crystal house, then the boy would cease to be a problem. And if he ceased to be, then Kron had to accept that. No matter how much he'd once cared for this child, Sal-thaath couldn't be allowed to steal other lives to sustain his own.

Kron had to call for Galia and Bella a couple more times before they finally dissolved the link. By then, the living bones had started to group together in combinations that would never work without magic. Skulls hopped on top of ribs, and limbs joined with other limbs at odd angles, as if Salth was creating living artifacts. Kron spat with disgust at the thought.

Bella grimaced as she approached Kron, and Galia's face bore a tinge of green. "By All Four, what's she doing?"

"I think these are her house guardians. Can you get me past them?"

Galia turned her head from side to side, surveying the sentinels. "I don't think we can handle all of them by ourselves."

"Then just clear a path through them."

Bella furrowed her brow, but she and Galia joined hands and pointed at the spot right in front of Kron. The half-creatures shuddered and scrambled over other ones to get away. Kron drew his clothing around him. As soon as a path was clear, he sprinted down it. Skulls snapped their jaws and legs kicked at him, but they couldn't reach into the protected path. He reached the crystal and uncoiled the end of the gold wire, then pressed it against the cold wall. It sank in, and Kron had to snatch his fingers away before they followed. How could he get the gold to stick to the crystal before the house swallowed it all?

This house isn't alive; it was made. It's an artifact. By All Four, it's an artifact. Why did it take me so long to realize that? Salth may have made this, but my magic should be stronger than hers for this.

Kron left the gold wire in place, flexed his hands, and deliberately pushed on the crystal. The artifact sucked at his magic like a babe at his mother's breast. Kron tried to follow his magic inside the house, hoping he could damage the artifact from within, but once his magic passed through the crystal, it changed, no longer feeling like him. It felt more primal, like the energy within the Avatars.

Of course. How stupid of me. I need their magic to destroy this house. Then he remembered he couldn't link with them or access their magic. Wasn't destroying this house supposed to be their task? How could they channel their magic into it when they could barely hold off Salth?

I should be the one facing Salth, not them. We need to switch places. Or at the least, he needed to guide them so they knew what to do.

Abandoning the gold wire for now—though he made sure the crystal house wouldn't swallow the rest of it while he was occupied—Kron checked on the Avatars. Incredibly, they'd linked through the three Springs, feeding the Winters with power from the Summers and Falls. But no matter how much lightning, hailstones, or even whirlwinds they sent at Salth and Sal-thaath, every weather pattern broke down before it reached the mother-son pair.

*This is hopeless. I can't shatter the crystal house, they can't defeat Salth and Sal-thaath, and I have no other artifacts that I can use against time. Unless…*he reached backward for the gold wire. If the gold was the only thing he had that resisted being corrupted by time, then he had to use it to break the stalemate.

Kron snapped the wire flush against the crystal, so smooth he couldn't even feel the broken end of the wire. He wound it into a coil about as wide as he was tall. Now came the tricky part: getting close enough to Sal-thaath to toss it over him. Without Galia and Bella to keep it open, the living moat had closed up again, trapping Kron next to the crystal house. If only he could jump across it, or fly…well, he had his boots. Why not turn them into artifacts too?

Kron directed the star magic into his boots. They bounded into the air, dragging him along for the flight. Kron struggled to keep his head above his heels. He aimed the boots towards Sal-thaath. Wind from the Winters' latest weather attack knocked him off course for a heartbeat.

As if he'd gained telepathy, Sal-thaath turned and gestured at Kron's boots. The stitches holding them together snapped, his boots fell off of his feet, and he dropped into a snowbank, an armslength from the moat. He jerked away from a skeletal hand and stood up. His feet burned from the cold snow, but Kron didn't have time to reassemble his boots. Instead, he flung his gold coil toward Sal-thaath. The child dodged with depressing ease. Then, with a pointed smile, he advanced on Kron. Kron, however, didn't focus on Sal-thaath. Instead, he beckoned the gold coil to fly forward, intending to wrap it around Sal-thaath. At the last heartbeat, Sal-thaath retreated, drawing closer to the Avatars.

"Watch out!" Kron called.

They didn't respond. By the way they had their eyes closed and their limbs wrapped around each other, they seemed to be completely ignorant of was what going on around them. But despite the cold, sweat dripped from their faces, and their bodies trembled.

"You know this is a hopeless battle for them, Kron," Salth said. She waved at the shell, and it cracked. Kron's heart sank. "Perhaps I cannot take their time—yet—but I can do other things with time, stretch out a many-hurtful moment of pain, or hurt them and not let them heal. If you care for them, Kron Evenhanded, you should bargain with me for their lives."

He suspected he already knew what she wanted, but he asked anyway, "And what would you have me give up for their safety, Salth?"

"Your life and your magic, Kron."

Unspoken were the words "to feed Sal-thaath."

None of the Avatars, not even his wife, reacted. Either they were so deeply engrossed in their magic that they'd lost all contact with the outside world, or they didn't care what happened to him. He knew that couldn't be true, but it was hard to believe that when no one spoke out against Salth.

"And if I were to portal away from here and leave them, what would you do?" he asked, more to provoke a response from the Avatars than to consider it.

Salth cackled. "You'd never do that, double-foolish Kron."

Domina shot a bolt of lightning at Salth, but she deflected it with no more than a gesture.

"Bella? Galia? Can you hear me?" Kron called. "Say something!"

"This shouldn't be a hard choice for you, Kron." Salth gestured again, and the water clock, now whole and grown big enough to hold a man, rolled toward her. Water streamed out of the middle row of holes. "Choose quickly, or your friends perish when the clock runs dry."

The water level dropped to the next row, as if Salth had sped up how fast the water would drain out.

Kron scoffed. "I'll believe that after you break through the protections I've given then."

Salth smiled and looked over the crowd. "It's not that hard to pick out the oldest Avatar, is it? And the oldest Avatar has the least time left to her...."

She closed her eyes. The tight knot of Avatars broke up, but Galia wasn't visible. The Avatars circled around her with concern evident on their faces. She staggered, one hand over her heart. The wrinkles on her face deepened, and clumps of her hair fell out, invisible against the snow.

Janno and Caye clutched each of her arms. With horror, Kron watched them age too. Bella stepped forward, but before she touched Galia, she turned to face Kron with a look of love and desperation. One by one, the other Avatars copied her, imploring him for help.

Any lingering doubts Kron had about the Avatars melted as Ocul and Magstrom took Galia's hands. The other Avatars formed into their groups again, all channeling their magic into her. But Kron knew that wouldn't be enough. Salth would first drain Galia of all her remaining years, then the rest of them.

"I love you," Bella mouthed before reaching for Galia.

Before she made contact, Kron said, "Enough, Salth!" He stepped toward the water clock. "I yield! Release them."

Salth's smile deepened.

"Kron, no!" Bella yelled.

As much as it pained Kron to ignore her, he had to if he was going to save them. Once he was gone, the Avatars would be helpless against Salth. Only if they returned to Vistichia, behind the Four's protective barriers, would they be safe. Before he could face Salth and Sal-thaath, he had to send them back, even if they hadn't finished their mission yet.

Kron put his hands behind his back. As he approached the water clock, he made circling motions with his fingers. He fed his power into the gold loop, enlarging it until the gold was thinner than a human hair. Even if someone stared directly at the circle, it would be difficult to detect.

"Sal-thaath, come here," Kron said. "I'll give you my power inside the water clock."

The boy looked at him warily, as if expecting a trick. Kron kept all expression off of his face.

"It's all right, Sal-thaath," Salth said. "The water clock is My symbol, My element. He cannot overcome it." She stared at Kron. "Leave your pouch and your outer clothes here."

He took them off slowly. As he released the pouch, something spilled out of it: the fire starter made out of the strange material. He covered it with his foot so Salth wouldn't see it. Although his toes were numb, he managed to coax them around the fire starter. Everything depended on this unknown artifact.

Pretending to limp, Kron stepped up to the water clock. The lip came up to his shoulder. He flexed his fingers, maneuvering the hoop into position and connecting it to the Avatars' courtyard. Then he pulled himself to the rim of the water clock. Sal-thaath levitated himself until he stood opposite Kron.

"On the count of four." *Spring, Summer, Fall, and Winter, I hope You can hear me. Take Your Avatars home and keep them safe, especially my wife.* "One, two, three…"

The hoop hovered over the Avatars.

"Four."

Taking a deep breath, Kron jumped into the pot. His feet seemed to stretch out as they entered the void. Before his hands became trapped, Kron released the hoop. He twisted his head to watch it. A flash of gold descended to the ground, but Kron focused on Bella, on her flecked eyes. For a heartbeat, her gaze met his.

Then she was gone, and the rest of the Avatars with her.

As the water clock swallowed Kron, Sal-thaath followed him.

CHAPTER TWENTY-TWO

The Water Clock

The water clock was bigger on the inside than it appeared. Kron found himself in a space as big as his workshop, the walls curving away from him. Water came halfway up to his knees, freezing his feet. He flexed his toes, using the fire-starter to warm the water. Rows of holes all around the pot appeared dark, but the opening let in enough light for him to see Sal-thaath hovering at eye level. He regarded Kron for a moment with sadness, as if part of him still regarded Kron as a substitute father. Then he smiled.

"You don't have to die right away, Kron." The boy's voice bounced back from the clay walls. "Mother already packed a lot of life energy into her crystal house for me. And I can stretch time out in this vessel. We can play for a very long time."

"I don't like your games, Sal-thaath."

The boy pouted. "Why do you have to be so mean?"

"There's a difference between being mean and being stern. If your mother had done a better job with you, you'd understand that."

Kron assessed the pot. It was well made, with thick, solid walls, a good choice for storing time. But it was an artifact too, and therefore something he could use. If he couldn't counter time directly, he could shape it. Or trap it.

Kron wiggled his toes, urging the fired clay to soften and become malleable again. The neck of the pot shrank in on itself, and the edges flowed into each other. The row of holes beneath water level closed up.

Sealing the water clock and destroying its capacity for storing time would not be an instant process. If Sal-thaath suspected what he was doing, he could halt or reverse Kron's changes. A distraction was needed.

"What did you do to that ball I gave you?" Kron asked. "How did you put a soul inside it?"

Sal-thaath stared at him with open eyes. "I wanted to make it into an artifact for storing life energy, something I could carry with me. Maybe if you teach me how to make something like that, I'll be nice to you and not hurt you for too long."

"Not if you're going to put another soul in there."

"Not just any soul. Bella's."

Anger made Kron lose his concentration for a heartbeat, or at least long enough for the top to reopen. He clenched his fist, willing the neck to close. Then he started on the rows of holes. The interior of the pot dimmed before Kron could enchant a stone caught in the clay to give off light.

Sal-thaath looked up. "What's going on?" For the first time, he sounded like a real boy, scared. Despite the wrench at his heart, Kron forced himself to ignore the child's fear and keep working.

Sal-thaath sprang over to the pot wall, but the hole in front of him sealed itself before he could poke his finger through it.

"Kron!" he whined. "This isn't fair!"

"Was it fair for you and your mother to torment and kill humans without magic?"

Sal-thaath pounded on the wall. "Mother! Help!"

Kron ruthlessly finished making the walls completely solid. Nothing could get in—or out. At least for now.

Sal-thaath turned from the wall, tear streaks gleaming on his cheeks. His expression hardened. "What are you doing?"

"You'll find out soon enough."

Kron normally made portals out of openings, spaces where someone could pass through. But this jar had given him another idea. What if he could use the jar itself as a portal? If he'd entered at one end, then perhaps he could create another opening and escape to somewhere else— back to Vistichia, where he'd sent the Avatars. But, what would he do with Sal-thaath? The Four wouldn't want the child in Their realm, and Their magical barriers might keep Sal-thaath—and Kron—out. Maybe Kron could seal Sal-thaath in the jar. What else could he do with someone who'd already died and returned back to life? It seemed cruel, but it was less cruel than letting Sal-thaath go free.

Kron swept his arm in a circle, and the walls thinned, then flowed toward the line he'd indicated. Sal-thaath glanced around and tried to push through the new divider before it became solid. *Oh no, you don't.* Kron borrowed the strength of the fire-starter's metal and placed it into the clay wall. The last he saw of Sal-thaath's face was the boy staring at him through a small gap, a forlorn expression in his eyes. The after-image lingered for a few heartbeats in Kron's mind once the wall was complete. Then the wall trembled as if struck. Would Sal-thaath be able to age it to destruction? Kron knew he had to leave before that happened.

He pushed against the outer edge of the jar, wishing now he'd left the water holes open so he could see where he was. *Don't be silly,* he reminded himself. *You just have to see the place you're portaling to in your mind.* He thought of the Avatars' courtyard as he'd seen it that morning—was it still the same day? So much had happened. He banished all distractions and pictured the walks, the garden beds, the apple tree in the corner. But the jar didn't open. It rocked back and forth, as if torn by Sal-thaath's own struggle to escape.

Kron tried to break the jar, but neither magic nor his fists prevailed. Even the wall separating him from Sal-thaath no longer responded to him. What was going on? He'd never had an artifact stop working like this before. Maybe the unknown metal was too strong. How much longer could he stay in here before he needed air? Did time even have any meaning when he was trapped in here with a magician who could manipulate time?

Kron rapped against the dividing wall, but the only response from Sal-thaath was to rock the water clock harder. It almost felt as if he wanted to push the entire jar to some unknown location. Perhaps if he reached the crystal house, he'd be able to access its power. That wouldn't be good for anyone.

Well, if Sal-thaath can move the water jar, I should try to move it away. Could I move it to Vistichia? The distance would drain his strength, but it would keep Sal-thaath from using his death-derived magic. Kron wasn't sure if Sal-thaath would be able to pass through the Four's barrier around the city, even if he was encased in a jar. But if he could, then Kron would leave him for the Four to deal with.

Kron reached out with his magic and grabbed the entire water clock. The effort made his vision dim. He focused instead on recalling every detail of the Avatars' courtyard. As before, he reached and reached without connecting with the location, even though he'd just sent the Avatars there. Had they arrived safely? Could their presence be affecting his ability to portal there? He hoped that was the case.

Kron tried recalling several other locations in or near Vistichia: the clearing in the woods where Salth had opened the portal, his first home with Bella, the marketplace, even the harbor where he'd found the shell. Nothing worked. He struggled to recall other places while the water jar rocked back and forth and he fought for breath. All he could think of was the Four's new temple, or rather the former palace where the Avatars had performed their soltrans.

SpringSummerFallWinter, help me....

At last his magical senses locked onto a solid location. Kron strained with the last of his strength to bring himself and the water clock there, even as the jar seemed to pull in another direction. A single heartbeat stretched into forever as he clawed with every part of his will for home. Then, with a loud crack, the jar split in two. Kron rolled out of his half onto a dusty stone floor and lay there, gasping for breath.

"I knew I felt Kron Evenhanded!" Spring's bright voice called. "Welcome back, old friend."

He eased himself into a sitting position. Standing in front of him were the Four Gods and Goddesses. Physically They hadn't changed, but They'd traded Their clothes for styles Kron didn't recognize. Spring and Fall wore long-sleeved, floor-length gowns of yellow and red respectively, Their dresses embroidered with flowers. Summer and Winter wore loose black leggings with white shirts and black overshirts cut down the middle. Although Spring smiled at him, Winter looked thoughtful, and Summer and Fall glowered.

Kron eased himself to his feet. "Spring, Summer, Fall, Winter." Part of himself urged him to bow to divinity, but he settled for nodding at each of Them. "I'm glad to see all of You, but I wish You'd returned sooner."

Winter turned His head, a half-smile on His face.

"There's nothing funny about this situation!" Kron shouted. "Why did You urge the Avatars to face Salth so soon? They weren't anywhere near ready! The whole mission was a disaster. I don't even know what happened to Sal-thaath. And where are the Avatars? Are they safe? Why couldn't I portal to their house?"

"So many questions." Spring stepped forward, hand stretched toward him. "You were right, Kron. The Avatars weren't ready for Salth back then, but they needed to learn that for themselves. The memory has given them reason to master their magic."

"That, and Chaos Season," Fall muttered.

"He's not ready to hear about that, Fall."

"Hear about what?" Kron asked. "And...memory? It hasn't been that long since we faced Salth, has it?"

The Four were silent, shifting so he couldn't get even an indirect look at Their eternal eyes.

Kron shuddered. "How long was I in that water clock?"

"Long enough that no one uses water clocks anymore."

"Spring..."

"It's been twelve lifetimes, Kron." She lowered Her voice. "Over eight hundred years."

Kron collapsed. Impossible. This had to be impossible, even for Salth and Sal-thaath. But the Fours' strange clothing and grave expressions confirmed Spring's story.

"The Avatars? Bella? What happened to them?"

"You might as well ask what hasn't happened to them," Spring replied. "They may be gifted with Our power, but they're still mortal, Kron. While you were trapped, their spirits have passed from body to body, life to life."

"You mean she's dead? Bella's dead?"

"The Fall Avatar you knew as Bella died thirty-four years after your ill-fated journey to Salth's realm. But she was reborn twenty-two years later. She's lived and died ten times since you last saw her."

Kron stared at Spring, trying to absorb what Her words meant.

Her smile became gentle. "Kron, Bella is currently named Ysabel s'Ivena Lathatilltin and will turn eighteen falls this year. We have arranged matters so that she is still unmarried, not even betrothed. You have the chance to win her heart again."

"Then where is she?"

"She lives at the other end of Challen—that's the name of Our entire domain. Do you remember that group of refugees you met on the way to Salth's realm, the first group of people to smelt steel? That's what they call the metal your fire-starter is made from. Ysabel's father is descended from them. These people have found ways to travel safely in Salth's domain, and you and the other Avatars will need this knowledge for your next attempt to break Salth's house."

"You still want us to try that? We accomplished nothing!"

"Oh, yes, you did," Winter said. "You drove a gold wire into her crystal house. She covered the end with crystal, but it's still there, an imperfection you can exploit."

Fall stamped Her foot. "And you need to get it right this time, Kron, so the seasons stop getting mixed up."

"Mixed up?"

"We think it happened when you tried to transport Sal-thaath into Our city." Spring's voice cooled slightly. "You two battered against Our barrier for hundreds of years, and you damaged it enough for Salth to send her foul magic through every few years. The Avatars have their hands full dealing with the problems it causes."

Kron glanced at the remains of the water clock. "Speaking of Sal-thaath, what happened to him?"

"We are certain he did not enter Challen," Spring pronounced. "Even the water clock was not enough protection to keep Us from sensing him. That's why it split: so We could permit you to return to Vistichia while keeping Sal-thaath out. The shards from his half of the water clock are scattered all over Challen, though." She tilted her head. "The question is, did he return to his mother, or did he go elsewhere? What other God or Goddess would accept him?"

"He had to return to Salth," Kron said. "He's...not really alive anymore, and all the time she stole is to sustain him."

Fall scowled. "And to attack Us."

Summer raised His head, and His cheeks grew greener, as if He was flushing. "Salth creates erratic time shifts in Our domain. The weather becomes unpredictable, My trees grow and shed leaves out of season, and Fall's animals try to hibernate when they should be active. Despite all that, Our Avatars keep the time shifts from destroying Challen and even make the country thrive." He halted and looked around, as if surprised He'd spoken so much. "Still, We want the Chaos Season to stop. Destroy that crystal house and take care of Salth and Sal-thaath."

"We will do the rest," Winter promised.

The Four Gods and Goddesses watched Kron as if expecting him to immediately promise to help Them—again. He sighed. "Maybe you say eight hundred years have passed, but to me, it all feels like the same day. I want to see Bella—"

"Ysabel," Spring said.

"I want to see my wife first before I do anything. And honestly, if my artifacts weren't good enough against Salth before, why would they be any better now?"

"The world has changed much while you were in the water clock, Kron," Winter said. "Mortals have created many new, stronger materials. An artificer like you could use them to create much more durable artifacts."

Despite all he'd been through, Kron's curiosity was piqued.

Spring came forward and squatted in front of him. Her eyes into eternity were obscured by Her hair, but the rest of Her face radiated concern.

"You have indeed endured much already, Kron Evenhanded," She said. "And you have much to learn about this new Challen and Wistica—that's the new name for Vistichia. Here." She touched his forehead. Energy flowed through him, as if he'd eaten his fill and slept for a day.

"Permit me to give you another gift, that of the modern language. No one will understand you otherwise, not even your Bella."

She must have sensed his agreement. Before he could speak, new words poured into him.

"You will be able to read as well," Spring said. "It is a common skill these days. In fact, it would be strange for someone as intelligent as you to be unable to read. I could give you all the history too, but I don't wish to overwhelm you. You may want to study at the University of Wistica so you can absorb a little of it at a time."

"University" was a new word for Kron; it was a place where young adults could study other disciplines besides magic. Pagli would have appreciated knowing something similar to the Magic Institute still existed.

"Some scholars at the University study the past," Winter said. "They would be very interested in the remnants of your water clock. I recommend you take it to them."

"But when will I get to see Bella?" he asked.

With a smile, Spring slid a golden bracelet off of Her wrist and held it in front of him. A young woman appeared in the middle of it, as if the bracelet was a portal. The girl's skin was darker than Bella's had been, and her hair was bound up and covered so he couldn't see it. But her eyes bore the same green-and-gold flecks he'd always admired in Bella. This new version of Bella sat in front of a wooden device, pressing white-and-black objects inlaid on the front of it. Her lips moved in time with her fingers.

"It's a new way of making music," Spring said. "I don't think music will be enough to shatter Salth's crystal, but she still enjoys it."

So different from my Bella, but so alike in many ways. Does she still remember me? What did she experience without me at her side? How did she feel when I didn't portal after her?

Spring withdrew Her bracelet long before Kron tired of staring at Bella. "The sooner you start your new life, Kron, the sooner you'll see her in the flesh. Gaila, Janno, Caye, and other Avatars too. Farewell, Kron. May the next time We see you be under better circumstances."

"Farewell," the others echoed. Then They faded away.

Kron raised himself to his feet. He knew the Four had only told him a little about the new world, but he felt overwhelmed. He took his time reassembling the water clock from the shards. At least this familiar task hadn't changed. Only half of the water clock was here, including part of the dividing wall he'd built. Even so, it was too big for him to carry. Kron shrunk the water clock down so he could tuck it under his arm.

He passed through the dusty corridors of the temple toward the front entrance. This area had been renovated, with sculptures and paintings in colors and poses he hadn't seen before. He spent several heartbeats studying the artists' techniques. Yes, the world had changed greatly while he'd been trapped. He hoped he still had a place in it.

With a deep breath, Kron finally walked out onto the front porch of the temple. Beneath him, the whole street had changed. Even in the evening light, he could see that the road was covered with a strange substance. The buildings surrounding him were stone, not mud-brick, and they towered over the old temple. At the corners and entrances to each building, poles bearing lights lit up the street. He couldn't tell what powered the lights. Few people were about, but they wore clothing similar to the Four's. Kron glanced down at himself and transformed his clothes so they resembled what Winter had worn. The Four might not have told him everything about this new world, but They'd given him what he needed to make his way here.

Kron stared out over Vistichia—no, Wisticia. Off in the distance, the Chikasi River still wound its way to the sea. So much had changed in eight hundred years that he was once again a stranger in this city. But this time he knew there were old friends out there, ready to be reunited with him.

The University would be the first place he needed to go on his journey back to Bella. He set out to find it.

Afterword

Thank you for reading my book; I hope you enjoyed it. Please consider leaving a review on Amazon or Goodreads to help other readers discover this book. It also helps me promote my work so I can eventually fulfill my dream of writing science fiction and fantasy full-time.

This novel is an expansion of my short story, "Demon's Diamond," which I wrote to develop the background of the Season Avatars' world. Thanks to my friend Aviva Rothschild for inspiring me to write it.

I would like to thank my beta readers for their input in helping me improve this story. They are Bert Hammerstad, Sheila Babcock, Susan Curnow, Elizabeth Hull, and Heidi Garrett. Maria Zannini of Book Cover Diva designed the cover, and the template for the interior book design (for both the paper and eBook versions) came from Book Design Templates. As always, special thanks go to my husband, Eugene, and my son, Alex, for their love and patience as I spent many hours at the keyboard writing, editing, and formatting this book.

If you'd like to know when the next book in this series will be available, you can watch my website, blog, or Facebook page for announcements. Or you can also subscribe to my newsletter (link is on my blog). I hate spam as much as anyone else, so I'll only send it out for announcements of new work and sales. Eventually, I plan to offer bonus stories to subscribers as well.

Thanks again for reading *Seasons' Beginnings*. I look forward to sharing *Scattered Seasons*, Book Two of the Season Avatars, with you soon. Please read on for a sneak peek.

Best,

Sandra

The Season Avatars of
Seasons' Beginnings

Group 1

Galia—Spring

Janno—Summer

Bella—Fall

Caye—Winter

Group 2

Magstrom--Spring

Carver--Summer

Sylva—Fall

Domina--Winter

Group 3

Tylan—Spring

Flilya—Summer

Hala—Fall

Ocul—Winter

Scattered Seasons
(Book Two of the Season Avatars)

Lady Gwendolyn lo Havil is an Ava Spring, born to heal others and lead the Avatars of her generation. When the current Ava Spring dies in a riding accident, Gwen must find the other three Avatars she will link with. Only a full quartet of Avatars can deal with the destruction of Chaos Season, times when the seasons all appear at once. But two Avatars are missing, and with Gwen's own magic is crippled by an ancient, cursed pottery shard, Gwen will have to use all of her skills to find the Avatars. Can she trust the stranger who claims to know the shard's origin, or is he her ancient foe returned?

Coming 2015—read on for an excerpt!

Lady Gwendolyn lo Havil fixed a smile in place as her head throbbed. She wished she could blame it on her future mother-in-law, but as dreadful as her taste was—witness the sickly sheep pattern on her wallpaper—something else had to be at fault. Gwen hadn't felt this much physical pain since she was twelve springs old and her healing magic had blossomed. What could be causing this? Something in her in-laws' mansion? Or did it have to do with her own Avatar magic?

"Gwendolyn, dear? Are you paying attention?" The false sweetness in Lady Shellinda's tone wouldn't have flavored her weak tea. "I was asking if you and William wanted my second-best plates for the wedding luncheon."

If she meant the ones imported from Fip, with the country's war eagle in the center of every dish, then no. Gwen could never forgive Fip for the war that had brought Challen into its empire. It had taken place several hundred years ago, but she still remembered that life, and all the injured people she'd treated, more clearly than she liked. Could her current headache have something to do with her memories of the past? Lately they'd been coming more frequently, stretching back closer to her very first life as an Avatar for the Goddess of Spring. Perhaps this was a sign from the dear Goddess Herself.

"Is it time?" Gwen murmured. "Time to find the others?"

"Whatever are you talking about, Gwendolyn? Are you ill? I thought you were supposed to be healthier than a horse."

Gwen drained the last of her hot chocolate, wishing the cup wasn't so dainty, and rose. "I think I need some fresh air, Lady Shellinda." William's mother complained flowers made her sneeze. Gwen had postponed trying to heal her affliction and was now secretly glad she'd done so. Maybe she could steal a few moments to be alone, cure her headache, and figure out what had caused it.

"Well, if you insist. But I wouldn't advise staying out there too long. There's simply too much to be done before the wedding next moon."

And if I don't hurry back, she'll choose something horrid for the lunch menu.

Gwen decorously lifted her skirt hem off the floor as she left the parlor and slipped out into the garden. Bright sunshine made her squint; it beat on her head as if to increase her headache still further. The roses weren't in bloom yet, but row after row of tulips marched like a squadron ahead of her, showing her the path she was meant to travel. Gwen's late mother had established a maze in their garden and changed the path through it every year. Gwen wished she was there now, someplace where she could hide instead of being exposed to watchers from the house. She forced herself to glide casually through the flowers. But although she took deep breaths, they didn't calm her. Something stirred at the edge of her magical senses. Something that didn't belong in Challen.

What is it? Is it close by, or do the reigning Season Avatars feel it too?

Gwen might be a Season Avatar for the Goddess of Spring, First of the Four Gods and Goddesses of Challen, but by herself, her magic was limited to healing. Linking with the other three Avatars—one each for Summer, Fall, and Winter—would allow her to share thoughts with the others, pool their magic, and spread it throughout the country. But there was already a quartet of Avatars taking care of Challen. They'd been in place for decades. Surely the Four meant for Gwen and the other Avatars of her birth year to replace the current Avatars soon. After all, as her father and aunt were fond of pointing out, she was already eighteen, old enough to be married and start raising a family. They didn't understand she felt more ready to be an Avatar than a wife. She remembered magic from her previous lives as an Avatar. As for what she remembered about her personal lives...she'd been married to the Summer Avatar more often than not. William was a sometimes childhood friend, sometimes childhood tormentor, but he was no Avatar. Plus he wanted her to start having children, and she knew she wasn't ready for childbirth, not after the way her mother died.

Gwen rubbed her head. This wasn't the time to be fretting over the wedding or children she hadn't conceived. She had to learn what was giving her a magical headache. Was it a Chaos Season, when all of the seasons appeared at once, and the Avatars had to return everything to normal? It had never given her a headache before. Besides, the flowers around her were still normal. But the air felt cooler now, bringing up goose bumps on her arms.

Gwen rubbed her skin, using her magic to feel warmer. As she did so, she surveyed the garden. A brown form lying in the path several yards away caught her eye. As she approached it, it resolved into a human figure. One of the gardeners, judging by his clothes and the trowel by his side. He wasn't moving, and the flowers around him were brown and wilted.

A mini Chaos Season. Maybe this is why my head hurts. What happened to the gardener? I'd better check.

Gwen stripped off her gloves, then knelt by the prone man. He was still breathing, but a gash on his forehead streamed blood into the soil. Perhaps he'd been hit by a hailstone. If so, it must have already melted. She pressed her hand against the cut, sealing it. Once that was done, she focused her magic inward, checking for more serious damage. The injury didn't seem serious compared to others she'd healed during her several lifetimes as Spring Avatar, but she would still recommend to the butler—Lady Shellinda would consider herself too far above her servant to be concerned about him—that the gardener be given a day or two to rest. Since this was a head injury, someone should watch him for any unusual symptoms so she could heal him again if necessary.

Not that it will be.

Gwen used a withered leaf to wipe some of the blood off of her hands before she accidentally stained her silk gown. As she stared at the soil, she noticed a pottery shard next to one of the frostbitten tulips. What would something like that be doing in the middle of a carefully managed flower bed? She pressed her lips together when she noticed a rust-colored edge on the shard. No hailstone had assaulted the gardener. But where had the shard come from? Maybe this Chaos Season had had strong winds, strong enough to fling small objects about. That was quite common. The shard, however, wasn't. It was lighter in color than the dirt, and it had marks on it that Gwen had never seen before.

Gwen picked up the shard to look at it more closely. The air was still, eerily still. She was careful not to touch the edges, but it turned in her hand as if it was alive. She let it go, but it clung to her.

By All Four... "Get away from me!" She shook her hand, but the shard bit into her palm. Gwen reached for it, then thought better of touching it with her bare skin. She covered her free hand with part of her skirt, then tried wrenching the shard free. The gardener stirred beside her, and Gwen wondered if she would need him to help her pull the piece of pottery away. Then it snapped. She could tell that a corner was missing—a corner shaped like the bulge in her skin. How had it slipped in? More to the point, would she be able to get it out? Normally that shouldn't be a problem, but this Chaos Season, though small, was anything but normal.

She drew a line over the bump, willing her skin to split. But for once, her healing magic refused to obey her. Pressure built in her head. If she wasn't already squatting, she might have fallen over. Was the pottery shard poisoned? She hadn't detected anything unusual when she'd healed the gardener. Still, something was interfering with her magic.

Have I ever come across anything like this before? Gwen searched her memories from previous lives. No, nothing had ever gotten stuck under her skin—or anyone else's—and refused to come out. However, the farther back she went, the more familiar the pottery shard seemed. She'd always considered her oldest memories the least trustworthy and least complete, so even this information didn't help her.

Goddess of Spring, what do I do now?

A trail of cold reached past her wrist and up her arm.

"Freeze it!" Never had swearing felt more appropriate. Gwen grasped her affected arm with her other hand and pressed down, trying to block the cold. For a moment, it seemed to work, but then the cold shot past her elbow, then to her shoulder.

"What happened?" Finally, the gardener opened his eyes. "My flowers! My precious tulips!" He blinked as he gaped at her. "Lady lo Havil? What are you doing here?"

Cold squeezed her throat closed. She gestured toward the house, even though no one there would be able to help her either.

Then the cold numbed her head, halting her pain—and everything else.

Other Works By the Author

Science Fiction: Catalyst Chronicles Series

Lyon's Legacy

The Mommy Clone

Twinned Universes

Fantasy: Short Stories

The Book of Beasts

Letters to Psyche

Silver Rain

Poetry

Life at Seventeen Syllables a Day: A Journal in Haiku

Fantasy: Season Avatars Series

Seasons' Beginnings

Scattered Seasons

Chaos Season (forthcoming)

About the Author

Sandra Ulbrich Almazan started reading at the age of three and only stops when absolutely required to. Although she hasn't been writing quite that long, she did compose a very simple play in German during middle school. Her science fiction novella *Move Over Ms. L.* (an early version of *Lyon's Legacy*) earned an Honorable Mention in the 2001 UPC Science Fiction Awards, and her short story "A Reptile at the Reunion" was published in the anthology *Firestorm of Dragons*. Other published works by Sandra include *Twinned Universes* and several science fiction and fantasy short stories. She is a founding member of Broad Universe, which promotes science fiction, fantasy, and horror written by women. Her undergraduate degree is in molecular biology/English, and she has a Master of Technical and Scientific Communication degree. Her day job is in the laboratory of an enzyme company; she's also been a technical writer and a part-time copyeditor for a local newspaper. Some of her other accomplishments are losing on *Jeopardy!* and taking a stuffed orca to three continents. She lives in the Chicago area with her husband, Eugene; and son, Alex. In her rare moments of free time, she enjoys crocheting, listening to classic rock (particularly the Beatles), and watching improv comedy.

Sandra can be found online at the following links:

website (www.sandraulbrichalmazan.com)
blog (www.ulbrichalmazan.blogspot.com)
Twitter (@ulbrichalmazan)
Facebook (SandraUlbrichAlmazanSffAuthor)
Goodreads (http://www.goodreads.com/author/show/5282664.Sandra_Ulbrich_Almazan).